Written by my cousins husband who lives in Wiltshire - a most enjoyable read.

Left for others to enjoy I hope.

Juliet Cook - 14.5.23
Hampshire.
U.K.

For Dad

THE GOOD MORNING GIRL

Craig Ennew

PART ONE

The young woman's body lay between the table and the seat of an upturned train carriage. The window cracked beneath her, her face inches from the old man's.

Focussing on her kept his mind at a distance from the stabbing pain through his upper thigh and lower back. He scanned her face for consciousness, aware that he could be the last person she might see.

Flickering carriage bulbs gave him zeotropic snatches of her features between the light and the darkness. He willed her to wake up.

Outside the carriage, across a deep layer of fresh snow, the trees shivered around the corpse of the wreckage. Ashes of debris drifted all about, indiscernible from the heavy flakes that crowded the sky.

Inside the carriage, everything had shifted by ninety degrees. The windows were the floor and ceiling; every surface a sliding cluttered shelf threatening to collapse.

A faint crackle came over the tannoy to die away. Simultaneously, in a brief rally, the spasm of lighting succumbed to silence and darkness as the snow continued to fall.

The old man no longer had sight of the girl but, at times, he could make out the rasps of her lips moving. Feeling for his stick, he shifted in his cramped position near to her, before pain cut through his cartilage and tendon like a blade.

His face tightened. Despite his own suffering, he could not fail her. He ran his tongue across his lips, and cleared his throat. "Young lady?" he whispered. "Can you talk to me?"

Silence.

He persevered. "Are you awake, my dear?"

His hand moved across his overcoat, to rest upon the inside breast pocket where a wallet contained a photograph of his wife while they had been on their honeymoon. On its reverse side, there lay scribbled an intimate love-note. He thought of their train journeys together: inter-railing as excited young lovers, taking the rickety, old night train from Mumbai. His Nancy, as she had once been.

He pulled himself back to the ragged breathing that had resumed nearby, his hand moving closer to where he imagined that of the young woman's to be. His fingers crawled through a sticky dampness and he rolled the thick liquid between finger and thumb. He could smell it. His own blood.

"I...I'm sure they'll come for us soon," he said.

A shrill noise began to flood the chambers of his brain. Clutching the top of his thigh, he felt the torn fabric, and the ruin of a raw, wet wound. Nausea rose from the pit of his gut; he needed to stay awake for the girl's sake, but fought for his own consciousness as the swirling, spiralling snow layered sheet after transparent sheet like a pall over the train carriage.

Only hours before, Oleg Kowalski had taken the last train from Waterloo, returning from a pleasant day trip in London. There had been a time when he had not travelled alone. They had called themselves 'The 1939 League': a tight bond of friendship that was named after the not uneventful year in which they were all were born. Their trips had been scheduled on the third Friday of each month: no excuses, all winds and weather. They would spend their journey laughing about old times; drifting between coffee houses, museums, exhibitions; putting the world to rights with the consummate ease and good humour that only the sage and the elderly possess. In the falling light of the setting sun, they would sit in the same snug of a tiny old London pub, diaries and half-pint glasses making a neat circle of promise for the next month's sojourn. For Oleg Kowalski, it was a brief reprieve from the solitude of old age.

Yet, as months and years diminished, so did their number. Harvey's duties as grandparent burgeoned as his daughter's career in the Home Office reached stratospheric heights; Jarvis never quite recovered from a failed hip replacement; and Jonners' jovial flame had been blown out by lung cancer. And so, in the lonely years that followed, Oleg Kowalski felt bound by loyalty to honour their close friendship on that third Friday, ambling around the same museums, sitting in the corner of the very same snug, nursing fond memories over a dimpled half-pint glass. Only now, he did so alone.

And so, upon returning from the capital, with the carriage hurtling through the evening towards the West Country, he'd pulled his scarf around his neck, and nestled his chin into it, settling into a vague drowse and lulled by the constant low hum and occasional clatter of the train on its tracks.

The train had come to a halt at some Godforsaken corner of the universe. He had jolted awake at the announcement of a stop at some blinked at the bleak deserted station, as the first few flakes of the snowstorm had fallen. For him, there had been something prescient about the expanse of concrete, the peeling posters, and the empty food wrappers skittering across platform.

He'd been the sole occupier of the carriage before he'd heard the automatic doors slide open. In a moment, it was filled with the busy presence of another. She'd struggled up the aisle, lumbering a backpack that bumped between the seats, stopping when she'd reached him. Hauling it onto the table with an inelegant thud, she'd slid into the double seat opposite.

At first, he had been difficult for him to get beyond her facial piercings. He liked to think of himself as liberal-minded, but was the first to acknowledge that, by the time first teenage rebel had made his or her mark on the world, he'd already joined the Rotary Club. And so he had felt a vague alarm when confronted by the metal that accosted the bridge of her nose, the ring that split her lower lip. Once past that though, he would discover the timelessness of her beauty that others had seen before and might after.

As an old man, he afforded himself the luxury that all old men have of taking in a pretty young woman. He knew he had a kind face, and not a lecherous one; but was not averse to looking despite there being little proclivity to take it further.

And so he'd watched her and was struck with the notion that she had been crying. Breathless, perhaps full of cold, her obvious distress had been sourced in something more substantial than missing a train, breaking up with a partner, or losing a ticket. Upon claiming the seat, she'd taken great handfuls of blonde dreadlocks, and scooped them back off her face to tie them in a ragged parcel at the back of her head. She'd returned his look, startled and wide-eyed, mascara streaking her cheeks. Searching his face for a moment, she'd attempted to settle herself back into the journey.

He'd continued to take her in. Her clothing was androgynous: greys and khakis, baggy, tied, and strapped. She'd rolled the arms of her top to reveal a whole sleeve of ink on a well-defined arm, and a wrist wrapped in festival bands and thin, leather straps. Beneath this alternative surface: under all of that hair she had the face of a Pre-Raphaelite angel – rounded, and pink at the soft edges from the cold world she had come from. Her mouth was full, the centre of her lower lip indented where that narrow silver band pierced its flesh.

He had watched as she'd taken in the darkening sky beyond their carriage.

After a while, she'd gone into her backpack and taken a slim book from one of the outer pockets. It had absorbed her. She'd run her slender fingers across the spine and over a bold red and white jacket; turning and turning it again as if to determine its worth. There were folded sheets of paper tucked within that she seemed preoccupied with, sliding them in and out of the book at regular intervals. But, as with the book itself, she'd chosen not to open them.

Finally, she'd rested the book on the table as the train's engines mustered some enthusiasm.

There had been another judder to the carriage, this time more violent. He'd been startled for a moment, but he'd returned to her, and had observed that her hands were covering her face. To his horror, he'd realised, that she was crying. At first, he'd wondered if it were more polite to pretend he hadn't noticed; but there had seemed to be a silent acknowledgement between them that they had moved past that moment. He had reached inside his satchel and pulled out a folded spotted handkerchief.

For a moment, she had been paralysed; but, much to his relief, she'd taken it from him, unfolding it and pressing it to her face, to blow her nose with abandon.

"Christ! What a mess - really sorry," she'd said, looking at him.

There had been a loose gesture in the direction of the book. "They fuck you up, your mum and dad."

He'd nodded and forced a polite smile. "Larkin."

She'd straightened herself in her seat. "Apparently, one of his favourites, the tosser..." Her hand had shot to her mouth. "Sorry!" He'd dismissed her indiscretion with a polite gesture.

Looking down at her handkerchief, she'd folded it again, smoothing the creases against the table;s surface. "Feel a bit bad giving it back to you like this," she'd said. "Perhaps I should wash it...?"

He had smiled again and had shaken his head. She'd broken into a raucous, open laugh that filled the carriage. "Yeah right. Like, that's going to happen." Wiping her wrist across her nose, she'd pulled herself together, becoming much more matter-of-fact. Holding out her other hand, she'd introduced herself: "I'm Hope. You don't mind me sitting here and making a complete idiot of myself, chuntering on, do you?"

"No. Not at all. I am Oleg. Oleg Kowalski. Chunter away, my dear."

"Very pleased to meet you, Oleg Kowalski." She'd paused. "That's an unusual name. Russian?"

"Polish."

"Oh!! She'd shaken her head. "It's good to talk!" She'd laughed that open laugh once more. There had been no secrets in her eyes. "Hey," she'd said. "D'you know what I did the other day? Well I'd been lying in bed thinking, one morning: what funny creatures we humans are. See, when I'm back home, it always falls on me to walk the bloody dog. Mum's too gone to do it, and God knows Spider – that's her stupid arse of a bloke - never ı walk the dog. And, you know, I walk the same path ᴵe water, the same route into town, through the streets ᵥver the park at the same time each morning. Been doing it foɪ years. I see the same people every time: some making their way to work, others to school, the job centre, a coffee house, whatever. There they all are, plugged in, watching their phones as they walk, faces looking at the ground. They never, ever *ever* look at you. And I start to wonder who they all are, these people. What are their names? Where do they live? What jobs do they do? What do they worry about? Are they in love with someone? You know?"

He'd nodded and waited. Rooting around in her rucksack, she'd pulled out a pack of cigarette papers and a small tin. She'd opened it up, to freeze, her fingers hanging above the packet.

"Oh," she'd said. She flashed an apologetic grin. "You don't mind, do you?"

"Of course not, my dear. And there is no-one else – not in this carriage at least. You go ahead." He had watched her as she'd initiated the well-rehearsed routine of preparing a roll-up.

Licking the edge of the paper, she'd continured. "You're very sweet. Give us a shout if you see the bloke coming." She had lifted the lid of the tin and made up her roll-up as she spoke. "Anyhow. So I'm lying there, and I think: *Do you know what? This morning, I'm going to smile at everyone I walk past and see what happens. I don't give a shit who they are – the postman, some homeless bloke, a perve, The Queen – they're going to get my full-on, one hundred per cent, bestest smile.*" Lighting up, she'd exhaled a large plume of cigarette smoke before dazzling him with a huge, exaggerated smile by way of illustration. "And I'm walking through town and it's a fantastic bright, sunny morning. It's like you can close your eyes and feel the morning air pass right through you and, despite all the crap that the world throws your way, you still feel connected. So I go for it. I smile. And what d'you reckon?" She pointed her cigarette at him. "What do they do when I smile at them?"

He'd shrugged. "I can only speak for myself: I would smile back."

She had nodded. "Yeah, some of them do. You know – that kind of startled look, followed by the little nervous laugh – like that thing old people do when you're both walking around a corner and about to bump into each other..." She'd stopped and was taking him in. "Oh. Sorry."

Oleg Kowalski had made a dismissive gesture, allowing her to continue. "So: others gave this big genuine smile back – like a habit thing, as if they'd always known me. They were nice. Faces totally transformed. Almost unrecognisable. And I was figuring how, seconds later, they'd be walking away in the opposite direction thinking, *who the fuck was that?* and drumming their brains for some memory of me that never existed. But after that I knew that the next time I smile at them and they smiled back, we'd have a shared memory, some knowledge of each other – even if it was for a fleeting moment."

"A charming thought," he had said. "I am expecting that you had some blank looks as well?"

"Oh yeah," she'd laughed. Fifty-fifty ratio of smilers to blankers, I reckon. And that's my guess as a glass-half-full kinda girl. But after that I was like - I'm not stopping there - I'm going to crack the ones who didn't smile back! So thenext day, I was there with the dog again: same time, same place, same people. Only this time, I slid in a *Good Morning* for good measure! It's easy ignoring a smile, or pretending that you never saw it. You know, the glance down at your feet – *here comes that crazy bitch with the dog again...* Not so easy to ignore a loud, cheery *Good Morning!*"

"And so they react how, your 'blankers'?"

She had taken a long drag on her cigarette. "This is the weird part. The ones who'd smiled back were fine with it. I mean, if you're grinning away at each other, what's the big deal about chucking in a *Good Morning* as well? But your blankers – well they did that weird thing, where they pretended they'd been in a world of their own." She'd mimicked their actions with an exaggerated jump. *"Oh... sorry! Morning...* They'd clocked me right from the start, of course - I could see them from miles away, keeping their heads down, hoping they could drift on past the weirdo. But that's the interesting bit- they were acting almost guilty - like kids who were found with their hands in the cookie jar."

"But that is as it should be," he'd said. "You, after all, were the friendly one. They were in the wrong – or, at least, impolite. They did not acknowledge you!"

"There you go! They knew I was right and they were wrong – making the world a better place by saying *Good Morning* to a stranger should be the most natural thing in the world!" She had given the *ta-dah!* gesture.

Oleg Kowalski had pondered this for a while. "D'you know, I think you make a very good argument!" he'd said. "I have lived in the same house on the same road for twenty-seven years. A creature of habit, save the odd exotic adventure in the old days. So, each day for many years, I am walking the same way to work, thousands of times over. My route takes me past the travel agent's in town. Every morning, year in, year out, I am seeing this little man with grand whiskers sitting behind the same desk, taking out his flask and his packet of sandwiches. He is of a similar age to me, this man. And it strikes me that there we are, we two: seeing more lines on each other's faces every day, whiskers turning grey at the same time, forgetting names and places at the same rate. And we are not knowing each other's lives or stories or names despite passing within a few feet of each other. Every single working day." He'd nodded. "When one thinks about it, it is quite extraordinary. We do not all have your courage, my dear: sadly, many of us choose to surround ourselves by strangers."

She had watched his hands, folding over each other like neat napkins on the surface of the table. Concern had passed like a light cloud over her face, as she studied him more intently. "Rude of me to ask, but...do you have someone else in your life?"

He had dropped his gaze. "No."

"Oh, I can't believe that." She had rested her arms on the table, inviting confidence. He'd looked up again. He had realised that he was not being polite or flattering – she simply hadn't believed him.

He had looked away, feeling like she was reaching inside. "No matter. Please: back to your story. Whatever became of them all? These people you were greeting with your 'Good morning'? Yes, they smiled, and some returned the favour. But did *any* of them eventually stop to talk with you?"

She had seemed lost in his loneliness for a moment, but continued nonetheless. "Oh yes," she'd said. "There were quite a few who stopped after that, usually to pat the dog, that kind of thing. When you're talking about the dog, both looking at the dog, the conversation is safe and neutral, yeah? *I grew up with that breed of pooch... Isn't she lovely? Had her long? What's her name?* And when you see them next time, you remember the dog's name, but never think to ask what the owner's is! Lots of common ground with pets. And with them, the smiling, and the *Good-Morning*-ing became easier each time – even if they'd started off as a blanker – until, as I say, it became the most natural thing in the world." A sudden memory made her smile. "Oh! There was this little old lady..."

"Go on..."

She'd laughed. "Tell me to shut up when you get bored. I go on and on sometimes."

He had shaken his head. "Suffice to say, my dear, we are nowhere near that moment as yet."

She'd laughed. "Well – she'd been one of the startled ones. You know – jumped out of her skin when I first spoke to her. And she wasn't putting it on either. She looked bloody petrified. I mean, who can blame her..." she gestured towards her own appearance, her dreadlocked hair. *It's alright*, I'd said. *I didn't mean to frighten you.* To be honest, I was a bit irritated by her – probably because that morning had been a morning of blankers. But then I felt guilty - she looked really sad, with this big old coat and her gloves still on, on a nice Spring morning, too. She had one of those little tartan shopping trolleys that you pull along the ground. So I said sorry, smiled and walked on. Next morning, though, I got this lovely smile back – and a *Good Morning* the day after that. After that comes the fourth morning, and, as I was about to walk past following the usual exchange,, she catches my arm and stops me in my tracks. *I wanted to say*, she says, *what a lovely girl you are. I mean, you're saying good morning to me each day.* She put her hand on my cheek." She had touched where the woman had touched, recalling the moment. "*A smile's worth a million dollars.* After that, she was gone. Never knew where she was coming from or going to. In fact: I never saw her again." She had taken one last pensive drag, before stubbing her cigarette onto the table, creating an orange burn on the cream surface. She'd looked at it, sighed and had stared out of the window.

The two of them had fallen silent.

The chill of the night had begun to steal into the frame of the carriage. The old man had pulled his coat tighter around his shoulders, as the bulk of the train started to reverberate once more with the same queer shuddering.

The girl had drifted back. He could feel that she had been looking at him out of the corner of her eye, weighing up whether it was wise to speak her mind or not. After a time, she'd spoken again. "This is going to sound really bloody stupid, but...well, bear with me..." She had been reaching for the red and black book again. She'd slid it from her backpack, to pinch the protruding sheet of notepaper between thumb and finger. Her movements had been slow, deliberate.

As the carriage had tilted into a left curve, a small tremor had juddered through the seats and floor. She'd noticed something too. She'd looked at him, eyebrows raised – almost startled.

When all hell broke loose, it began with an almighty jolt. There was another, followed by a third. A violent shuddering vibrated with an escalating violence through the shell of the carriage and the bodies of its few passengers. It must have been no more than twenty seconds, but the sheer turbulence had made it seem longer.

An eerie silence had followed: stillness more terrifying than all that had passed before; one that, in that instant, held the very fabric of the world to ransom.

And so it was that now, some unmeasured time later, Oleg Kowalski found himself clinging, in the darkness, to this girl's face as he listened to the decreasing circles of her breathing. For a brief moment, a faint light from outside of the carriage caught the whites of her eyes. He could hear her hold her breath, straining with the effort of speech.

When it came, it was a cracked whisper that slid like a tiny snake through the bible black vault of the fractured carriage.

"My...book," she said.

He remembered the red and white jacket, the sheets of paper tucked inside. He whispered: "Where, my dear?"

She made to answer, but was interrupted. He'd heard it too: the faint but terrifying click... click... click of something massive giving way beneath them.

They listened as the sound gained momentum: a huge old door yawning open, a rusty cog struggling round as, second by second, it gathered pace into an ominous creaking and straining that groaned and whined through every nook and crack of the train's sixty-tonne carcass. The strain on the branches that groaned beneath the great iron cradle was palpable: the dread of something massive being hauled from beneath them.

He tried to shut the catastrophe out, to pray to a god he'd never trusted before. Wrapping his left arm around a table leg, he felt the carriage shudder.

Everything began juddering downwards with unimagined violence in terrifying fits and starts.

He gripped tighter still whilst trying to block out the agony of his throbbing thigh. More stretching, cracking, straining, and another sudden drop – maybe six feet, perhaps more; his body sliding sideways; his skull cracking against the metal bar of a window; his arm almost yanked from its socket by the sheer force of the movement. The table had split away and now fell through the carriage into a doorway, shattering the glass.

Their centre of gravity shifted, and the carriage's contents – random items of litter and luggage – hurtled down the hollow length as laundry inside the last throes of a drum.

The shell of the train threatened to split, but all became still once more.

The situation remained that way for some time. On occasion, a fuse box spat out random sparks of contempt, and the old man was given a brief but terrifying view of the ruin of plastic and glass, draped in smoke and night mist.

Everything beneath his waist felt numb, and a drilling pain bore into his temples. He opened his mouth to cry out for help, but no sound came – merely the stultifying silent assault of the snowfall, wrapping the world in thick beautiful swathes, the arcing wings of angels...

...Now he was on a bandstand in a snowy park. Nancy was there beside him. Where were they? Prague? Budapest? A beautiful white storm whipped and swirled around their blissful shelter; and from somewhere, the strings of an orchestra lifted up, up into the branches. He had let her smile engulf him while the tempest circled in, encompassing them both in a thick cotton blanket of swelling choruses and tiny, spinning perfect flakes...

As he lost himself in blissful delirium, spoken words reverberated around the hollow caves of his skull: "The book..." He remembered: the young woman.

Time moved on. Although still not fully conscious, he became aware of change. The air was busy with purposeful activity: low, urgent whisperings into radios; silhouetted uniforms taking quiet notes; floodlights hoisted between bare branches. Beyond, the lights of emergency vehicles swept over the snow-laden tracks, and the wintry landscape stretched away into the bleak but beautiful darkness. He was breathing into an oxygen mask, feeling the pinch of an intravenous tube as his weight was lifted onto a stretcher and delivered into the back of an ambulance, cocooned in thick blankets. But where was the girl? He glimpsed figures on temporary platforms, cutting into the wrecked torso of another carriage and, in the distance other bodies, some with faces covered, were being carried away from the scene.

No more than thirty feet in the distance, he saw her backpack. A policewoman had hoisted it around one shoulder as she strode towards a police van. HJe saw the slim red and white volume in her hand

He'd stretched out towards her in vain, but the policewoman and the backpack disappeared from sight.

Within minutes, Oleg Kowalski was in the back of an ambulance, flanked by medics. They carried him, he knew, towards safety, but away from the one thing that he might have done for the Good Morning Girl.

PART TWO

Two: France. The Previous Summer – Saturday 4th June 2016

On a terrace in a village in Southern France, a thickset, middle-aged man perched beneath a parasol, deliberating over a book which had never been opened. For four days, the slim red and white volume had sat in a locked drawer inside his villa, sealed in a plain white jiffy bag, addressed to him.

Before him, the sprawling valley at the feet of the Alberes Mountains stretched towards the horizon, where threads of carriageway carried lorries, campervans, cars towards the Spanish border. From deep inside the villa, came the distant strains of a Disney soundtrack.

Jimmy Dunbar knew his own hands well: they were those of a man who had known manual labour and booze-fuelled skirmishes a long time ago: imperfect, strong but now card for. On the side of his third finger, a smooth callus had worn, through years of brushing against the surface of paper.

He pinched his heavy, bearded jowls. After a moment, he shunted his glasses to the top of his head and sat upright. Holding his smartphone at arm's length, he squinted at the touchscreen before jabbing speed-dial.

He stood as the call was taken. His voice was low, with the slur of a thick, Glaswegian accent. "Lefevre? Hallelujah…"

The voice of a Canadian responded - breezy, if somewhat

distracted. "Ah, James. I'm guessing you received the proof copy." He heard the rustling of papers, the clicking of keyboard keys.

"I've had the proof copy for the best part of a bloody week. Getting hold of yous has been a bugger. Where the hell have you been?"

"Hang on. Cassie didn't call you back?"

"Aye, she did. But you'll not fob me off with one of your minions, Lefevre…"

"You know how it is, James: the devil finds work for idle hands and all that…"

Jimmy glanced back towards the villa and lowered his voice. "What matters is I've pinned you down, you bastard. 'Bout the book: truth be told be told, I'm a wee bit stumped by the red and black stripey shite on the cover? I mean - I cannae remember us talking about any o'that." He pushed his glasses to the top of his head and moved his face closer. "It looks like some fucking Neo-Nazi manifesto…"

" James. We had a long conversation about the concept art. You were all good with it, remember? You wanted to rush it to bring the publication date forward: the decision may have seemed rushed."

Jimmy flipped the book and examined his own likeness on the back cover. Taken over a decade earlier, the black and white portrait spoke of a time before any sly streaks of grey had infiltrated his trademark auburn locks and ragged beard; a time, in short, before a successful writing career had been subsumed by marriage, fatherhood and mild self-neglect. His mouth loosened with compromise, but he felt reluctant to make his publicist's job too easy. "I dinnae remember that. I was expecting something a wee bit more - I don't know - floral? Red roses an' shit?"

"Red roses?" Lefevre whistled. "Woah. I'll give you one word, James: *Striking*. Striking is what you pay me and my people to produce. On somebody's cell phone, that jacket appears teenier than an English postage stamp, my friend. One click to purchase on Amazon. I may know nada about poetry, James, but I do know what sells books. You can ask your wife about that."

"Aye, well…" Jimmy skimmed over the cover, but could not resist the lure of his own accomplishment: he opened the volume to the contents page and slid his finger down the list of titles. His poems. He knew that this was his literary swansong.

There was some impatience at the other end. "So. Are we done now?"

"I'd be encouraged if you could sound a wee bit more arsed, Lefevre. This is a big deal for me."

"I know, I know. And with a good wind on your back, my friend, we can get you back to the top of your game. But it could help if, for once, you start to have some faith in people who are trying to support you."

Jimmy paced towards the edge of the terrace and gripped the railings. "Faith? Let me tell you about faith, sunshine. I googled myself the other day. D'ye wannae hear summat? That wee poem I wrote for the Dundee coach disaster is still getting way more searches than anything else I've written in the last twelve years, let alone this new book. How does that happen?"

There was a pause. He'd like to have thought of Lefevre composing himself at the other end of the line: a twiddling of cufflinks; a fixing of the knot of his tie. The Lefevre he knew, though, was smooth and unperturbed: "Not all of us can be quick learners, James. I get that. But I'm hoping that this is the last time I have to give the lesson on search engines and algorithms. Let's try again: when you googled yourself - who came top of the list?"

Jimmy squinted over the valley. "Well... the missus."

"Boom! Top search: Katherine Kennedy. And I'm guessing second too? And, whoop-de-doo, there the lovely lady is yet again at number three and four until somewhere, right down at the bottom of the fifth page you finally get to the YouTube clip with 1.6 million hits for you reading out your poem for the Scotch kiddies who got killed in a coach."

Jimmy frowned. "Your point being..?"

"Multiple points, James. Whose idea was it to write the poem?"

Jimmy rolled his eyes. "Yours, I grant yous that, but..."

"Exactamundo. This is what you pay me for. And my people take care of these analytics over and over again. Every. Single. Week. It's what I pay *them* to do. And here's the thing: your amazing wife, Katherine Kennedy, has been on British screens for the best part of a decade. Find me a single street in the UK that doesn't have at least five copies of her bestsellers on the shelves of their kitchen. Harsh as it sounds, baking, cooking - whatever you want to call it - will always sell more than poetry: a sad indictment of our times you may argue, but a fact nonetheless." Now, he sounded like he was on the move: an elevator door, the noise of traffic and rapid footfall. "What I'm saying here, is that it's my job to capitalise on trends, not set them. People like your wife do that." Jimmy heard a car door slamming, and an engine start. "Look: I really gotta get going..."

Jimmy cut in: "Hawd your wheesit."

"What was that?" A brief pause. "No matter. Listen: my turn. This is the last thing, I promise..." Jimmy baulked at the Canadian's capacity to turn the tables. "The Capital Arts Festival on the 30th? The launch and book-signing? I've got some business in the London that week. Here's what I'm gonna do for you: front of house, like the old days. I'm going to put running a multi-million dollar conglomerate to one side to facilitate the renaissance of your literary reputation, James. How does that sound?" Another pause. "But, hang on – before you answer - Cassie told me you never confirmed the final number of airplane tickets you needed to get over to London. Two returns, right? You and Katherine?"

"One. Kat's no' coming."

Any activity at the other end of the line ceased. "But Katherine is aware of the book launch, right?"

With haste, Jimmy tucked the proof copy back into the envelope. "She is not." He squinted up at the brazen midday sun as it scaled the sky.

"Forgive me if this sounds impertinent, but you two do actually communicate, yeah? You know, like man and wife?"

Jimmy looked with longing towards the pool on the lower terrace. He needed to cool down. "About work? If we do, it usually ends with us both of us growlin'." He afforded himself a chuckle.

"Okay. I'm not going to pull punches: we need Katherine at this gig. What we have is a damned big hall to fill. If she is there, I promise you that the audience - and subsequent sales of your book – will double, even treble." He sighed. "I need to be blunt, James: the number of returns to invites has been modest so far, to put it politely. Persuading Katherine to be there will turn that around. Sincerely."

Jimmy's slow Scottish burr ground into the mouthpiece. "Listen, Lefevre: this event is no' about Kat. It is about me. *My* poetry. *My* words were in print when her ma was teaching her how to make cucumber fuckin' sandwiches. Let's keep Kat, as gloriously bloody talented as she is, separate from what I am trying to achieve here, huh? Can we no' do that for once?"

Lefevre appeared oblivious to what Jimmy had said. "Hold it right there... she's aware of the new work, right? Tell me she has read the poems..."

"Of course she hasn't read the bloody poems. She never reads the bloody poems. She's a bloody cook, for Christ's sakes."

"Sheesh." Lefevre sang under his breath: "*There may be trouble ahead...*"

"What you talkin' about?"

Lefevre was able to recite, word for word, the blurb on the back cover of the new collection of poems: "*Through witty yet poignant verse, and more candid in middle age than ever, Dunbar extrapolates his celebrated yet notorious climb to literary success. The brawls, the affairs, the missing days are all faced head-on with self-deprecating...*"

Jimmy cut in, "Woah, woah, woah! Hang on there, pal. I do recall that playing up the autobiographical angle was your idea?"

"With the naïve assumption that, if you were going to write confessional verse about past indiscretions, you might think about running it past your good lady first? Or did you assume that this was also my job?" He snorted. "I do PR. I do not do family mediation." His lowered his voice. "Look: I need to get on. Tell me we're done?"

With the conversation over, Jimmy rested his phone on the table before ambling down the incline that brought him level with the pool. As he tugged at the buttons of his shirt, the white-blue stolid flesh of his belly spilled over the waistband of his trunks. Kicking off his flip-flops, he stood, flat-footed at the poolside, toes curling over the edge.

He breathed the wide valley in: the distant hum of traffic, the irked yelping of a mutt from an anonymous neighbouring villa.

Holding his breath, Jimmy propelled his body into the deep end of the pool. His fingertips, his arms, his shoulders, his torso crashed through the water.

Beneath the surface, his hand pulled back against the water, his heartbeat slowing. He stayed under for a while, allowing the currents to pull his limbs this way and that.

Within ten minutes, he was back on the lounger, and in the shade of a poolside canopy. He turned onto his front. As his fingertips dripped onto the hot terracotta of the tiles, he watched the heat dissipate each tiny pool. In under a minute, he was in a light sleep.

Now, he was twenty-five years away, in a dark converted warehouse apartment.

Night. The air was cool. He was slumped against the door frame of a metal fire escape high up in the eaves of some industrial building. He nursed a half-empty bottle of Smirnov by its neck. Ethereal female voices lifted from below.

He bent his frame to place the bottle at his feet. The world span and titled, and he staggered against the wall, a shoulder connecting with the black steel brackets of a fire extinguisher. The bottle span on its shoulder.

The talking ceased. He held his breath, then they resumed.

Someone had put a record on – one of his own collection. The plaintive strains of The Cure's *Disintegration* became a backdrop to their muted words.

He crawled across the mezzanine walkway until he had sight of them: two silhouettes held in an intimate conversation, their whispering lifting into the vastness of the old, industrial space. Their words became clear.

"You're sure about this?"

The second silhouette nodded, and spoke through tears. "I'm positive. I've missed my period."

He recognised the calmer voice as that of Roo, the South African friend of Jasmine, his girl – the second speaker.

The sound of wine being poured hitting glass.

"OK. So, you're gonna to need to talk to him." Her voice was matter-of-fact, practical. "Like, very soon. While you still have some control. Tomorrow morning – promise me you'll talk to him tomorrow morning, Jas? When he's sober."

There was a small sob. "We're talking about Jimmy, Roo. He's not exactly Mr. Commitment."

"He might surprise you, love. But even if he's true to form, the guy deserves to know at some point."

Unseen high above them, Jimmy watched through blurred vision as Jasmine rose, her profile etched against a tall window frame with the lights of the waterfront glittering beyond. His eyes traced the edges of her fragile beauty: the curve of her cheek, the slenderness of her naked arms. He watched as her hand moved round to her front and slide over her stomach. "I need more time to think..." She rested that way for a time.

She turned, moved back to her friend and sat down again, this time much closer. A match was struck, the brief flame revealing both intense faces. Jasmine, took a long, deep drag of a joint before lifting her face and blowing a long plume of smoke into the metal vaults above. Her face found the other woman's once more, her whisper floating upwards. "You know what the biggest bastard is in all of this?" Her voice caught. "I think I've fallen in love with him."

Jimmy leant his head back against the wall, his mind reeling. The voices were swimming in and out of his head and he felt sick and hot, like he could pass out any moment. Now he knew that he needed to get out of that building.

The next he knew, he was stumbling along the river path, away from everything that he had heard minutes before.

As he staggered forwards, sirens wailed across the city, the oppressive night air was stifling him, robbing his lungs of oxygen.

With scuffing footfall, he slowed to a halt, bent double, wheezing. The nausea lifted from the pit of his stomach, up through his chest to burn through his throat. With a loud wretch, he vomited onto the grass at his feet. His gasps slowed to slower heavy panting, and he wiped his sleeve across his wet mouth.

He found himself staggering into an alleyway beside a Lebanese restaurant. Slithering down against the brick wall, he became aware that he was not alone. Before him, was a tiny figure, no more than a silhouette. A child. The child began to whisper, a small sound at first, but a noise that swirled around and around in his head, gaining momentum:

"Daddy, daddy, daddy..."

Behind the child, there was light: meagre at first, but strengthening in intensity until he had to shield his face with his forearm until the screaming abated...

He took his arms away.

Above him, the coarse fabric of his parasol flapped in the forewarning of the *Mistral* which rolled as a burgeoning wave across the North of the valley.

Jimmy blinked: the sky was hidden by a dark-skinned boy with a mop of curly brown hair. The child looked down at him with huge, auburn eyes. His thick lips were curled into a petulant pout. Fumbling for his phone, Jimmy saw that he'd been asleep for around forty minutes.

The boy clutched a plastic sword, and was waving it back and forth in front of Jimmy's face.

"Daddy!"

Coming to his senses, Jimmy rubbed the bridge of his nose and slid his thick-rimmed spectacles back in place. As the wind gathered momentum, an inflatable skidded across the surface of the pool as, at the far side, another parasol tipped over to clatter on the tiles.

Frowning, Jimmy regarded the child who danced from side to side. "Alfie. How long have you been there?"

"The film just finished," said the boy in a low, gruff voice. He pointed at the pool with his sword. "Can we do some swimming?"

Jimmy checked the time again. "It's too hot, son," he said. "Maybe later."

The boy made a whimpering sound. "But you always say that! *Please*, Daddy?"

Jimmy eased himself up onto his elbows, with a grunt and pulled his shirt around his shoulders. "No, laddie."

Without warning, the plastic sword slapped across the dough-like white flesh of his belly, leaving a red welt behind. Yelling, Jimmy leapt to his feet, the lounger skittering backwards.

"Jesus Christ, son!" he roared "How many bloody times?"

The boy skipped backwards, pleased with the dramatic reaction. "Jesus Christ!" he mimicked.

Jimmy lunged at Alfie, but the child was too quick for him. The offending plastic sword clattered on the tiles as he fled for the far side. Jimmy grabbed hold of it. In fury, he attempted to hurl it towards the centre of the pool; instead, the light plastic caught the breeze before resting on nearside of the pool's surface, where it bobbed with indifference.

Screeching with delight, the child scampered back up the path towards the villa. Jimmy buttoned up his shirt and lumbered in the wake of his son's victorious hollering.

In the valley below, the *Mistral* gathered force, sending a hundred more sun loungers across tiled surfaces, tipping a hundred more spindly parasols.

Up where the path met the wide terrace of the villa, stood the boy's mother, Katherine Kennedy. She watched the scene unfold without passion. Her figure was slender, almost boyish and her expression neutral. As the child came running towards her, she let a light shopping bag drop from her grip and, with long, slender fingers, tucked a dark strand of hair behind her ear.

"Mummy!" yelled the boy, arms and legs flailing. "Daddy's thrown my sword into the pool. And he won't go in with me."

By now, Jimmy had now made it back to the terrace. He doubled over and tried to communicate through a series of dry wheezes. Droplets of sweat fell onto the terracotta tiles in flat, heavy slaps. "The little shet wacked me in the stomach with his bloody sword!" he gasped. "I was asleep, for Christ's sake!"

Katherine Kennedy pushed her sunglasses to the top of her head, and rested a hand on her hip. A full length black maxi-dress hung over the lean contours of her body, its sheer fabric swaying with each slight movement. She surveyed the scene with a cool feline prescience. Acknowledging her husband with the briefest glance, she focused on her son. The corners of her mouth curled upwards with affection.

Two arms stretched towards him. "Alfie, sweetheart? What have I told you about going out in the sun at this time of the day? Have you had sun cream applied?"

He came to her and she pulled him in, her manicured, unpainted nails scratching the soft down at the nape of his neck. Alfie buried his head into her breasts, making small nuzzling noises. Her fingers moved, with affection, around his head.

Without looking again at her husband, she spoke in a low, clear voice. "Has he eaten?"

From the corner of his eye, Jimmy caught sight of the padded envelope that contained the proof copy of his book. It had remained on the terrace table all this time. Taking a step towards it, he raised his voice by way of a diversion. "Did you no' hear what I said? Aren't we going to deal with his poor behaviour first?" Alfie peered from behind his mother's with a guileful expression.

Kat took the boy's shoulders and turned him around to face his father. The boy's face was sly as he took in his father. "Alfie, my big, clever five-year-old boy," said his mother, "What can you count up to now?"

"Thirty hundreds," said the boy.

She smiled. "So tell me: how many children are here on this terrace right now?"

The child responded with glee. "One – me!"

"There's my clever little brown berry! And how many grown-ups are there? Take your time, sweetheart."

Alfie's face split into a furtive smile. "One. Two," he counted. Breaking free from his mother, he thrust his head forward and blew a loud raspberry at Jimmy's face before fleeing back into the villa.

With incredulity, Jimmy made a feeble gesture after his son. "Are we going to let him get away with that?"

Katherine Kennedy took slow catwalk paces towards the edge of the terrace where a towel had slipped from the railings. "We? We? If, Jim, there had ever been a time over the last five years when you were prepared to take some responsibility for the welfare of our child, I would happily have that conversation with you. We tried joint-parenting – it wasn't your style, remember?" She folded the towel against her body.

Jimmy spread his arms in protest. "Hang on there, a wee minute. I do my bloody share!"

Kat lined up the corners of the towel "You take him riding once a week. You drop him off at school each morning. Occasionally, you might pin a few of his clothes to the washing line. Let me know if I've missed anything. Everything else is done by me or one of the staff. The tiny amount you do, Jimmy, I allow you to do so that you can feel that you've done something." She took three paces over to Jimmy's writing desk. "Enough, already. I need to eat."

Dropping the folded towel on the desk, she spoke through a sigh. "I've got a Skype meeting with the production company at four and the vlog to record at five. Maria isn't due here until Alfie's supper-time, so you'll need to think of what you can do with him before that. Christ only knows what he's been watching on that i-Pad while you've been doing God-knows-what out here..."

She stopped. Her attention was caught by the small, brown package that said on the table, equidistant from both of them.

He spoke quickly. "Ah – I forgot to say: Lefevre called. He wants me over in the UK, late November. The publishers have some ideas about this new anthology..."

Katherine had not taken her eyes off the envelope.

Jimmy added, "Plus a production company's doing some kind of documentary about Dundee. You know, the anniversary's coming up. They want an interview."

His mind returned to twelve months before. It was two days on from the horrific road accident in which thirty-two passengers and the driver of a coach had lost their lives on a carriageway to the North of Dundee. Jimmy had been appalled as, even before the victims turned cold, Lefevre was suggesting the writing of some epitaph to unite a grieving public. Not long after, Jimmy and Kat found themselves sitting in the middle of a corner sofa as they watched the evening news. In a report recorded earlier that day, Jimmy was reading his poem outside the locked gates of school. As he spoke the words, his voice cracked with emotion as everyone pondered on the wreck of blood and tissue and shattered bones inside a twisted tin-can of a coach; the bones that had made the same journey each day, week year without fuss. The parents, the teachers, the brothers, sisters placing their cheap garage flowers and scrawled eulogies on the bank of the carriageway, staring with hopeless grief into the eye of the camera.

Watching it play back on the Channel 4 news, Kat's fingers had found his as she stared ahead, tears brimming. Despite everything, he'd felt a stab of pride knowing that his words could reach her, and something of the admiration that each felt for the other's talents was rekindled, if only for a moment. It had been one of the last moments of intimacy between them that he remembered.

Now, almost a year on, after one last long look at the package on the table, Kat was turning away and heading back into the villa. In her wake, the French windows slammed against the villa walls as the Mistral gathered strength.

She called back to him. "Your November thing. You'll need to look at how that works with my schedule." Stopping, she turned again. "Actually - what is Lefevre thinking of? Surely he, of all people, is aware of how busy I am right through to the end of the year..."

A low growl of thunder rumbled deep in the throat of the Alberes Mountains and the French windows shook again. The sky had darkened and the first few fat drops of rain smacked the earth.

She shook her head and turned away again. Jimmy snatched the parcel from the table and tucked it against his side before following her into the villa. "Look, lassie: I know you're the one earning the big bucks. But there could be a lot resting on this London gig. It's a chance tae get my name back up there with the others. I do have a career too..."

She dropped her sunglasses down onto the marbled work surface of the kitchen island and moved to the refrigerator. "I struggle with your definition of 'career'. If it means you sat on your arse watching Sky Sports whilst occasionally putting pen to paper, there's a slight sense imbalance, don't you think?"

"Now come on, love - that's hardly fair..."

She pulled at the door. "Oh, it's 'fair', Jim. We could start by comparing working weeks? And then, perhaps, we could move on to remuneration. Does that sound 'fair'?"

Jimmy slapped his thighs. "Ach, what's the bloody point?" He turned from her and skulked towards a large cream-coloured corner sofa.

Turning back to the fridge, Kat piled various packages of cheeses and cold meats into her arms. Alfie had returned, clutching the iPad. Although he came close to Kat, the focus of the boy's attention was still his father. He slammed the tablet down on the surface with a clatter. "Daddy forgot to charge the Pie-Pad again."

She plucked a saucisson slice from its packet, and popped it into the boy's mouth. Taking the tablet, she walked back past the island and tossed it onto the cushion beside Jimmy. She looked over to the boy. "Never mind, sweetie. Daddy was telling me that, after lunch, the two of you were going to do something nice together while Mummy gets on with some very important work." She reached into a high cupboard for some plates. "Preferably, something that *doesn't* involve you sitting, zombie-like, front of inappropriate cosplay videos on YouTube for most of the afternoon."

Back in the kitchen area, she slid a cool bottle of rose wine from the wine fridge. Pulling the cork from its neck, she poured herself a generous glass.

The sounds of liquid hitting crystal filled the space. Jimmy imagined the translucent ribbons of pink rolling round the hips of the glass. He thought of vineyards and rolling hills, of getting drowsily drunk under a wide-brimmed hat.

Pulling himself together, he focused on the parcel. He slid it halfway under a cushion before reached for the remote to click on Sky Sports. But before he even knew it, his wife was on the move. She'd made her way to the TV to switch it off at the set. "I refuse to let you ruin the one moment of peace in the day that I have." She stood before him. Jabbing with a breadstick, she made little stabbing motions with each stressed syllable. "Who pays for Sky Sports, Jimmy? Whose business acumen allows us to keep up a second home here in France? Whose salary funds Alfie's pre-school and au pair bills? Whose hard toil enables a certain semi-retired 'writer' to lie by the pool on his derriere most afternoons while his common-law wife puts the fucking baguettes on the table?" She leaned over him. "I mean... can we, for a single moment, get real?" She allowed space for a retort, but he found himself with nothing to give. She shook her head. "Shit. I've had it with you! I really have! Floating in this childish, self-centred bubble of bullshit. If you insist on being the centre of attention, you do it on your own time – not on mine. And not on Alfie's either..."

She paused. Her focus trained in on a tiny corner of the envelope that was protruding from the cushions. Now angered, she chose her moment. In an instant, she had hold of it. "So what is this?" she asked, lifting and turning it. She looked at the front, where Jimmy's name and the address of the villa sat beneath the familiar smart logo of Lefevre's publicity group.

Jimmy was on his feet, reaching out. "It's nae bother," he said. "Just stuff to do with the London meeting I was talkin' about. Interview schedules, that kind of pish." He moved forwards and took a corner.

Without warning, the TV screen beside them burst into life, the plaintive tones of Mr. Tumble filling the living space. Alfie was hanging over the back of the sofa, the remote dangling from his fingers.

Kat ripped the package from his grasp threw it back down on the sofa. She stared hard at him for a moment and then turned. Her voice was cold as she walked away from him. "I don't trust you, Jimmy."

Three: London – Wednesday 30th November 2016

The lecture theatre was a daunting space. Standing at the front, a trim man on the easier side of middle age adjusted his cufflinks as he looked down upon the small boy stood before him. The man was clean-shaven and erudite, his dark, razor-cut hair shot through with distinguished streaks of silver. He looked, for a moment, as if he were about to reach out and ruffle the boy's tight brown curls; but something in the child's surly expression made him think better of it.

The man looked to the front of the theatre, where his client deliberated over the printout of his notes. He eyed the hunched figure of James Dunbar with a curious expression of detachment, but transformed into something more becoming when the big man looked up. "So here we are: no Katherine and, erm, one small child, I see."

Jimmy's pen paused over his notes. He ran his eye over Lefevre's dark, tailored suit; the neat little bow tie. Glancing down at the lapel of his own shapeless jacket, he was reminded that he forgot to remove the mayonnaise stain from the previous evening. Frowning, he said, "The laddie has a name, Lefevre."

The younger man reached into his jacket and checked the time on his phone. "Of course he does. Don't they all?" He affected a polite smile. "So. Given we're all systems go in – what, twenty-nine minutes? - any suggestions as to what we do with erm...?" He looked back down at the boy.

Jimmy banged the pen down on the surface. "Alfie, Lefevre. His name is Alfie."

Lefevre tapped his temple with his index finger. "Of course! Alfie! I knew it was something mildly Victorian. Gotta love you Brits and your names." He stepped closer, to manoeuvred himself between father and son. "James, if I may...in a little more than fifteen minutes, I'm hoping that this lecture theatre will be crammed top to toe with your adoring public. The child: what say I get Cassie in to take him away and keep him occupied?"

Jimmy looked across to his son. Truth be told, he could do with a break. The trip across London had been defined by a series of bribes to stem relentless questions that revolved around returning to his mother.

Initially, Alfie had lulled him into a false sense of security during a First Class early morning flight followed by a series of visits to the big museums that had passed without incident. Confronted with sprawling dinosaur skeletons and frozen Neolithic hunters glowering behind glass, Jimmy was, for once, finally making a decent stab at fatherhood. The boy had even asked some questions that betrayed a modicum of curiosity - he'd even asked to go back and see one of the exhibits for a second time. It was during that second visit to the Natural History Museum, though, that defeat was snatched from the jaws of victory. On their way out, just inside the shop beyond the foyer, a large, porcelain model of a t-rex had caught Alfie's eye.

"Let's have a look at this, son!" Jimmy said, whilst attempting to prise the model from Alfie's clutches. "This is your King of the Beasties - the T-Rex! But remember what I said: no touching unless we're buying. Let's pop the wee fella back on the shelf where he belongs..."

"Can we buy it, Daddy?" The boy would not relinquish the model.

"We cannae, laddie. Not today. I'll tell ya what: we'll park this fella back on his shelf, and you can choose one of those wee plastic ones in the basket over there to take away."

Still not letting go, Alfie had cast a sceptical look to the baskets on the shelves. Clearly, he was less than impressed. "Those are teensy ," he said. "I want this white one. *Please,* Daddy?" His voice took on that bleating whine that he often affected when he wasn't getting his own way – the whine, JImmy knew, to be a precursor to full-on meltdown. Jimmy clocked his cunning with growing dismay. He was aware that heir raised voices were already catching the attention of the other people in the shop, including a supercilious assistant in a toupee behind the till, who had been keeping his eye on them for some time.

With some effort, Jimmy managed to prise the porcelain T-Rex from his son's clutches. Basking in the victory of the physical struggle, he had, unfortunately, overplayed his psychological card. "Let's put it back, now." Walking over to the corner of the shop, he had placed the T-Rex back on its pedestal. Pointing back to the shelves, he'd said, "Off you go, and choose one of the other wee ones..."

In a swift riposte, Alfie had ducked down to get between his father's legs in an attempt to find the quickest route back to dinosaur of choice. Jimmy's instinct was to jam his knees around the boy's ears.

Looking down to see his Alfie's gawping head, Jimmy had steeled himself for the explosion he knew was to surely follow. The calm before the storm. The boy's mouth extended as wide as it is possible for a five-year old mouth to go, emitting a silence that could only precede the horror that was to come. And come it did: a blood-curdling scream that ripped through the entire building, an all-eradicating tsunami of sound that had every adult within a fifty-metre radius stopping their ears. The attendant was now taking short, mincing steps in their direction, his hairpiece quivering at a jaunty angle, arms stretched before him.

"You've hurt me! You've hurt me!" screamed the boy, sinking to the ground, arms curling over the top of his head. Jimmy had cast an uneasy eye about the shop before crouching down to his son's level. "Now listen to me laddie…" He spoke in an urgent whisper. " - that was an accident. But, if you'd have listened to what your da was saying…" As he spoke, he tried to prise Alfie from his spot on the floor, but the child was stuck fast. He cast another quick glance around. "Fuck. We need to leave this shop, son. Right. Now"

"But you've hurt me! *And* now you've said the fuck word. I hate you. And I'm telling Mummy" wailed Alfie again, miraculously finding more volume. "I'm telling Mummy unless you get me the glass dinosaur."

The whispering took on a more sinister cadence: "I want you to look at me and calm the fuck down, son…" He'd grabbed the boy by the arm. "If you haven't shifted your *wee arse* by the time I've counted to three, we leave this shop with nothing and I take you straight back to the hotel room. You can forget about Old MacDonald's. You can forget about ice-cream for all of next week. Capiche? " He began the count. "One…" The boy remained still. Two…"

Five minutes later, Jimmy was watching, in grim silence, as the man in the toupe gift-wrapped wrapped the porcelain T-Rex. He shoved his credit card across the counter, cowed by the indignity of having to pay twice – the first time for the model that had ended its short life in four pieces on the shop floor.

Walking back out of the shop, towards the lobby of the museum, Alfie had paused by the basket containing the multi-coloured plastic dinosaurs. "Don't you even bloody think about it," Jimmy had growled.

The man in the toupee held the doors open for them with a smug smile. "And you can fuck off too," Jimmy had said.

Now, stood alongside Jimmy in a cavernous lecture hall at the Southbank Centre, Lefevre was unremitting in his need to press the point home: this was not the first occasion upon which he had mentioned that this venue would not be suitable for children. "I've said it before, but, darn it's a shame that Katherine can't be here." He cast a quick glance towards the exit. "She could've taken care of the kid...and there are disappointed people out there with armfuls of copies of her books to sign. Everyone would've been a winner. As it is..." He shrugged his shoulders, hopelessly.

"I've told yous," grunted Jimmy. "this is ma wee bash here. Can we no keep Kat off-topic, just for this once?" He looked up through the tiered seating to where Alfie weaved in an out of the rows of seats. He was being a fighter plane, arms stiff and horizontal as his lip made fat, burring sound that filled the hall.

Lefevre cocked an eye at the boy. Turning on his heel, he breezed over to the side entrance. The noise of the crowd outside penetrated the hall as he opened the doors.

From beyond, a well-presented young woman now stepped before Lefevre, awaiting instruction. Jimmy noted how she held eye contact with him a little longer than was necessary; how she played with hair as she spoke. Most women found Lefevre attractive, he knew. But it fascinated him how the Canadian, without exception, remained polite yet ambivalent. As far as Jimmy knew, Lefevre had been celibate during the seven years or so they had worked together.

Cassie passed Lefevre a tablet; and he signed something off before they both turned towards Alfie. "Keep him busy until this is over, Cassie? There's a gift store in the basement. Anything he wants can go on expenses." Cassie smiled at the boy, tilting her head.

Jimmy frowned and looked Cassie over. There was a time,

when he wore thinner man's clothes, that his gruff charm could have won over the attention of a younger woman; but he had conceded that, for the best part of a decade, that horse had long since bolted the stable.

Cassie reached Alfie and whispered something in his ear. They looked across to Lefevre, and a wide grin lit the boy's face. She stood back up, reached out her hand, and the boy went to her. As they walked past Jimmy, Cassie checked if it was okay to take Alfie to the shop. He looked at his watch. "Aye, if y' like. And good luck to you if you're expecting to avoid spending any money."

She smiled. "Fifteen minutes to go," she said as she passed Lefevre. "We could do with hurrying things on. The press are outside already." She stopped in her tracks. "Oh – I almost forgot. I heard Security talking about a couple of dodgy characters who were hanging around outside the building. They looked like they meant to cause trouble."

Lefevre looked up. He walked towards the door and peered through, mimicking her accent. *Dodgy?*"

"Yeah The guard at the door said that there was this tall guy who'd been winding up one of the guards. And he thinks a younger woman was there too. But I'm sure it's nothing Security can't handle. We could do with getting everyone in as soon as we can, that's all."

Lefevre glanced back towards Jimmy. "If there's any trouble, I'll get out and deal with," he said, disappearing through the doors.

Cassie called back: "Can I bring you anything back from the shop, Mr. Dunbar?" She gestured towards his water jug. "Anything else to drink other than water?"

He pushed his reading glasses to the back of his head. He held the glass up. "I'll stick with Adam's Ale, missy. Although these gigs always used tae be easier after a few wee swallies."

Cassie grinned again. "Come on, Alfie," she said. "Let's see what we can find…"

When they'd gone, Jimmy took the place in. Nearby a life-sized cardboard mock-up of a younger version of himself cast a pensive glimpse into the mid-distance, past the rows of empty seats. Behind him, in bold, black san serif, stretched across the giant screen was a single word:

Anamnesis.

He rubbed the coarse copper hairs of his beard. In moments of self-doubt, he'd worried about the word being some pretentious catch-all. At other times, he'd forgotten what it meant entirely, and had found himself reaching for the dictionary app on his phone again.

Jimmy tipped the last few drops of water from the jug into his glass and drained them. The minute hand on the clock at the back of the hall crawled nearer the hour. In twelve minutes, for the first time in years, he – James Crawford Dunbar - would be centre stage once more. His final chance to prove that he was back and on top of his game. He rubbed his hands together.

He read through the notes again. Three minutes passed. The doors opened again. Lefevre had returned, phone clasped to his ear, shoulder curled around it. "Time to throw open the doors. Good to go, James?"

Jimmy nodded. "Did yous find the trouble-makers. You know: Mr. Dodgy?"

Lefevre shrugged. "Nada. Must have got bored and left." He put his phone away and pinned the doors back against the wall, beckoning those outside to come in. A small group armed with cameras and recording equipment came first, and took the front row. Squinting, Jimmy thought he recognised a couple of his old adversaries from the press, some of whom he had once graced with verbal assault. Memories of those times were patchy but he felt an off surge of pride when recollecting them. Now, as a gesture of reconciliation, he nodded and remained reticent.

Six minutes to go. A steady stream of punters were trickling in.

Jimmy became aware that one of the newcomers hadn't taken a seat, but had chosen to linger nearby instead. A slight, shambling man of around his own age before him. With his jaunty pork-pie hat and wide, lop-sided smile, he rattled a few memories in the back of Jimmy's brain. Jimmy found himself examining the dysmorphic, fairground-mirror of a face.

The man took his hat off, revealing a close-cropped, grey-white skull. His watery eyes blinked back at Jimmy with benign acquiescence. The penny dropped "My god! Hereward Double-Barrelled? Is that you?"

The other man grasped him, the skin on his palm was cold and paper-thin, his hands red and mangled. Jimmy could almost hear the bones crack inside.

Hereward's accent was broad East End, but he enunciated his words with unnatural caution. "Watcha, Dunny, old boy! Saw you on a poster in the Working Men's Club. Thought I'd pop along and take a butcher's...been a long, long time, mate!"

Jimmy slapped the other man's shoulder. "Years...even decades! Good to see ya, man - I'm a wee bit ashamed of myself that I've no' got in touch sooner." More people were coming in now. The entrance was becoming a bottleneck, and there was a disconcerting sound of raised voices in the foyer beyond them.

Hereward was oblivious. "I know," he grinned. "No need to tell me: I 'aven't changed one ayota! He grinned with a resolute cheeriness.

Jimmy stole a quick look at his wristwatch. "No, no – looking good," he lied. "So good to see you after all this time, H. Really good...."

There was some shouting in the foyer now, and many of those coming in had turned back to check the disturbance.

Meanwhile, Hereward was unravelling a knitted rainbow scarf from around his neck. Pointing to the life-size cut out to Jimmy's right, he winked. "It's all going well again, mate? The writing like? I kept an eye out for you, but it all went a bit quiet. I always said you were the one out of all of us who would go the distance!"

Through the crowd in the foyer, Jimmy could see a disturbance: the odd flailing limb, or shout of protest   "Aye, that you did, H..."

Hereward forced a wider smile. "And you got yourself hitched, as well, I see? To the cookery lady on the telly!" Hereward paused, placing a skinny gnarled finger on across his lips. "Not Nigella. The other one..." His eyes lit up. "Jackie Kennedy!"

Jimmy looked again at the clock and knocked the pads of his fingers against his thumb. What was happening outside? And where was Lefevre? In four minutes they were supposed to start. "Aye. That'll be Katherine. Katherine Kennedy. Seven, eight years now. Somethin' like that." He straightened hid body and gathered his notes together. "Look, Hereward: it's great to catch up..."

Hereward Double-Barrelled leaned in. "So what happened to Jas? Always thought you and her would be a permanent item?"

Hearing her name, Jimmy looked up. It had been a long time since it had been given voice – longer still his own. Without looking up, he said: "Not seen her for years, pal. Hey - why don't you grab yourself a seat before they're all taken?"

Hereward stared at him for a moment. He seemed disappointed by their encounter. He draped his scarf back around his neck and rested his walking stick on the bench. He began rummaging around in his pockets for a time, his tongue lolling about his lips. After a time, he retrieved a dog-eared business card clenched between his knuckles. "Keep in touch, this time, me old china, hey?" He jerked his head towards the auditorium. "I'll fuck off now."

Without reading it, Jimmy tucked the card inside his jacket, as Hereward hobbled towards the rows of seats.

With two minutes to go, there was still no sign of Lefevre. Whatever was happening outside was ongoing. Curiosity getting the better of him, Jimmy headed for the entrance.

He looked through the gaps between the heads and the shoulders of the onlookers. At the epicentre of the disturbance, a sharp-elbowed streak of a man goaded two security guards. Lefevre was there too.

The newcomer was an anomaly. His movements were angular, twitchy, disconcerting, like he was conducting some demented orchestra.   The sides of his head were shaved; he wore a shapeless flat cap, the peak of which cast a shadow over his face. Ribbons of cord-like ginger dredds snaked down his denim vest.

Fixating on the largest security guard, he shoved the guard's shoulder with long, rigid fingers. The guard held both his gaze and his position with an impassive expression as trouble-maker continued to jig around him with a queer, taunting expression on his face. As Jimmy watched, the tall man's left elbow caught one of the display stands, spilling copies of Jimmy's books across the floor, a catalyst to further trouble.

Jimmy saw Cassie, Lefevre's PA, and Alfie now appearing at the top of the stairway leading off the foyer. Alfie had his fist scrunched around a carrier bag – Jimmy guessed that it contained purchases from the store on the lower floor. Jimmy moved to step forward, but noticed that Cassie, clocking the intruder, had begun to usher Alfie back down the stairwell.

But the boy was curious and resisted. The gangly, unkempt man was a crude, vociferous freak show, a cartoon baddie. Alfie shrill laugh stopped him in his tracks. There was a moment when the boy and the intruder locked eyes – slight but nevertheless significant – and the tall man's face split into a knowing, leering grin.

His was a face that, even from a distant vantage point, Jimmy found unsettling: a broken stick of chalk for a nose, with a disconcerting distance between the cavernous, flared nostrils and a thin upper lip. A large jaw cradled a jagged rim of stained teeth, ugly groynes on a storm-savaged beach. Beneath the jawline, inked spiderwebs tangled with the raw sinews of his neck. His gaze flitted over the crowd, basking in the chaos.

He spat his words into the security guard's face: "What's with your shit, mate? You askin' everyone that, or only us?" He was slapping his own chest and swinging round on an inoffensive middle-aged woman who, to her misfortune, had arrived late. "Go on: ask her too." He bent down and grabbed a copy of Jimmy's book, copies of which now lay scattered across the floor of the foyer. "Here, Lady: you gonna buy a copy of this shit? Cos Hitler here says otherwise, you can piss off - ain't that right, pal?" His head jerked in and out as he spoke. The woman stepped backwards, the curls of her permed head bobbing in alarm.

For once restrained Lefevre observed the man with folded arms and a frown, allowing the tableau play out until he picked his moment to intervene. Jimmy willed him to move events on - he should have been be addressing the audience by now. Glaswegian roots tugging his core, Jimmy inched forwards with curled fists, compelled to pitch in when, without warning, he caught sight of another player joining the stage. With arms raised to calm the aggressor, a young woman had come to the fore. She stood with her back to Jimmy, her bare arms and cascading blonde dreadlocks suggested she might be a companion to the intruder. Her voice and movements, though, were more those of peacemaker. She spoke in a low, urgent voice that penetrated the affray: "Spider, leave it…"

Her companion wasn't listening. He was still preoccupied with the larger security guard, prodding him in the chest, goading further. The security guard took his upper arm and his response was to grab the guard's shoulders. In a sudden sequence of ungainly grapples, the two men were staggering backwards, the tall man grasping the security guard's waist as they fell through a series of imperfect circles - a twisting tangle of limbs that crashed to the ground.

The crowed around them pulled back, and Jimmy could see past.

Now the second guard was pitching in and their combined efforts had the man under control in no time: one pinning his arms behind his back, the other pushing the side of his face to the ground. Like the playground bully's, his grin straddled between humiliation and fruitless defiance.

The second guard hauled him upright. Now sitting up, his chest rose and fell, his mouth still hanging open. Lefevre chose the moment to intervene. Unbuttoning his jacket, he crouched down. He moved his head in close and met the tall man's eye, the two of them measuring each other's worth. The younger woman was still there; she was saying something to her companion, and he turned towards her, a sneer curling over his ugly wide mouth. With reluctance, he slumped into acquiescence.

The guards released their grip, and the tall man shook himself, like an unrepentant stray dog. He allowed Lefevre to take his arm and lead him away from the lecture hall. The young woman, still with her back to Jimmy, followed.

Jimmy caught a very quick action – perhaps Lefevre stuffing something into the breast pocket of the denim jerkin – it was hard to tell. He headed back into the lecture theatre, where he'd wait for Lefevre to join him.

Lefevre did not take his time. In minutes, he was breezing back through the doors, buttoning his jacket back up. Jimmy looked at his watch again: five minutes past the hour. He gestured towards the doors, now closed to the foyer. "What the hell was that all about? That idiot was wired tae the moon."

Lefevre looked around the packed theatre, with his fixed smile. "I'll tell you another time. It's all taken care of." He grabbed Jimmy's water glass, emptied it into the jug and knocked a fork against the rim. He took in the audience. "I – erm – hope you enjoyed the entertainment that we laid on for you in the foyer, ladies and gentlemen…" There was a polite peal of laughter as the audience settled. "I'm sure that there are thousand dazzling conversations going on out there that I am rudely interrupting – but we are now running a little late…"

Lefevre was a confident compere: his Ivy League charm won over a crowd with ease. Listening to his smooth baritone and erudite vocabulary, Jimmy was, not for the first time, struck with the oddness that it was he, the roughly-hewn Glaswegian dockhand's son, that the audience had come to see. There was the matter of soul, though. His was a poet's, through and through. He suspected Lefevre had sold his soul some time ago.

Following a series of rehearsed housekeeping points, Lefevre eased himself into a flattering portrait of his subject that had evolved over the years of their acquaintance. Much of this was familiar to Jimmy, and some moments bore resemblance to the truth. But it was while Lefevre was still speaking, that Jimmy's peripheral vision caught a small chink of light appearing beyond the top row of the auditorium. A door slid ajar, and it grew to a vertical beam, dazzling him at first, like morning sun finding a gap in the curtains.

Although no more than a mere silhouette, the late comer was the very same young woman who had accompanied the trouble-maker in the foyer. To his relief, she was now unaccompanied. The ease with which she tripped down the central stairway threw up sharp contrasts with the uncoordinated chaos caused earlier by her companion - her steps were quick and light, and she walked barefoot, a battered pair of Doc Marten boots held between her fingers. A frayed, hand-knitted tank-top slipped to expose the smooth brown skin of her shoulder.

As she descended, she asserted herself as an incongruous yet compelling addition to the large space: her aura was ebullient and busy. Heads turned as she passed.

From his vantage point, Jimmy could see three, perhaps four available spaces. He wanted to point them out to her, but daren't interrupt Lefevre's flow.

In time, she spotted somewhere to sit. Her movement across the row was more clumsy than it needed to be, her choosing to either greet or apologise to everyone who half-stood to let her pass.

She sat down and Jimmy was brought back by some loud applause.

"Mr. Dunbar?" Jimmy looked to Lefevre. His publicist's face urged him on: *this is where you take over, buddy.*

"Aye... aye... of course..." He waved in the direction of his publicist. "Sorry to be caught off-guard. Sometimes I resign myself to the fact that he's never going to shut the fuck up." There was an affectionate ripple of laughter, during which Jimmy unbuttoned his jacket. Without looking, he groped for the object of the moment: the little red and black volume of poetry spelt out his latest take on modern life.

He cleared his throat. "It's certainly, erm... a great honour to be here at Southbank. It's been a wee while."

His tried to dismiss thoughts of the young woman There was, he conceded, a need to distract himself; to get back to business; and he and forced himself to look across to other faces. The demographics of his audience were disappointing: predominantly white, ageing and middle-classed. Feminine rather than masculine. There was a time when he would have glared at them with contempt: *look on my work, ye mighty, and despair.* He would have given them what they craved: challenge, controversy, ambivalence. Now, with a few lost and unproductive years between him and them, he felt more beholding.

There was a tremor in his fingers as they fluttered over his notes. He cleared his throat. "You know, for me, this talking bit – the part where I introduce my own poems – is something that, at best, is superfluous, at worst ironic. I didnae mean to offend anyone by that." He frowned. "But what I mean to say is: the words, *my* words - I feel they should speak for themselves. I always have. As soon as you feel the need to start to explain something, you take away that mystery –right? It's like, I dunno, a stand-up having to explain a joke..."

It bothered him that the audience was silent. He took a slow slug of water, and felt his eye drawn to where the young woman was sat. For reasons his mind couldn't fathom, he found himself going off-script. "There was a time way back, when some deluded sod considered my poems good enough to get into this wee anthology for schools." His face creased into a smile. "I say 'wee': nearly every school in the bloody country had to endure it. Ten thousand fifteen year-olds forced to answer exam questions on my random ruminations. Anyways, I remember this wee lassie – fourteen, maybe fifteen years of age - once the gig's over, and every other bugger's wending their way home, she trots down to the front. *Mr. Dunbar?* she says. *Excuse me.* Good manners. *Yes, love?* says the less polite, Glaswegian hackett. I'm looking at my watch, thinking the pubs are about to open. She says, *That poem.* She names one of my poems she's been studying – I'm pretty sure it was *Waste Paper.* She looks at me with this keen young face. *I know it's all about writing,* she says. *But how do the references to 'pulp' and 'sap' fit in? Are they linked to another deeper meaning?* she asks." Jimmy pulled a face. "Deeper meaning? What does that even bloody mean? Deeper than what? But she's dead keen. So I say to her: *What d'you want the poem to mean, love?* This poor wee lass: she stands there. She might have coped with *What d'you think it means?* but *What d'you want it to mean?* So I go on, *If you want straightforward answers to questions and me to explain why I've used enjambment in the third stanza, you need to catch up wi' your teacher on the coach.* I shrug my shoulders at her, poor lass. *I write it down as it comes,* I say. She goes away, none the wiser, and I stand there feeling like a right cunt." Jimmy sighed. "But I guess a point of sorts was made." He frowned and straightened up. "And this is my theory…" He held the red and white volume above his head. "Once the words are out there, whatever you have written cannot be destroyed. In fact, it has to multiply. Two people who have read the same stretch of verse will, create two different readings. It's like alternative dimensions. Sliding doors. Afterwards, it becomes theirs: their version of my poem. I think that it's kind of symbiotic, the relationship between writer and reader. There is no need for any kind of prologue, introduction or preamble." He pointed again at the book. "I go into more detail about this in the forward." The audience laughed and Jimmy felt able to relax a little. The connection with the audience, he remembered, was one of things he had missed most when he'd stopped writing. With an audience, there was no answering back, no guilt-trips...

He breathed out.

He'd almost managed to forget the young latecomer, when she chose that very moment to raise her head.

She was looking straight at him now.

When she'd first entered the hall he had been struck more by her presence. Now, for what was an immeasurable amount of time, he saw only the eyes: startling and clear, the deepest green; a thin metal bar piercing the bridge of her nose between them. Wide-set and intense, and now tearful, they held him until he could scarcely breathe. Her face was heart-shaped, her chin slender; her mouth full and petulant, a silver ring tight around the centre of her lower lip. She held her upper frame so still, only the slight rise and fall of her exposed collar bone betraying animation. Her arms were strong, their muscles defined. Whatever he said, wherever he chose to look, he kept coming back to her over and over.

Filled with an inexplicable panic, he tried to look away. Finding his own notes again, he scanned the meaningless rows of type, and he felt his throat tighten. He straightened his glasses, fighting in vain for composure.

He moved his book over to the lectern, and stood behind it, grabbing each corner. As he pressed hard, his nails turned a dark crimson.

A polite cough nearby startled him. Lefevre was sat on a high stool to one side. He dropped his gaze back to the little red and black book before him. He looked over at Lefevre and raised his eyebrows.

"*Read a poem,*" Lefevre mouthed.

"So," Jimmy faltered, "M'laddie here says I should stop gabbling and read some of this stuff out..." He had corners of the pages he'd intended to read from folded over, but now the integrity and honesty of the words on the pages felt more like the plaintive cries for attention of some dying diva.

He gave voice to the eponymous title: "Anamnesis", thinking how hollow it sounded to his own ears. A silence fell over the auditorium. The girl's eyes still burned into him, he knew. He searched the far corners of his memory. She had to be too young to be one of the shameful conquests in his blackout days of yore? Groping its way across the early lines, his voice cracked and faltered at the doorway of the second stanza.

He had to find his way into this.

The stub of his forefinger trailed across the marks on the page and he began to read.

Moments passed and he found that, by some minor miracle, he had staggered into the final page of the poem.

A stillness hung over the auditorium. For a long time, he dared not look up from the page, expecting to see an ocean of disappointed, disparaging faces. Often, moments of success were mere punctuation marks to statements of failure. When he did look up, he felt compelled to find her - the young woman with the extraordinary face. But there was a space where she had been. Jimmy stepped forwards and looked up the steep flight of steps, before glancing back towards the side exits. He scanned the rows, one after another, trying to find her face. Nowhere. There was a space where she had been, and the top door swinging on its hinges. He felt a flutter of panic.

From a high open window, the hum of the Southbank traffic kicked in and someone in the front row blew their nose. His old pal, Hereward, was still there, his own copy tucked under an arm, on the verge of tears. A lady behind him joined in with enthusiasm, only pausing to dab at her face with a handkerchief. The applause gained momentum to roll around the vast space like a Summer storm, summoning a strange energy and momentum. Someone got to their feet. Someone else followed.

Jimmy allowed himself a slow smile: they liked the poem.

Now, Lefevre was walking towards him, hand held out.

"The girl," Jimmy whispered, as the other man reached him. "Did you see her?"

Lefevre looked down. "I didn't see a girl." He turned back to the audience, his expression switching in an instant. Taking Jimmy's arm, Lefevre waited for the applause to die. "Ladies and gentleman..." He beamed at the crowd, shouting over them. "I give you Jimmy Dunbar: those words! Truly humbling. Sincerely."

Still on their feet, the audience applauded again. When it had died down, Lefevre became more matter-of-fact. "I know you'll all be thrilled to hear that this most talented of poets has agreed to take questions about his extraordinary new publication. And, I think we'll be treated to some more readings. Yes, Mr. Dunbar?"

Jimmy blinked. "Aye. Of course." He sank back down onto his stool, caught between confusion and relief.

Lefevre beamed. "Oh – and the plug - if you haven't yet

purchased 'Anamnesis', we have lots of shiny new copies, at a reduced price of course, outside in the foyer. Mr. Dunbar will be signing copies once we're all done in here." He grasped Jimmy's shoulder. "Now: who'd like to start the ball rolling with some questions for the main man-of-the-moment?"

The questions came quick and fast – polite at first: why was he writing again after a hiatus of five years? Had the public response to the Dundee tribute poem rekindled the relationship with his readers? What did *Anamnesis* actually mean? Was he planning to tour as he used to?

For a short time, the reporters bided their time, queuing up like vultures on a telegraph wire, high above the dying old beast. Finally, one of the younger hacks pitched in with a loaded question.

Jimmy took a deep breath and handled it. He was used to these and had learnt, the hard way and through some tuition from Lefevre, that it paid to anticipate. They would do this, Lefevre said; they would try to shake his cage until the Jimmy Dunbar of old – hot-headed hellraising no-fucks-to-give Jimmy Dunbar, ripped through the skin of this tired, greying and overweight effort of a man before them and all hell broke loose. "Like The Hulk," Lefevre said, by way of literary allusion.

Jimmy sighed. No, he said: he couldn't give a shit if the literati sneered at his poetry. It was poetry for the masses, he said. Sure, he always appreciated a new, younger audience; but was way too uncool and lazy to change his style to please the next generation, he said. "Self-deprecation would disarm the haters," Lefevre had told him.

With inevitability, questions of a more personal nature followed. Yes, Katherine Kennedy *was* wholly compliant in his desire to use this latest poetry as both an expose and exploration of forays into past relationships and heavy drinking. No, the absence of his celebrity wife today should in *no* way be seen as an indictment of his writing or his choice to bear his indiscretions.

"Look," he said, grasping the lectern and leaning forward. He was careful to address the whole audience, not the aggressive faction of it. "Katherine's a busy lady, okay? She has four or five companies to run; she's promoting the pilot for a new series; she'd finished adding the final details to her latest book and schools' project; hell, at a guess, she's propping up the Forth bloody Bridge as we speak..." It pleased him to draw a laugh from the audience. He held the book up again, as if to remind them why they were there. "She's cool with all of this. We're open about our pasts, the two of us. And I'm here because of this, not because of her. *Anamnesis* is, in part, about another Jimmy Dunbar – one that belongs to another time, another set of rules. The poems were an opportunity to exorcise a few daemons: for the new me to come to find some peace with the old me. .."

One of the journalists pressed him: the poem he'd read – who was the subject? Jimmy scratched his beard. For a split second, the years rolled away and he thought of Jasmine again, the sounds of her sobbing as he stole across the fire escape and away from her burden. Despite that familiar cold breeze snaking up his spine, he did his best to sound calm and reasonable. "You cannae stop folk speculating," he said. "But the subjects deserve the dignity of anonymity. I'd like tae move on if you don't mind?"

A young woman with a high pink fringe sat among the reporters. She had thick rimmed glasses, an arch, disinterested face. She caught their attention. "Mr. Dunbar? Danni Brennan, Belfast Literary Review. Forgive my brutality, but even a noted misogynist writing about famous ex-lovers couldn't be naïve enough to believe that your readers aren't going to speculate? And doesn't controversy, after all, sell more copies? Your last collection sold, what, under two thousand copies, compared to half a million back in the late Nineties?" Jimmy made to speak, but the young reporter persisted: "I actually quite liked the poem; but it doesn't take a great leap of the imagination to recognise your subject as being the artist Jasmine Kelly?" Jimmy's stomach turned over, and he gawped like a fish, trying to get a word in edgeways. "Weren't you the working man's Ted Hughes and Sylvia Plath of your day... kind of?" She looked down to her pad, a tiny smile playing on her lips. "Kelly disappeared from the art scene what: ten, fifteen years ago at least? What's there to lose from being honest with your public?"

She had paused for an answer. But the damage was done. Lefevre was looking down at his itinerary, pretending not hear any of it. Jimmy knew what he was thinking: *I warned you that this would happen, buddy.* At least Kat wasn't there to hear it...

Jimmy pursed his lips, unnerved by the rise of a spirit from past times. It had been two decades since he'd heard her name spoken in public. He swallowed. "I'm sorry to have to repeat myself: I won't be drawn on who any of these poems are about. Famous or otherwise, these are all real people, with real feelings." He tapped his chest. "As am I. Hey - I'm happy to talk about how I felt, what I was going through. Just not who it was with." He eyeballed the reporter with a faint hint of Glaswegian menace. "I'd like to park it there, missy. Okay?" She tilted her head to the side a little with a sardonic smile. She moved her head down and she was writing again. Shit, he thought. Missy was a feminist to boot.

A short while later, a snake of people were forming a polite queue around the edges of the foyer, most with copies of the book and a half-filled flute of sparkling wine. From his desk, Jimmy scoured the foyer. Of the young woman, there was still no sign. He looked up into the eager face of someone who must have been pushing retirement. "It's Claire," she said, looking at the promise of the empty page. "I love the way you write."

Jimmy smiled. "You're too kind." He resumed his round-shouldered crouch and scribbled her name over the flyleaf in a large, unruly script.

He remembered Lefevre's words after Kat had connected them, over ten years earlier. "See the signing as the key opportunity to make a connection with your fanbase. Look the punters in the eye. Meeting you is a big deal to many of them: they'll tell their folks about it when they get home."

For Jimmy, it never shaped up to be the ego-trip that he'd looked forward to. For a start, there were always the amateur writers: *Oh! So you write too? Well, good luck – keep plugging away! Do you mind if I don't look at it right now – I have this wee queue to work my way through! Pop it down there, and I'll pass it over to my agent.* Often, ten or more ragged, stapled and unsolicited efforts would pass his way at such events. In all the years they had worked together, neither he or Lefevre had taken them further than the nearest waste bin of the particular venue they happened to be working.

Jimmy signed more books and the time passed quickly enough. Alfie, who had been distracted by another MacDonald's sojourn with Cassie, now found his way back, squeezing around the boxes of books, and pushing ahead to wriggle onto his father's lap. He smelt of fries and was was wielding a grease-smothered plastic *Happy Meal* toy, already broken.

The boy's bony bottom dug into Jimmy's thighs. "Well, wee man," Jimmy said. "What you been up to?" He ruffled the boy's hair, and planted a kiss among his untidy brown curls. He smelled of sleep.

Alfie picked up Jimmy's marker pen and the cap, clicking on, off, on, off. "Daddy? Can we go back to our hotel now?"

Jimmy took in his surroundings. Most of the boxes around him were empty – sales and signings had exceeded expectations, perhaps because Lefevre had done little to contradict the ill-founded rumours of Kat's presence. Behind them, Cassie slit open one of the remaining boxes with a pair scissors. "A wee while longer." He felt the boy's body tighten in protest. "If you're good, I'll find you a wee treat."

"A hot chocolate?" said the boy.

"The third today but aye, if you like."

Jimmy continued signing the books with the boy on his lap. As the queue dwindled, he yawned, and stretched his arms out straight in from of him, as another copy was pushed his way over the table. The recipient was obscured by the Alfie, and by now, Lefevre's tips on how to keep engaged with punters rang hollow – he couldn't even be bothered to look up. "Who am I making this one out to?" he asked.

He hovered over the blank flyleaf and watched the edge of the table as he waited for an answer.

He saw her fine fingers first of all. Olive-skinned, with sepia henna vines curling around each to snake over the wrist. Heavy jewellery, bangles, leather wristbands, unpainted, bitten nails.

Without looking up, he knew it was her - the young woman from the lecture theatre.

His grip on the pen tightened. He felt his arms slide away from the table and curl around the boy's waist as he sensed her taking both of them in in. He sensed her body bridle, and heard an intake of breath before she spoke .

Alfie stared up at her, mesmerised. Jimmy lifted his head until his vision was fixed to a point beneath her mouth. A silver stud pierced the flesh above her chin.

He tried to sound normal. "What d'you want me to scrieve, lassie?"

For a moment, he thought she was moving to leave, but something in his voice stopped her in her tracks. She came back again, her arms falling to her sides.

As Alfie slid off his lap, Jimmy found himself getting to his feet to meet her. She was still barefoot.

She was shorter up close than how she had appeared when coming down the steps, but this took nothing away from her presence. She looked from Jimmy to Alfie: startled, but attempting to regain her composure. Pulling her shoulders back, she reached down and pushed the book back between them once more.

Her voice was low but sure. She glared at him with fury. "How about *To my darling daughter, love Daddy*?" she said.

Four: London -the evening of Wed 30th November 2016

Jimmy Dunbar watched his son sleeping on his side in the hotel bed that they'd been sharing. The boy wore the clothes of the day before and his shoulders rose and fell as his lips burred with little snores. The corners of his mouth were stills stained with ketchup.

Jimmy flicked the ash from the tip of his cigarette into a coke can. He recalled his last words to Alfie before sleep: "We'll give your Ma a call in the morning, son. Promise."

Shit. That wasn't going to happen.

He took a long drag, and, as he had done so many times over the sleepless night before, he replayed the fateful moment in the lobby.

To my darling daughter, love Daddy.

Before waiting for any response, she had turned to leave. He had grabbed her wrist.

Now, Jimmy rested his cigarette across the lip of the can, and grasped his own wrist. He was a strong man - had he hurt her? Even at the time, he'd been in awe of how fragile she felt, her bones beneath his fingers. How would he know? He had never held her hand to lead across a busy road or away from a school pick-up. He recalled how her body had stiffened, how her fingers were rigid and splayed. He'd held on long enough to be able to scribble his number across the flyleaf of the book. Only after that had he let go. She'd stared at him, aghast. Whether she was appalled by his force or the audacity of her own action, it was impossible to tell; but he felt shamed by her reaction nevertheless.

Whatever she had felt, she had decided to take the book with his number scribbled inside.

Turning away, she'd pushed back through the throng of people. Jimmy had become aware of the rippling controversy that spread outwards: her devastating words echoed around the space, a fierce contagion spreading across the lips of onlookers, mobile phones held aloft to make a permanent record of the moment.

Without thinking, he'd called out to her and there was the briefest glimpse of her as she looked back over her bare shoulder, making her way towards the lift at the far side of the foyer. She was jabbing at the button, mascara streaking her cheeks.

The lift door had opened. Inside, unsuspected, the tall man from the earlier altercation stood waiting for her.

Other people crowded his line of sight, but he knew she was there for a moment, struggling to enter the lift, whilst her companion tried to prevent her from leaving. Jimmy had moved from behind his desk but, by the time he could see the lift door again, she and the other man had gone.

Now, in the quiet of the hotel room, the shrill ringtone of his mobile jolted Jimmy back to the present. Once Alfie had fallen asleep, he had been staring at it until a grey dawn penetrated the thin curtains of their room. For hours, he had waited, in vain, for her call.

Now, as it rang, the boy stirred. Jimmy smuggled his phone into the en-suite. He looked at the screen, but it was a blur: he'd left his glasses by the bedside. He lifted the phone to his ear.

"Hello?"

"Jimmy: what the fuck, is going on?"

"Kat?"

He cupped his hand over the phone and peered around the

corner of the door to check on Alfie. Jimmy felt grateful that he was still sleeping. He listened again. For a moment, he thought she'd hung up, but the ultimatum, when it came, was clear and abrupt. "Never mind. I want you to listen to me. I want you to bring my son back on the next flight home. If you don't, there will be consequences."

Jimmy sank down on the toilet seat and leant forward. "Hang on, Sweetheart! What are you talking about..?"

"Shut up. I haven't finished. You get a taxi to Heathrow, and you get him on the next flight available. Whether it's Perpignan, Toulouse or Gerona – I don't bloody care, as long he gets back to me fast. And after you've done that, call your solicitor." There was a brief pause. "I want a divorce." The line went dead.

Jimmy stared at the phone for a while before moving back into the bedroom. *Call ended.* He walked back into the room, and stood over the sleeping body of his son. His arm was curled around his favourite blanket, and it rose and fell with his breathing.

In less than a minute, a text followed the call. Kat again – no message save a URL link to a news story:

Jimmy Dunbar: Chapter and Verse

Dundee Disaster Poet confronted by woman who claims to be estranged daughter during book signing in Southbank

Gracie Wenn 22:00 GMT, 30 November 2016

Writer and broadcaster Jimmy Dunbar was unavailable for comment last night following an incident at a Southbank book launch during which a woman, reported to be in her late twenties, approached him claiming to be his estranged daughter.

Dunbar, 45, was promoting the publication of new poetry – his first following an eight-year hiatus – entitled **Anamnesis.** *The collection is purported to amount to a veiled confession of previous misdemeanours over the years, including his tempestuous relationship with 'Cool Britannia' artist, Jasmine Kelly. He had been giving a short talk at the Miller Lecture Theatre at the Southbank Centre ahead of signing copies of the new publication. No stranger to controversy, Dunbar achieved notoriety by making a series of drunken appearances on various late-night chat shows in the late nineties. In 2007, he hit the headlines by being arrested for drunk-driving having publicly declared himself to be a recovering alcoholic three months before. He proved himself capable of winning back the hearts of the British public, however, with a moving poem attributed to the victims of the Dundee School bus Tragedy of April last year.*

Preceding the controversy between Jimmy and the young woman, reported to be one Hope Kelly, aged 28, from the Brighton area, there were unconfirmed reports of an earlier scuffle with security guards at the event involving two members of the public, identified by those involved to be Kelly and an older male, as yet unnamed. Eye-witnesses claim that Dunbar was not present when these earlier altercations had taken place.

Kelly is reported to have confronted the writer while queuing for books being signed. Witnesses said that she left the building after that.

Dunbar, who lives with his wife, celebrated TV chef Katherine Kennedy, in the South of France with their five-year-old son, Alfie, left the venue following the incident and refused to answer any questions. His publicist, who also represents Kennedy, refused to comment on the claims made by the young woman, adding that he was not expecting his client to make a statement to the press in the near future.

Related Content

- **BBC announces Katherine Kennedy Christmas Special** 23

Oct - London

- **Katherine Kennedy wins ratings war with cookery crossover show** 1 Jul – Manchester
- **Profile: Katherine Kennedy** 5 Feb 14

Poet: 'How Katherine Kennedy helped me battle my demons' 10 Oct 09

Five: The South Coast – Thursday 1st December 2016

The following afternoon, Jimmy Dunbar sat on the sand, his back against the sea wall. He looked to where the pebbled slope of the shoreline curved into the horizon. There, three figures - two men and a boy - stood a short distance apart, connected by a canary yellow kite that dived and strafed in defiance against the slate December skies. One of the men passed its reel to the boy, crouched behind him, and took his wrists to help feed the bright diamond head back towards the heavens.

As it soared, shouts of victory lifted into the air to be lost amongst the screaming of the gulls that circled the heavy underbelly of clouds. The boy turned around to face Jimmy and waved with youthful vigour.

Jimmy acknowledged him with a raised hand, his expression unchanging. The cold crept through his clothing and into his bones, and he pulled the collar of his jacket about his neck and tucked his scarf inside.

Jimmy had fished out Hereward's business card not long after the phone call from Kat. He needed a bolthole, and the evening before, Hereward had offered one. His old friend proved himself to be a man to honour a promise: there was always room for a mate, he'd said. And, true to his word, he'd been waiting in the hotel lobby for at least half an hour, his stick resting between his legs, as the morning staff hauled cages of fresh bedding to and fro. Even though he'd seen Hereward some twelve hours before, the drama that had interceded in the meantime had meant that it had taken Jimmy a while to realise that the old man reading the fire regulations was the very same 'H' whom he'd known all those years ago.

Upon seeing them in the lobby, Hereward had eased himself to his feet with a grimace. A grin through a life map of leather skin. "Not gonna lie, Dunny: well chuffed that you took us up on the offer so quick!" There had been a spontaneous hug. Jimmy could feel the bones of his spine through the cheesecloth shirt.

Taking the line southwards from Waterloo, they'd kept to the same side of the river: two men and a small boy travelling in silence, fighting an incoming tide of grim-faced, plugged-in commuters. An hour and twenty minutes later, a dented cream-coloured Land Rover had picked them up from the short stay car park outside Brighton station. A man, shy of forty and donning an ill-fitting combat jacket rested against the passenger door. He sucked from a stubby roll-up that he pinched between his fingers. Seeing them approach, he tossed the butt into the gutter.

"Dunny – this is Cliff," Hereward had said, tossing his stick onto the well beneath the front passenger's seat. He added, "Cliff helps me out back at the hostel." Jimmy took him in: dark, close-cropped Action Man hair, a plasticine nose, a shy mouth cut into the side of his face and dark, and doleful amber stare. With his rounded shoulders, and arms bent at the elbows, he gave the impression of a featherweight boxer caught on the ropes in the final rounds.

He had made to greet him, but Cliff, was already turning away. Walking with a pronounced limp, he had addressed Alfie with a high raw whisper of a voice. "Alright, man? What's your name?"

"Alfie."

Cliff nodded, and zipped up his combat jacket. "I'm Cliff."

Once they were inside, the vehicle had growled and spluttered away from the station car park. Jimmy had stolen a look at his mobile: four more missed calls from Kat, another three from Lefevre. Nothing from the girl. He wondered if he had written his number correctly. Looking up, he saw Cliff watching him through the rear-view mirror. He had tucked the phone back inside his pocket.

After half an hour, they turned off the dual carriageway and into a coastal town a few miles East of Brighton. As they drew near, Hereward jutted his stick towards the unforgiving, grey sea that had come into view, and smiled back at Alfie. "Want a butcher's at the seaside, little man?"

Jimmy nudged the boy. "Course he would. Wouldn't you, laddie?"

And so, here they were: a short stretch of beach where Jimmy Dunbar, cradling a polystyrene coffee cup, looked out to the three figures on the sand, by turn hobbling and leaping in the mid-distance.

Out across a pale, muted ocean, gulls screamed their insolence and the air turned cold. Jimmy rested his coffee against the wall. Reaching inside his jacket, he extracted a pocket notebook and pen.

Jimmy hung over a blank page for a while. He looked out to where the sea met the sky.

The young woman. His daughter. Without doubt, she was his. He saw himself in her face, heard his voice in hers; he knew that the anger and the fear and the passion that drove her came from the very same source as his own.

When he looked down, the page was filled with words he could not recall writing.

Jimmy ripped out the page, folded it, and tucked it into his top jacket pocket. Getting to his feet, he looked for the three figures on the sand again. Alfie had seen him stand, and was calling out, but the sea-breeze carried his words over the waves.

Jimmy blew on his hands, cupped them around to his mouth,

and yelled. "Put your scarf back on, laddie! You'll catch your death o' cold!"

As he stepped forwards, he could hear Alfie's words: "Dad! I flied it on my own. Did you see?"

"Aye," Jimmy walked towards his son. "But you've nae got the right clothes on to be outside for so long. Your ma would have a blue fit if she could see yous." He addressed Hereward as he got nearer. "D'you nae think we should head off soon before it gets any colder?"

Cliff was taking off his own coat and giving it to the boy. He wore a t-shirt underneath. Alfie pleaded, "Can we stay for longer? Please?"

As Jimmy came near, Cliff turned to face the sea. He fished out a battered tobacco tin from the back pocket of his jeans and rolled a cigarette.

"It's too cold," Jimmy said to Alfie. "And you're tired. We all are" He watched the boy's face fall, and it struck him that the two of them had never flown a kite together. He gave a weak smile and ruffled his son's head. "We'll come back again soon, eh? Maybe when the weather's better..."

Hereward rubbed his hands together. "Right," he said. "Let's get you back to our gaff. A hot drink, and a guided tour!"

The evening was falling. They followed a deserted main road for fifteen minutes before turning onto a lesser road that narrowed to become a wide track. Either side, the South Downs rolled away, scattered with windswept trees, shrubs, small dwellings and looming wind turbines. The sea beyond this was a flat ribbon of grey.

The Land Rover hauled them up a steep incline. At the track's

THE GOOD MORNING GIRL

end there was a hamlet. They pulled into a steep drive, and Cliff pulled hard on the handbrake. He sat still for a moment before pulling his keys from the ignition. Before them, a tall three-storey building with tall arched windows and a sturdy green door stood proud. Scattered across front yard, maritime paraphernalia - driftwood, lobster pots, large battered orange buoys, all tangled in frayed blue rope – added curiosity.

"Welcome to The Old Schoolhouse Hostel," said Hereward. He reached for the passenger door handle. "Let's get inside. Bloody brass monkeys, innit?" Once outside, he rested his stick against the car and rooted around his person to find the keys. Reaching the building, he wrapped his hand around the brass handle and rattled the key around the lock for a while. Cliff stood behind him with their luggage.

Once inside, they encountered a small lobby, cluttered with curios and artefacts. Alfie mooched around, touching every object. Leaning towards him, Hereward said, "At the top of the stairs, we've got a treasure chest packed with dressing-up things. And a brass telescope that used to belong to a pirate."

Cliff dropped the bags and pointed towards a cast iron stairway. His speech was slow and deliberate. "Come on. I'll show you." He turned towards Jimmy, but made no eye contact. "If that's okay with your dad."

"Aye. Sure," said Jimmy.

The guest room was small but not without its charms: long and narrow, it was lined with scuffed skirting boards and mis-matched, garish cushions and rugs. A bunk bed with a lower double occupied one end; a tiny en-suite with dripping shower-head the other. Alone in the room, Jimmy lifted their weekend bag onto the lower bunk and began to unpack. He pulled out Alfie's ironed and folded Captain America top, his green fleece, those little rolls of socks and held on to warm thoughts of the boy, his sturdy little body, the flawless brown skin. It seemed no time since it had been nappies and baby-grows and booties. He found himself thinking of the clothes she, his daughter, had worn – clothes he had never seen: party dresses, nativity play costumes, new uniforms...

All of a sudden, he felt tired. Pressing his fingers into the hollows of his temples, he sat down beside the case. Back at the hotel, he had congratulated himself for resisting the mini-bar. Were he beside it now, he was not sure that his resolve would be as strong.

Buzzing in his jacket pocket made him start. He fumbled for it as it got caught in the lining. Lefevre.

"James? The hotel told me you'd checked out? Where are you?"

Jimmy walked over to a Velux that was positioned above a small sink in the centre of the room. With the phone held to his ear, he ducked his head so that he could see out. He squinted, watching the dark hull of a container ship drag across the horizon. As evening fell, the little bunk room was beginning to take on a queer light. Objects indiscernible by day, now winked on the edges of the horizon. The distant shriek of an unidentifiable bird scratched the evening sky. "I'm staying with an old mate near Brighton. The laddie and I could do with a wee bit o' space."

"Right." There was an intake of breath. "James – we need to have a conversation."

Jimmy frowned. "What d'you mean?"

"Everyone's looking for this girl. It's all over social media." Jimmy braced himself. He knew what was coming next. "What she said. Is it... true?"

Jimmy stroked his chin. "Christ. I don't bloody know, do I? Aye, maybe…" His voice tailed off and he felt the blood drain from his face as shame engulfed him.

Lefevre wasted no time. "You had a conversation with Katherine yesterday, I hear. She's been trying to call you since. It's kinda embarrassing to have to point out that she's worried about the boy?" Another pause. "I'm presuming he is there with you…"

Jimmy shivered. A thin draft from the window passed across the back of his neck. He clicked a small bedside lamp on and drew the Velux blind down. "Of course he's bloody with me. " He straightened himself. "Tell Kat from me that Alfie is absolutely bloody fine. If she wants him back sooner, she'll need tae come for him. I'm no' leaving the UK at the moment. Not wi' this pish tae deal with."

"Listen James: I don't get paid to be a mediator between husband and wife. When she calls, it would be good if you took it, so I don't have to deal with all this crap." A period of silence ensued. "Look: I have a clash of interests here. I represent you. I also represent Katherine. Katherine is the lucrative client. To be brutal, you ain't."

Jimmy frowned. "What in the name of fuck are you going on about, Lefevre?"

Lefevre sighed. "There's never going to be an easy time to say this, James. I'm afraid that I can't represent you any longer."

Jimmy pulled a face. "Hang on a wee minute, sunshine. In the space of twenty-four hours, I've been confronted by someone claiming to be my long-lost daughter. I'm now being accused of kidnapping my own son; and on top o' that, I now find myself being pied by my publicist whilst on the verge of being served bloody divorce papers. You tell Katherine this: I'll do what I want when I'm bloody ready to do it, matey…" He threw this phone down on the bed in disgust. "Christ, the pompous wee shet!"

He got to his feet. He needed a drink.

Six: The next morning – Friday 2nd December 2016

Jimmy awoke to the screeching of gulls that scraped out the insides of his skull. The morning light sliced through a slit in the curtains like a merciless assassin.

He became aware of a polite yet insistent tapping at the door.

Turning away, Jimmy found his movements restrained by clothes he'd worn the day before. On the bedside table sat an empty Bourbon bottle and a drained tumbler.

He had been sober for eight months. Jimmy fumbled for his phone, his sight taking a while to adjust to the tiny text. More missed calls from Kat. He read the most recent text:

Carry on ignoring me. I'm coming to get my son.

"Shit," he muttered.

Beyond, the door had crept ajar. Hereward lingered on the threshold, bearing a mug of tea. His hand shook, and the liquid slopped over rim.

"Thought you might like a nice cuppa to sort you out, mate?" He glanced at the bedside table. "You found the booze cupboard, I see?"

Putting down his phone, Jimmy squinted at Hereward and reached out for the mug. "Aye, thanks. Sorry about that. I'll buy a replacement, of course." He knew he never would. He gazed about the room. Raised himself to a seating position, he planted his feet upon the floor. "It was only supposed to be a wee nip..." He scratched his beard, now aware of the quietness of the room. "Where's his lordship?"

"Alfie? Oh – he's had breakfast already. Cliff's taken him out to walk the dogs."

Jimmy nodded. He remembered waiting for the boy to drift off to sleep, sneaking out to find a drink. Beyond that, events got blurry.

He saw the open case on the upper bunk. "You... erm... found his clothes?"

Hereward nodded. He looked around the room before settling on Jimmy. "It's all good. Look - I'll leave you to sort yourself out, me old mucker. I'll be downstairs doing the brekkie, if you fancy a bite. Might take the edge off."

Jimmy was eying the bottom bunk as he slurped the tea, contemplating another hour, when Hereward popped his head back round the doorway again. "Oh – I almost forgot - the reason I came up here. I remembered something."

"What was that?" asked Jimmy.

"That lanky geezer creating a palaver at your do in London yesterday: it was bugging me all night. I've seen him around before. Sometimes he hangs about outside the one-stop in town – reckon he might be up to no good. But I seen him with your American guy as well."

Jimmy looked up. "Lefevre? Hang on... You saw Lefevre with that jalky from yesterday? When was this?"

Hereward shrugged. "Dunno. A month ago? Seeing them both together yesterday stirred something up here." He tapped the side of his head. Catching sight of Jimmy's frown, he dismissed the matter with a gesture. "I might be wrong. The old grey matter ain't what it used to be."

Jimmy repeated, "That cannae be right..." As he spoke, his

mobile rang from the floor, beside his bed. Stooping to retrieve the phone, he pushing his glasses back onto his head as he pulled faces at the screen. He let the call ring out without answering. "The missus again. She wants me to take Alfie back to France." He sniffed. "Oh – and I missed the best bit: she also wants a divorce! I'm on a fucking roll at the moment."

Hereward eyed him warily as he turned in the doorway. "I'll see you downstairs, yeah?"

Jimmy listened to the sounds of his slow shuffle moving down the corridor. He seemed to take forever. Collapsing on the bunk, he covered his face with a pillow.

Half an hour later, a brisk shower had him feel as though he had a claim, albeit slight, to be a part of the human race once more.

The Old Schoolhouse kitchen was an imposing high-ceilinged affair: a busy yet handsome space of sea-green metro tiles, an assortment of hanging pans, and gleaming brass surfaces. Hereward was sat on a high stool wearing soiled chef's whites. He was leaning on his elbow and resting his head on the heel of his hand, his hat pushed to the top of his head, with thin strands of long grey hair spilling through his fingers. Before him, lie scattered loose papers and open folders.

Jimmy cleared his throat. "Cooking the books, H?"

His friend looked up. He shut the two folders that were lying open, and moved them closer. "Not really, mate. Other business."

Jimmy shuffled over to a deep Belfast sink, and rinsed his mug in it. He filled it with cold water, and knocked it back. He thought of the empty bottle of bourbon back in the room, and fought the persistent tickle of craving at the pit of his throat. "Never had you down as running a gaff like this," he said. "How long have you been here?"

Hereward placed one folder on top of the other and folded his hands over them. "Been almost seven years."

Jimmy moved nearer, and, with some effort, heaved his body onto the stool beside Hereward's. His elbow jogged one of the folders, which fell to the flagstones below. Hereward let Jimmy retrieve it, and as he stopped to do so, he caught sight of pages of Hereward's awkward handwriting, and sheets with the letterhead of Brighton Social Services. As he returned the folder, a moment of awkwardness passed between them: questions that covered between the best part of three decades stood between them.

As he tidied his paperwork, Hereward decided to talk. "Funny thing is, the one bastard thing that almost done for me turned out to be a Godsend." He looked up. "Ten years ago to the day, I had a stroke. Didn't realise what it was at the time. First one felt like I'd been proper knocked out or something. Bit fuzzy afterwards, but I didn't think no more about it. Should've gone to the doctor's; couple of months later, along comes the proper job. I couldn't speak. I couldn't walk." He tapped the side of his head. "Totally scrambled up here."

"Christ," said Jimmy. "I'm sorry, H. I never realised."

Hereward continued. "Lucky for me, the business had been doin' well: I had the dosh to go private. Great team pulled me through, plus support from mates. But by that time, there was little point going back to publishing. I had people who could've taken over, but the clients weren't standing still, and the brain was too fried to deal with the stress. 'Time for a change, Hereward, old man,' I thought. Considered going abroad for a while – a little place by the sea in Spain, maybe, but it seemed to me that that would be a waiting-for-death scenario, which ain't like me. An estate agent mate gave me the wink about this gaff. So I came and had a butcher's." His eyes moved around the kitchen and glistened with pride. "The Old Schoolhouse was a tired old gal, but it was still love at first sight."

Jimmy looked around. "I dinnae get it, H. how does renovating a building ever get to be a slower pace of life than running a publishing business?"

Hereward scratched at his stubble. "It needed a kick up the arse: rewiring, lick of paint." He laughed. "I say all of that – I didn't intend to do any of it - knew I was too buggered to take it on myself, so I first came down, I got asking around at the village boozer nearby to see if there was anyone who could help. That's when Cliff's name came up."

"Oh yeah?" said Jimmy.

"Turns out he was renting a room above the post office. He wasn't a geezer for talking – he got on with the jobs, worked cash in hand. You see, Cliff's an ex-squaddie. You probably worked that one out. Poor bastard saw some serious head-fucking shit in Afghanistan, and on the Iraqi border before that. You can't even begin to imagine the stuff he went through, man. Bottled it all up for a while but it caught up with him. They ended up paying him off to get out. He bumbled around for a bit, fell into bad ways. Rode a bike while pissed and lost a leg in an accident: you might have seem his limp. And when he fell, there was no safety net. Nowhere to stay, no work. Knocks at every turn. They give you more support now, but not back in the day. He spent a couple of months on the streets until, some mates from school recognised him and helped him out. Got him a roof over his head, lined him up with a few odd-jobs. Even got him connected with a charity for veterans that helps out with counselling and the like. And that's about the time I met him. The work he did for me was first-class. There was nothing he couldn't do: sparky, chippy, plumbing, plastering, building – Cliff grafts until the job gets done. An' after a while, he was here so much, there didn't seem no point in him going back to anywhere, all alone like. So he bunked up here at the Old Schoolhouse. And here we still are. I'm front of house; Cliff gets stuck in down in the engine room, fixing leaks, painting windows and chopping logs. At nights, when the guests are all in their rooms, we lock the place up; we light a fire. Sometimes we sit there, listening to the logs crackle, and the rain hit the roof; sometimes Cliff gets his army stuff off his chest, and I listen. Yeah… it's comfortable." Hereward's coarse brown skin split into wrinkles of affection, cheekbones sharp and angular, lost for a moment in pleasant reflection.

Jimmy watched him for a moment before tapping the breakfast bar with his fingertips. He did his best bright-and-breezy voice. "Well that's a good thing, my friend. Shacking up with a pal; finding a common purpose." He paused, inviting Hereward to elaborate, but the other man was not forthcoming. "Hey Hereward," he said after a time. "Can I ask you summat? And tell me to piss right off if it isnae any of my business."

Hereward grinned. "Piss right off," he said.

"Back in the day, when we all rubbed along together – you, me, the rest of the gang… There were a lot of lasses – way more than I can remember. Tell me if I got the wrong end o'the stick, like – but I cannae remember seeing yous with anyone. You know: a wee girl, like. You were always the guy guarding the fort, or smoking a joint downstairs, listening to the records – you know – holding fort, like while the rest o' us did the deed."

Hereward pulled his arm out from behind his back and stretched both arms high, his bones cracking. He blew out through his cheeks, pushing his little pork-pie hat to the back of his head. He fixed Jimmy with a look. "You wanna know about Cliff, right? Go on. Ask me the bloody question: which one's biting the pillow, right?"

Jimmy pulled himself up. "Hell no, mate! That's nae business! I was just…"

"That's what you wanna ask, though, ain't it?" Cocking an eye, he thrust a finger at Jimmy, he said: "D'you remember what is was like back when we was young? You, Danny, and Danny's mate - the one with the tattoos – whatsisname? You clicked yer fingers and the birds came running. I was the one with the squeaky voice who got ditched at the start of the evening 'cos I looked too young to get into the pub. So the birds thought I was cute. I got all the cuddles, took all the jokes about pressing me face into their tits. But you were the cocker they wanted, mate. Bloody Braveheart, Rob-Roy - the Jock-with-the-Cock. "

Jimmy laughed. "Aw, H; it wasnae that way…"

"Yeah it was, Dunny." Hereward folded his arms. "It was always that bleedin' way. But, you know what?" He flashed a brave smile. "I weren't bothered. You see, I was never into birds. Not back in the day, not now. But it's not the kind of thing you admit when you're a nipper - you'd get called queer, or a poofter, or a bender. And there was AIDS, of course. Nope - it weren't no time to be shouting it from the rooftops."

"Aye, true enough," said Jimmy. "A man can see that."

"So, yeah - Cliff…"

"Then… yous are together-together?"

"We go to bed at the same time; wake up together in the morning. He brings me a cuppa tea at six every day, come rain or shine. There's no how-your-father if that's what you're getting at. Don't think either of us are that bothered" Hereward took in the folders in front of him. He had been shielding them, but now seemed to draw away. He tapped the top file. "And this stuff, too."

Hereward opened a ring-binder folder, and extracted a thick pile of plastic wallets, each full with paperwork. He was deliberate, letting Jimmy into his confidence, word by word. "Forms, letters, paperwork."

Jimmy raised his eyebrows. "I saw the thing from the bloody Social Services. What you been up to?"

"We're thinking about adoption. Or maybe just fostering."

"Hang on...you're fostering Cliff?"

Hereward laughed. "No, you daft cunt!" He shook his head, tapping the papers as he spoke. "We'd be the foster parents. Me and Cliff."

"Foster parents for who? I don't get it."

Hereward sighed. "Listen: Cliff and I got no family. My sis has moved to New Zealand. Mum passed away ten years now, God rest her soul. An' Cliff – well, they all run a mile when he came out the army." He leant forward. "We reckon we could give someone a good life." He leant in towards Jimmy, his eyes bright. "You seen Cliff with your Alfie? He's a bloody natural with kids. Since he's begun getting his shit together, what with counselling and stuff, we thought we'd give it a go. Having a kid we could raise here, on the South Downs. Nature. Sea. Where better to grow up?"

Jimmy's mind flitted over his own past record as parent. Hereward didn't seem the judgemental type, he wondered if he'd already made a lousy impression as parent. He managed to muster some enthusiasm: "That's pure sound, H. It's a great idea. Why not?"

Hereward pulled a face. "A cripple and an ex-con. Hardly the bloody Partridge family, but we'll give it a shot." There was a moment of contemplation. Without looking at Jimmy, he asked, "And you, mate?"

Jimmy took his glasses off. He got up and walked over to the other side of the kitchen. He wiped the lenses in his top. "What d'you mean?"

"You know. Last night. The girl in the queue."

He held his glasses up towards the vast the skylight in the centre of the kitchen. "Oh? What about her?"

Hereward leaned forward, his face crumpled concentration. "I was workin' it out last night. Let's say this girl – or young lady as she is - is in her late twenties, or thereabouts. It would have been when you, me, Jas and the gang were all hanging around together in the Big Smoke."

"Maybe. I dunno." Jimmy avoided eye contact. He moved the arm of his spectacles back and forth, back and forth.

Hereward cupped his jaw, running the pads of his fingers around his stubble. "Funny what you remember. It's up there 'cos I did that six-month stint as a roadie for Maiden afterwards. Got back to find you and Jas had split up and all my mates had gone their separate ways. It was like, without you two holding us all together, we weren't a unit. All changed after that."

Jimmy walked back to Hereward and took his seat once more. "Aye," he said. "But life goes on." He weighed Hereward up. "Anyways. We didn't split up. I buggered off."

Hereward pushed his little pork pie hat to the back of his head. "You left her? So hang on – you left her?" He frowned. "So... when she was, like...?" He made a motion over his stomach.

Jimmy's mouth straightened into a grim line. Hereward gave a long, low whistle. "Jeez. Poor Jas."

Jimmy said, "She didnae know that I knew. You remember Roo – the gobby South African bird? Well, I overheard them talkin'. Turns out Jasmine was gonnae tell me the next morning, like. I wasnae ready for any o' that. I mean, the wee lass meant a lot to me and all... but a wean?" He shook his head. "Have tae tell you, H: I was bloody petrified. Turned and ran. Cowardly, I know..."

Hereward kept his eye on the other man. "So what next?"

Jimmy's voice took on the tone of confession. "Every day for weeks, even months, I waited for a knock on the door; to see Jas and some little bundle on the doorstep. But she never did. So I kinda blotted it all out. Carried on as normal. It was about the time the poetry was taking off big-time. First major publishing deal, the South Bank Show feature...It was easy to put the personal stuff to the back o' my heed. But after, when I started tae make a name for myself, the fear came back. What if my past came back to bite me on the arse? How would it look – that I'd left this woman in the lurch to bring up a kid with no support? We were on the threshold of the new millennium. *Let's all meet up in the Year 2000* and all that crap. New Year's Eve 1999 – that was it. My curiosity got the better of me. I decided tae find out what had happened to Jasmine and to the baby. So I did some snooping around. I tried the artworld at first, but it turned out Jasmine had dropped out of the scene years ago. But it didnae take long, though, to find her again - she was leading a quiet life in this little terraced place near Greenwich."

"So did you go and see them?"

"I wrote a letter." He couldn't look Hereward in the eye as he said it. "Ach, I know it sounds crap. But it was better than nothing. Or so I thought at the time."

"Did you get a reply?"

"Nothin'. Waited and waited. So that was that."

"What? You didn't follow up? Go to see her in person? What if she never got the letter?"

Jimmy pulled over a salt cellar from the far side of the surface and started worrying it. "Oh, she got it alright. I put it through the letterbox myself. And I saw her come to the front door tae pick it up." He shook his head. "So the way I saw it, was the ball was in her court from there on."

Hereward's voice rose in pitch. "But the gal? Your daughter? You wanted to see her, right?"

Jimmy abandoned his salt cellar, got up again and turned away. "Christ, H! I don't know what I wanted back in those times, honest to God."

Jimmy walked over to a large window. It overlooked a steep bank that fell away from the Old Schoolhouse. Beyond the ridge, he saw a small dog, tail wagging in furious joy, scampering after a ball. A second mutt, much older, limped in its wake. It was pursued by two distant figures, man and boy, silhouetted against a livid red morning sky. Jimmy recognised the movement and shape of his son. He willed them both to reach the kitchen before he had to complete his conversation with Hereward.

He half-listened to Hereward as the watched them. "Dunny... the thing you said about being bitten on the arse... It's happened, yeah?" The legs of his stool made a jarring sound as they scraped against the kitchen flagstones. He was standing, gripping hold of the surface. "I'm not one to tell a bloke what to do but...you gotta face up to it. What if your little lad finds out he's got a big sister and you haven't told him nuffin'? You thought about that?"

CRAIG ENNEW

Jimmy ran his fingers through his hair. "Aye. Kinda. But what's if it all a bunch of pish? Someone trying tae blackmail me, or the like. You saw that other guy she was with…"

Hereward cut in: "I think we both know that that ain't the case mate." He took a few steps closer. "Look – I should have said this a while back, but I didn't wanna freak you out; what with all this other stuff going on…." Jimmy looked up. "Jas: I've seen her about."

Jimmy turned back towards him. "Jasmine?"

Hereward nodded. "A few times. Maybe three, four occasions over the last twenty years or so? There's this place I go for a coffee. Once or twice we had a quick chat about nuffin' in particular; other times, a nod. The last few times… well… she 'asn't been looking too clever mate."

Jimmy shrugged. "In what way?"

"The years 'aven't treated her well. The last time was a lot worse. She could even string a sentence together. All over the place. I reckon she was on something. I mean. I've smoked the odd joint to steady the shaking… but you gotta be on more serious shit to end up looking that rough."

Jimmy stared at Hereward for a moment. "Christ. So where is she?"

"She's living on one of the houseboats on the estuary. There's a row of four or five of 'em near the footbridge that crosses over from the town. I could show you? You could speak to them - Jas? And maybe the girl if she's there too?"

"A houseboat?" He shook his head. "Want tae hear something ironic? Where I come from, a houseboat is Weegie for a posh gaff. Not owned by the council."

Hereward smiled. "We're not talking posh 'ere," he said. So... what d'you reckon? You up for it?"

Ach, I'm no' sure..." Jimmy drew his shoulders up, and felt for the back of his neck.

Jimmy was rescued by the sounds of a doors opening, a purposeful bustle of bodies clattering into a space. Relieved,he walked towards the entrance of the kitchen. The claws of a small dog could be heard tapping the polished wooden floors until he found the entrance to the kitchen and beetled over to Hereward, tail wagging. Hereward groaned as he bent to greet her. "Hello, old girl," he wheezed, tugging her dirty white ruff. "You're bloody freezing! That snow on your coat?"

Cliff, Alfie and the second dog were now in the kitchen too. "Dad! It's snowing, it's snowing, it's snowing!" cried Alfie. He was dancing around the room as if still beneath some spectacular flurry. He ran up to Jimmy and uncurled his fist. A squat Firestarter flint lay in his palm. "And Cliff's shown me how to make a fire!"

Jimmy ruffled his hair. "Well look at that," he said. He looked over at Cliff. "How long does it take the fire brigade to get all the way out here?"

Cliff looked at Jimmy for three long seconds, saying nothing. There was, for Jimmy, something critical in his silence.

He wasn't banking, either, on Hereward's persistence. He had moved closer to him now, and his hand was on Jimmy's forearm. "I gotta say this, Dunny. That girl, yesterday: she was the spit of you, mate. The absolute spit. There's no denying." He applied a gentle squeeze. "I'll drive you over to that houseboat. Cliff an' me take care of the boy. He'll be in safe hands with us. Promise."

Seven

Within the hour, both men were travelling in silence towards the South Coast in the cabin of Cliff's Land Rover. Above the dual carriageway, the sky darkened as a band of low pressure swelled from the West. Snowflakes, that had been light and tentative when they the set out, now fell heavier.

Cliff had agreed to occupy Alfie while they looked for the houseboat. "I'll try not to be long, son," Jimmy had said, but the boy had already turned his back on him, taking Cliff's hand.

As they travelled, Jimmy sank a little further into his seat as large, wet flakes of snow hit the windscreen to disappear as soon as they'd come. Pulling his collar around his face, he folded his arms and stared ahead, deep in thought. After a short while, he pulled the phone out of his pocket and stared at it, swiping the screen upward at intermittent intervals. "Doubled the number of followers on Twitter since last night's shenanigans hit the news," he said. "Guess every cloud has a silver lining."

Hereward said nothing. Keeping his eyes on the road, he stepped on the accelerator before pushing up a gear.

After twenty minutes, they swung into a small parking bay near to small harbour. Following an undignified scramble on the passenger's side, Jimmy placed a foot onto the ground, the sole of his boot slipping across the thin carpet of snow. He looked up at the sky, now a thick, dark throw of uniform dark grey. A few flakes rested on his cheeks and beard.

Walking around the front of the vehicle, Hereward looked out across the river where, through a dirty curtain of sleet, four or five dark shapes hugged the bank. "Reckon Jas's houseboat must be one of those," he said, waving in that direction. I can't think of anywhere else it could be."

They both stared across to where blocks of darkness blotted out the glinting lights on the water. Behind them, the shabby town sat hunched in a crestfallen stupor, a blur of half-hearted Christmas lights against a soundtrack of rush hour traffic.

Jimmy cocked an eye at a dismal mock-Tudor pub that sat some way back from a developers' site, cordoned off with battered wire fences. He ran his tongue around his lips. "I might have to rely on a wee bit of Dutch courage afore I go over," he said.

Hereward turned the car keys over his gristly red knuckles. He hung on the driver's door. "You go ahead if you think that's a good idea." He eased himself into the driver's seat, closed the door and wound the window down. "You got my number. Give me a call when you're done and I'll come back and pick you up."

"Thanks, pal. I appreciate this." He took a few steps, to turn back. "I think," he said with a sly wink.

Hereward turned the keys in the ignition and manoeuvred the Land Rover out of the car park. Jimmy headed towards the dull yellow lights of the pub windows with his head down.

***

By the time Jimmy had resurfaced, the light had disappeared and another inch of snow had fallen. The temperature had dropped by another five degrees.

He let the pub door close behind him, muting a brief burst of raucous laughter from within. He half-turned back with nostalgic longing. New-found friends were a much more attractive option than that which awaited him across the water.

Pinching the film from a cigarette packet, he extracted one with his lips, struck a match, and lit up. A plume of smoke rose into the night air. He breathed the night in before pinching the tab between the tips of two fingers and his thumb, and tossing it to the ground. Brushing a gathering layer of snow from his shoulders, he pulled the hood of his duffle jacket over his head.

As Jimmy made his way onto the bridge, the warmth of the final double faded. Reaching the walkway, he discovered it yet to be gritted; as he stepped on, the soles of his boots slipped across its surface. He grasped for the rail, his fingers blue with cold.

When he was half way across the bridge, he hesitated.

Peering through the gloaming to where he imagined the houseboat might be, he was startled by the incongruous bird-like shrieks of a ragged affray of kids, excited by the snow. He clutched the handrail and inched his way forward. Ahead of him, a female figured wearing a beanie and rendered shapeless by winter layers, walked a short distance ahead, small dog in tow. Jimmy hung back until she had reached the far side, and then moved forwards again.

Beyond, a small path followed the curve of the estuary. Along it, the keepers of the boats had laid claim to their strip of land beyond each berth, with a series of ramshackle metal spikes or split fence panels. Motley detritus littered each stake: nail-studded palettes, burnt-out incinerators, mouldy plastic toys, even the burnt-out chassis of a Vauxhall Astra. Amidst all, an embarrassed cross of St. George was draped atop a slanting flagpole. All was rendered analogous by the gentle onslaught of fresh snow.

Jimmy stopped short at a small wooden gate, no higher than his thigh. It hung on a single hinge, languid grasses breaking through the layers of snow at its feet. From there, a narrow jetty stretched over the ridge towards a huddled row of low, box-like structures that bobbed on the water: the houseboats.

A short distance ahead, he heard sounds. He recognised the dog-walker from moments earlier. Shen seemed oblivious, and he held back, not wishing to give her the impression that he was following her.

The figure moved beneath a streetlamp, crouching to unclip her dog from its lead. It strained with impatience before scampering off into some undergrowth as soon as it was loose.

She straightened her body, lifted her head upwards, and pulled off the squat beanie in one fluid movement.

There, in the half-light, Jimmy watched her blonde dreadlocks tumble over the shoulders of her combat jacket to fall down her back.

It was her.

He held his breath.

With grace, she lifted her face to the dark blanket of sky, head tilted upwards, feeling the snow settle on her skin. The fluorescence caught her profile, the soft feathery flakes settling to melt on her cheeks, the strong chin, the small, snubbed nose.

All around, houses, churches, locked-up factories, clung to the rolling South Downs, hunkering down against the stealthy soft snow that added layer upon layer. She alone embraced it. Jimmy wondered if he'd ever seen anything quite so breath-taking as the snow falling on the face of his daughter.

She seemed to come to, calling after her dog. "Echo? Echo!" Her face turned in his direction, and he shrunk back against a group of thorny brambles.

She froze for a split second, but the dog joined her, and she moved on. Jimmy traced her steps, to pause where a ripped sofa, stacked high with plastic crates marked the entrance to a second mooring. He heard the sounds of heavy footfall scuffing on decking and moved forwards until he could see over the brow of the bank.

She stood still, holding a key to the lock of the door, listening for life within. Turning the ley, she glanced over her shoulder once and moved inside. A light click came on within the cabin.

Jimmy watched, holding himself very still. This was where his daughter and her mother were living.

Eight

As Jimmy drew closer, a silhouette moved across the curtained window. The odd word lifted out of the fragile shell of the cabin and into the evening, but they were disconnected and evasive. That said, the tension between them was plain. One voice was hers. It was lower, more controlled. The other was languid and higher in pitch.

Jimmy Dunbar felt unwell. A cloying heat spread through his throat and neck, and the dampness of his jacket seeped through to his clammy skin. He thought of the pub on the other side of the river with its musty carpets and dirty beer towels across the bar and wondered what had possessed him to listen to Hereward in the first place. Here. Now. Head-to-head with Jasmine for the first time in the best part of three decades, with a grown-up child and fortunes that taken starkly different paths.

From within the boat came the slithering sound of something heavy bumping off a surface, and being lugged across the deck. The weaker voice came again: "Please don't go, love. If I did anything wrong, it was for your sake..."

Everything in Jimmy's psyche screamed at him to run for his life. He heard Hope's voice: "Jesus, Mum – since when? You're doing my head in! If you can't even be arsed to give me a decent explanation... Look: I need to get away for a while to have some space to think this shit, okay? It's not like I won't come back. I always come back."

Jimmy held his breath. Fuck it all. There would never be a good time. He half-turned to leave, when the door to the houseboat opened.

He was in the shadows, so she didn't see him at first. Lugging her back-pack over her shoulder, she stepped onto the deck.

Jimmy felt himself stepping forwards. She raised her head as she was pulling the door to. Father and daughter were face to face.

She glanced back towards the door. "Shit!" she hissed. "How did you find us here?"

Jimmy's voice was low. "I just did." He cast an eye past her to the window, before returning to her. "Why didn't you call?"

She stared at him for a moment, allowing herself an ironic smile, before hitching her backpack over a shoulder. "I was leaving." Her boot rested on the edge of the boat. "I need to get past."

Jimmy's bulk blocked the only exit she had. "Hold on just a wee minute. *You* came to find *me* the other day, remember?"

Her gaze remained fixed on the decking. "Look: I don't want any more crap. It was a mistake, okay? Let's just say I acted on bad advice." Her eyelashes flickered and she took a deep breath. "Please get out of my way."

A voice came from within. "Hope? Is that Spider come back?"

"No. It's alright, Mum." She looked hard at Jimmy. "It's nobody."

The light behind the door changed. The shadows of another crouching figure were appearing behind the orange glass pane, fingers gripping the edge of the door's frame. Illuminated by the bulkhead above the entrance, they were as near to skeletal as something encased in skin could be. Taught and angular, they moved like the legs of a spider, the nails of each brittle finger long, dirty and uncared for.

A face, the most part obscured by shadow, followed. More petite than her daughter, all that remained of Jasmine Kelly was skin and bone. Her hair, dyed jet black, was scraped back from her face. Where the roots had shown through, a pale, light grey tramline crossed the top of her skull. Beneath pencilled eyebrows, eyes shot through with specs of blood, kept an exhausted vigil. Sharp cheekbones pulled her thin lips and jutting chin into a curl of distrust and regret. The blood drained from Jimmy's face as he saw what his lover had become.

Stepping onto the decking, Jasmine Kelly, like a child, took in the falling snow as a thing of wonder. After a time, she found Jimmy, fitting pieces of a puzzle she had thought long-lost. Without taking her wide, terrified eyes off him, she whispered to Hope: "Get him away. Please, darling, get him away..."

Hope unhitched the rucksack from her shoulder, to let it slide down her leg and onto the decking. She shifted her it back inside the porch of the door and took her mother's arm. "Come on, Mum," she said. "It's way too cold for you out here."

Following her mother inside, Hope turned her head. "Please," she said to Jimmy. "Just go."

The two women disappeared into the houseboat once more, the door closing behind them. Jimmy watched them. If he stayed, he was harassing; if he left, he was the perennial deserter once again.

Between where he stood on the bank, and the edge of the boat, the water glinted with dark menace. With grunting effort, he stepped over and planted two large, clumsy feet on the deck. He paused for thought before tapping on the door. Hope's face appeared. She came out again, closing the door behind her. Pulling her coat tighter around her shoulders, she spoke again. "What do you want?"

"To talk about stuff," said Jimmy. "That's all."

She weighed him up for a moment. "Wait there," she said.

When she came back out, his heart jumped as he saw that she

was clutching the red and white book – the very copy bearing his scrawled number on the flyleaf. He wondered what she had made of what was within. She pulled a sheet of paper from it. "This," she said. She held it, her arm straight so that it was directly in front of his face.

Jimmy took it from her, and carried it to the window of the cabin where there was more light.

A voice came from within. It was frightened, fragile. "Hope? Is he still out there?"

"It's okay, Mum," Hope shouted. She looked back to Jimmy, biting her nails.

Crouched against the window, Jimmy read the letter. He looked across to his daughter, astonished, before returning to the note once more. "I wrote this – what? – ten, fifteen years ago?" He looked up. "Why are you showing this to me now?"

She walked up to him, eyes cast down. She took the letter from his hands, and slipped it back inside the book. "Because the first time I saw it was two nights ago."

"What? You mean she never...? But that was addressed to you. She had no right..." He made a move towards the door of the houseboat.

"Wait," Hope put herself between Jimmy and the door. "You hear me out." Her mouth trembled. "You need to hear this. That bitch the other night? The one who confronted you when you were signing those books? That wasn't me ..." She shook her head. "I mean... I'm never like that...never." She swallowed. "I'd managed to shut it all out for so long – the version of you that Mum put into my head. But recently, Spider, Mum's bloke, he's been stirring it up again. *Let's take him on,* he says. *Him and his rich wife. He owes us.* And I was half-way through a bottle of voddy, and I thought: why the fuck not? I mean..." She gestured across the full length of the houseboat, and the words spilled out of her. "...look at what we've got. We're not exactly living in the lap of luxury are we? And I was all fired up. Spider told me about your French villa. So I was kind of fired up for taking you on about it. But when I was in that queue, and I got closer, and I saw the little kid as well – Jesus! – my half-brother! I thought, like, is this bloke the total bastard that Mum described? So I said my bit, but after that, I bottled it – which made Spider mad. I had to find out more. I knew that Mum keeps a box with old stuff in, and while she was out of it, I ransacked the place. Eventually I found it." She shook her head, looking down at the letter. "You think you have a handle on stuff. But something always comes along and fucks everything up."

Jimmy stepped forward. "What did you mean by 'version of me'? What has she said?"

"Imagine the worst, and add some more. The kind of stuff a daughter doesn't want to hear about her father." She looked him straight in the eye.

Jimmy felt an indignation burn inside." Jesus Christ." He pointed towards the door. "We need to have this out..."

"Hope?" They both froze. It was Jasmine's voice again.

"You can't go in there." Hope blocked the door with her body. "You saw her: she's in a fragile enough state as it is. You being here like this'll push her right over the edge. Please."

Jimmy frowned. "I'm sorry, love; but there's no fucking way I can let this lie."

She shook her head and her mouth tightened.

Jimmy moved in. He gripped her arms above the elbows, and

pushed her to one side.

Inside the cabin of the houseboat, a stove threw long shadows over the panelled walls and the deep crimsons and emerald greens of scattered rugs and throws. A few feet from where Jimmy now stood, Jasmine Kelly had eased herself onto a battered Chesterfield, tucking her legs beneath her slight frame, and hugging herself, her body wracked with involuntary shivers. Both livid and terrified, she was aware of him as soon as he appeared. Around her, a sea of painted canvases occupied every space: propped against the furniture, stacked in piles on the floor, peeping from beneath tired furniture. Many Jimmy knew from their time together. But not one occupied wall space. And there was no sign of an easel, or palettes or brushes.

Jimmy closed in on the tiny frail figure on the sofa. On the coffee table before her, among take-away cartoons, half-drunk cans of cider and unopened bills, sat a small square of burnt out foil and a disassembled biro. Jasmine clawed the objects towards her, and scooped them onto the floor. She hissed at him. "Don't you dare judge me."

Jimmy glared at her. "I will too. You know what she's told me? She's told me about the letter. The letter I addressed to her over fifteen years ago. The letter that you buried. Why did you never let her have it? And what filthy lies about me have you poisoned her mind with, huh?" He thrust his head forward, standing over her.

With her arms wrapped around her legs, and the shawl tucked around her slight frame, Jasmine looked like the survivor of a recent atrocity.

Hope came behind her and touched his arm. "Please don't do this. Not now…"

But Jimmy wasn't listening. "C'mon!" he said, his voice rising.

"What was I like, hey? Did I sleep around? Was I handy wi' my fists? Maybe I was a kiddie-fiddler, too?" He was taking her arm, thrusting a finger at Hope. "What filth, in the name of God, have you put into the lass' head, woman? Whatever you've said, you bloody take it back, you hear me?"

Jasmine cowered back, pulling her arms about her face and head. "I...I don't remember."

"You're a liar," Jimmy yelled.

She lifted her face and withdrew her arms. Seeing something in her face, Jimmy stopped in his tracks. In a rare moment of lucidity, she found her voice. "There's only one lying shit in this room, Jimmy Dunbar. All those years ago, you told me we were meant to be. I was 'the one', you said. And bang! Without warning, you were gone. How could you have left me if that's what you believed?" She swivelled her slight frame around, dropped her legs down, so that the tips of her bare toes touched the floor. The brittle fingers clawed at her own face, as she sobbed through them, rocking back and forth. "You took everything away: my friends, my stability, my life. Everything fell apart." Jimmy looked on in horror: her face, so near to his, was scarred, ravaged, hollowed out by long years of misuse, neglect and disappointment.

She had risen, half-standing, half-crouching, her elbows bent back and her face thrust forwards until, with a final effort, she stretched and straightened herself to be as near his height as she could.

Hope clutched her arm and tried to pull her back down, "Mum: you need to keep calm. It's not worth it..."

Her lips drew back to expose long, dirty teeth and bruised gums, and she blinked the tears away. She hissed the words. "And you send a letter suggesting you can saunter back in any time you choose to take my Hope away from me. You haven't even got the guts to come in person." Her voice rose to near hysteria. "A bloody coward, hiding behind words. That's all you'll ever be, Jimmy…"

She was trembling now, a raw anger building inside her. For a moment, she appeared to compose herself. "Get out," she whispered, looking for all the world like she might kill him. In horror, he watched her mouth tremble, her head shake. The trembling grew as the rage flooded down the wasted years to torrent through every fibre of her being until she was howling and screaming like a banshee into his face: "Fucking *get out!*"

Jimmy recoiled as she lashed out: a claw that ripped across the flesh of his face. Now he was careering back into the low sideboard, piles of her small canvases and other detritus crashing about him.

Horrified, he put his fingers to his stinging cheek and could already felt the warm, sticky blood that she'd drawn.

Hope wrapped herself around the convulsing body of her mother like some human straight-jacket. She was the stronger of the two, and it took little effort forced Jasmine down onto the sofa. Hope's restraint turned into a comforting hold, and the older woman's screaming and thrashing lessened until they were mere whimpers and sobs.

Hope cradled her mother's skull, holding the head close to her own. "Hush…" she whispered, rocking her back and forth. She planted small kisses on the top of her mother's head. "Hush…"

In the arms of her daughter, a torpor overcame Jasmine. Her breathing became less rapid, and the muscles in her body relaxed. Hope looked up at Jimmy. "You need to go."

He stood aghast, feeling the sting of his wound, the blood

soaking into his beard. "Listen to me…"

"Go," she repeated.

When, twenty minutes later, she came out of the houseboat carrying her backpack, Jimmy was still waiting on the bank opposite the mooring, a dusting of snow upon his hair and shoulders.

"You're still here," she said. She was looking at his cheek.

He could see that she'd been crying. "Aye." He pulled the cigarette from his mouth, and trod it into the Earth.

She was carrying the backpack. She hitched it up over her shoulder and buttoned up her jacket. Pulling a beanie over her head, she tucked her dreadlocks inside. She looked up again, dragging her sleeve across her nose.

"Where ya headed?" he asked.

"Anywhere that's not here. I'll get a train." She sniffed. "My head's all fucked up. I need some space." In an attempt to sound less dramatic, she added, "I got mates down in the South West. I'll maybe go there for a few days,"

Jimmy's arms hung by his side. "I don't want to you to go," he blurted.

Her face tightened a little. She composed herself. "Shame Mum never got the chance to say that to you all those years ago." She nodded across the water. "Not that you're worried, but the guys in the boat next door'll take care of her when I'm not around. They're nice people."

She stepped across the decking and down onto the bank. As she walked past him, her arm brushed against his. "See you around," she said.

Jimmy turned after her. "Hope?" He felt taken aback by his own voice: this was the very first time that he had called her by her name. But she walked on and he knew that she didn't want him to see her tears.

Jimmy glanced back to the cabin of the houseboat. Errant flakes of snow skittered around the bulkhead over the door. All was quiet, but he felt he should check.

Inside, he looked at the mother of his daughter. Despite everything, he felt pity and guilt. The glowing ashes of the stove threw a meagre light across her vulnerable form. He threw open the cast-iron door and tossed another log inside, before pulling the blanket up and around the still woman. She stirred. "Don't leave me, Hopie," she murmured without opening her eyes.

Stepping back out into the winter evening, the air was cold, and the tiny, forlorn lights of the other boats nearby bobbed on the water. It didn't take long for Jimmy to find the towpath once more. He headed off, his palm pressed against his wound. The snow was heavier now, all visibility diminishing. Cupping his hands around his mouth, he shouted, with a loud, booming voice into the void: "Hope…"

With less conviction, he called again. "Hope?"

But Hope was long gone.

England: the South West

03 December 2016

Driver Killed in Train Accident

The incident took place on the South Western line between Overton and Whitchurch on the 18:34 train from Clapham Junction yesterday evening.

Emergency services were called to the scene at 19:30 hours, where they found the front three carriages had derailed and fallen down a steep embankment into a canopy of trees. It is not known what caused the derailment, although heavy snow had been falling across the region for a prolonged period of time.

Two fire engines from the Hampshire Fire and Rescue service were tasked with cutting open the carriages so that casualties could be removed.

Sergeant Kate Cooper-Hayes said, "Sadly, a 56 year-old man, believed to be the driver, has died as a result of this accident. The emergency services recovered all other passengers, a number of whom are now hospitalised, where they remain in a serious condition. We are appealing for anyone who saw the accident to contact us."

All services between Basingstoke and Salisbury have been suspended as an investigation into the accident is being carried out. A spokesperson for South Western Trains has said that a bus replacement service will run in its place 'for the foreseeable future'.

PART THREE

Nine – the morning of Saturday 3rd December 2016

The following morning, some eighty miles West of the houseboat, an old man lay still beneath the starched sheets of a hospital bed. A blanket was pulled beneath his chin.

Since his admission the evening before, Oleg Kowalski had achieved the status of minor celebrity within the Spinal Unit of the district hospital. From the moment the emergency services had cut his body from the twisted hulk of the carriage, his survival had been declared nothing short of miraculous. Junior doctors had braved the cold weather to start their shifts early in order to marvel at the octogenarian; the local press had harangued the receptionists for access.

Now, the old man's fingers were intertwined like some benign sarcophagus. He was a picture of calm in all situations, despite the fact that he neither slept, nor did his brain cease from turning over.

Some fifty yards away, near the entrance to the ward, one of the staff on the ward spoke with a police constable. From time to time, they glanced over to the old man's bed.

After a while, they came over.

The police officer's face was still raw from the outdoor chill. A clear poly bag dangled from her fingers.

Once beside the bed, she and the nurse ruminated on the inert patient. "Is he awake?"

"He has been," said the nurse. He looked at his watch. "Can't believe how he's bearing up..."

"What's the extent of his injuries?" She glanced around the ward. "Guessing it's not great news if he's in here."

The nurse was looking at the notes on a clipboard at the end of the bed. He pulled a face. "They think paralysis from the waist down, but it's too early to say. But he's been very brave." He caught a scent of the young policewoman's impatience. "Not gonna lie: I'm pretty reluctant to disturb him unless you feel it's necessary? He only came in last night."

The policewoman took a notepad from the inside jacket of her puffa jacket. "Okay. I guess it can wait. Has anyone been in to see him yet? Family? Friends?"

The nurse folded his arms. "He said that he wasn't expecting anyone."

The constable took off her hat, and rested it at the foot of Oleg Kowalski's bed, along with the sealed bag. "Hope I've got someone who comes and visits me when I'm that old."

The old man's eyelids flickered.

The policewoman flipped her notepad over and went to write, licking the tip of her biro and shaking it with great vigour. "Bloody thing," she said. "So has this gentleman said anything else to you about the accident?"

"The ambulances brought seventeen in, in total. One died at the scene: the driver. Another, a woman in her mid-forties, died an hour after being admitted. Most of the others, bar three or four with serious injuries, should be discharged later, but not Mr.

Kowalski here." He spoke through a yawn. "Lord, it's been a long old shift. I finish at ten." He gestured towards the bed. "He was awake for a while in the night but was a bit fuzzy. Do they know what caused the accident yet? Was it something to do with the weather?"

"That's part of the reason why I've come here. The train derailed at around 7pm last night. We think that he driver was killed instantly. Nothing official yet: too early for full toxicology results – but the guv thinks it's likely that he fell asleep at the controls. If it had happened earlier it would've been complete carnage – it's one of the main commuter lines..."

There was a gentle movement beneath the bedclothes. They both looked down.

A frail voice came between them. "How is she?" Oleg Kowalski had opened one doleful eye. He waited for his answer, watching the policewoman with an intensity that belied his fragile state.

She exchanged glances with the nurse. "Sir. Sorry. We didn't think you were with us. I mean, I didn't realise you were awake..." She held up the plastic poly bag. "Here to reunite a few bits and pieces with their owner, sir. Found in and around the train." She rested the bag near to him. "Your little book's in there. One of my colleagues saw you reaching out for it while you were being stretchered from the train. We'll need a signature. When you're up to it, obviously..."

He glanced down at the package and shook his head before repeating his question. "But I need to know - how is she? The young woman that was on the train. In my carriage," He swallowed. "She is... alright?" His face was ashen.

The policewoman turned to the nurse and spoke in a lower voice. "There was only one other person recovered from his carriage: young woman, late twenties." She turned back to Oleg Kowalski, and spoke as if to a small child. "Was she travelling with you, sir? The young lady?"

The old hesitated. "No – at least... we met on the train." He went to move himself further up onto the pillows, but only felt a massive weight pushing down on his body.

"Steady on, Mr. K," said the nurse, reaching around the old man's back. "There's no trying to move yourself for the time being. You need to let us do that for you."

Their attention was caught by the crackle of a police radio. The WPC ripped it from her duty belt. "Mike Whisky. Sierra four-four. Go Ahead. Over."

Ignoring the distraction, Oleg Kowalski tried again: "It's important for me to know, you see?" The nurse nodded and flashed a small, kind smile, his attention caught between his patient and the police radio.

Turning away, the policewoman covered one ear. "Mike Whisky. Affirmative - I'm in the adjacent building. Yes, the old part. You want me there or should I wait for back-up? Over."

"Sierra four-four. Negative. Please proceed: patrol on way and able to assist. Support is three minutes repeat three minutes away. And Sierra four-four? Warning: subject may be violent. Over."

"Received, Mike Whisky – may be violent. Out." She grabbed her jacket and hat, and fumbled with the notebook. "Better be off. Can you tell me where Eggerton Ward is, please?"

"Out the ward and down the corridor till you get to the link bridge to the new building. After that, it's second floor, first on the left." He shot a brief glance back at his patient. "Hang on, I'll show you. I'm pretty sure it's the ward that the young woman from Mr. K's carriage is in..."

The policewoman was already at the door of the ward. "I know. She's where I'm headed."

"Wait!" The old man's voice was a plaintive croak. "She is here? In this hospital?"

The nurse looked over his shoulder as he hit the exit button and disappeared through the double doors. He called back. "Fill you in later, Mr. K. I promise."

Oleg Kowalski watched the doors swing back in on themselves. He listened to the trail of footsteps die away down the corridors until the sterile space was consumed with silence once more. His eye was drawn to the clear sealed package near his twisted, arthritic fingers and, in particular, to the modest red and black book within. His lips made the tiniest movements.

"Well, well, well" he mumbled.

* * *

Much later that night, In the quiet of the spinal unit ward, Oleg Kowalski's face hung as a death-mask. Framed by the white cotton of a single pillow upon which he was propped, a halo of pure white wisps of his hair circled his head. On occasion, the gentle night-lights of the ward caught the suggestion of a movement; but for all that, the old man's mouth remained open and dry at the corners. He mumbled the words he had heard the evening before.

I smile at them and they smile back, we'll have a memory of each other; we will know each other – even if just a bit.

Thinking of the girl on the train comforted him. It was little more than twenty-four hours earlier, yet it seemed part of another life. He allowed himself the gentlest of smiles, and drifted into a light sleep during which the past blurred into the present in his dreams. He had met his Nancy in a train carriage, and he saw her again now: petite gloves folded on her lap, a straight back and a shy smile. Just staring, for a while, into each other's faces...

It's good to talk...

In through a dark tunnel and out into a snow storm where the girl with tattoos and piercings waited. *Chunter away, my dear*

He peered again, to darkness. He wasn't sure whether he was sleeping or awake. Over time, he became aware of a figure sat by his bedside. She was in a wheelchair, her hand clutching a portable drip. The moon was out, and the criss-cross of the branches framed by the window cast shadows across the contours of one half of her face. The other half was concealed.

"Nancy?" he said in a high, quavering voice.

He could hear the figure swallow and struggle, at first, to find words. In the quiet of the ward, her words were whispered "Afraid not. Just me. How are you?"

He saw the alarm of purple bruises in the half-light, a stitched wound running from the outer corner of her eye, down her cheek, pulling the flesh inwards.

So here she was: the Good Morning girl from the train.

As she leant forwards, the smallest gasp of pain escaped from her lips. Her hair, he saw, had been cut short, the long blonde dreads gone. She held her body rigid.

He spoke with the stoicism of a man of advanced years. "Oh I am sure I will be fine. And anyway, I am old." He realised that what he'd said was facile. They were, after all, in the spinal ward. "And you, young lady? How are you?" He looked over her wheelchair, the intravenous drip going into her forearm.

She shrugged. "Oh, I'm okay. They're all making a lot of fuss but I'll live."

"How...how did you get down here."

"I asked them if I could see those walled gardens next to this ward? Said I'd make my own way back." She paused. "I'm out of here tomorrow, anyway, so I wanted to come here to say thanks, first."

A look of concern flitted across the sharp features of the old man. "They are letting you go?"

"Not exactly. There's stuff outside that I need to take care of."

"You have yourself to take care of, my dear. You must listen to the doctors. If you are not well, how can you be of use to others?"

Her head shot up, like she appeared fearful of him knowing something he should not. "Others?"

Realising he had opened a raw wound, he pursed his lips and changed tack. "You spoke of thanking me. For what, may I ask?"

"For being there with me. On the train. Your talking kept me awake. And safe." Her fingers crept from within the layers she had shrouded herself in, and she took the frail bones of him in her own grasp. Her lips parted, and she hesitated. "They say that shared experience of terrible catastrophes like disasters or accidents kind of bring people closer, don't they? You know: like soldiers in the trenches and stuff? The accident – it seems so long ago already but it was only – what - the night before last? Since, I've had wires put into me, been stitched up, poked and prodded... and a load more grief besides. But I *knew* I could talk to you. I have no-one else. I wish...I wish we'd had longer to talk..."

"I remember you being upset," he said, "You were running away from something?" She remained silent. "Forgive me – it is none of my business."

She raised her head. "Oh," she said. "Something else. I asked about the book I'd lost. The policewoman told me that she'd thought it was yours, and passed it on to you?"

"Ah." He slid a frail wrist from beneath the covers and he pointed at the bedside cabinet. "You will find it in there, my dear."

It took her a long time to get her wheelchair beside the cabinet – and he realised how much effort it must have taken her to reach his bedside. She wrapped her arms across her stomach. He heard her curse through gritted teeth. "Oh shit!" She held her breath.

He looked to where the emergency chord hung. "You must allow me to fetch help my dear."

"No!" The way she said it startled him. "I'll be okay in a minute," she whispered. "It goes after a while." She froze, holding her breath until the pain abated.

He listened to the drawer glide back, the skin of the volume slithering out of the polybag. She couldn't read it in the low light of the ward, but she needed to feel it. Out came the two sheets of paper before she closed it back up without speaking a word.

"Have you looked inside it? If you have, I don't mind..."

"I must confess: after the policewoman who brought it had gone, I asked a nurse on the ward to assist me in checking that it was indeed the book that you showed me. In truth, curiosity had defeated me, but I had not the strength to digest the contents, so instead I concentrated on considering how to return it to its rightful owner. And now, Fate intervenes! It returns to its rightful owner." He paused, before adding, "If you will permit me to ask, though: the author? The gentleman on the back cover? I could not help but notice the resemblance. And, of course, I remember you citing Mr. Larkin..."

Her laugh descended into a cough, shaking her frame. She clutched her middle for a while. Composing herself as he looked on in concern, she nodded her confirmation. "My father. One of the reasons for running, when we met on the train."

"I see. A disagreement between father and daughter is not uncommon..."

She smiled a quiet smile. "It's not as though there was a lot building up to it. It was only the second time in my life that I'd spoken to him." Oleg Kowalski raised his eyebrows. She moved in her seat, trying to get comfortable. "Wanna hear about the first?"

"If you would like to tell me. It's not as though either of us have anything better to do!"

She sighed. "Maybe if I start at the beginning? Talking helps take my mind off the pain. I'm telling you: I'm all for the NHS and that, but the painkillers they're giving me are shit."

"I feel nothing. At least not from the waist down. It is a very odd." She looked down to his legs for a moment. "No worries," he said. "Please do begin your story."

"Well we're going back eleven, maybe twelve years. I'm this awkward fifteen year-old. My mum's struggled with stuff all her life, but by this time she's almost given up. We're living on the houseboat at that time. I get a chance to go on a school daytrip and I can't believe my luck. I mean – this is something that has never happened to me before. We either couldn't afford it, or Mum was too out of it to fill in the forms.

It all starts one lunchbreak when my form tutor, Mrs. Waller, catches me stealing an exercise book from her cupboard. She looks in my desk for more evidence of my chavvy ways, and she finds this whole pile of stolen books with my random thoughts scribbled all over them. I use them as a kind of diary? Later in the day, she comes up to me. I'm prepared for a massive bollocking, but it's not the way it goes. It turns out she's read what I've written. *You have a real talent,* she says. She talks about this trip that the year above are going on the following week. They're going to listen to some poets that they're studying for the exam. The poets talk about their work, read some stuff out, answer questions– that kind of thing. She says she can fill in the forms if my mum says it's okay.

"So I end up going. I remember the coach on the way up, on a double seat alone. Getting out of that city for the first time in my life felt like heaven. And when we get there, it's so exciting. We've been doing this poetry anthology in school and I've actually got into it. I've gone over and over the words until I know them by heart, and now I get to see and listen to the people who write them.

"When we get there, the event seems like an anti-climax at first: this huge, dirty old hall, heaving with noisy, sweaty, over-excited kids that seem a lot younger than me. God, the stench of the place – I can smell it now: Tango, Coke, Frazzles, Smartie tubes rolling about in the aisles. For them, it's a right laugh. Our Day Out. No interest in the poetry at all. And, you know what? Despite my own shitty upbringing, I feel so embarrassed for them all. You see, by this point, I've been taking care of Mum for what, three, four years? I've had to grow up quickly.

"There are these five people stood at the front – the writers – most of them looking like they want to ground to swallow them up. I mean, would you choose to open your soul to a crowd of self-obsessed kids who don't give a shit for anything other than themselves? And they're trying to be heard over a din of, like, giggling and shrieking and the pop of Pringles tubes.

"So after this young guy has tried his hardest to kick the whole thing off by introducing the writers one by one, an older lady is the lucky one who gets to go first. She's a tiny little cartoon granny – all fussiness and knitwear – and I'm betting her house is crawling with cats. The other writers sit down on chairs to the side, and she steps up and starts reading. She has this lovely Welsh accent, but you can't hear it through the din that the kids are making. But I manage to focus on her, and blot them out to let her in.

"She's reading her poem about a mother and a daughter sometimes rubbing along, sometimes clawing at each other's faces, but loving each other fiercely nonetheless. Although she's reading it out like it's the football final scores , it's kind of moving – probably 'cos it's so far removed from how things have ever been with Mum and me." She sighed. "But none of those other kids hear it. So she finishes reading and stands there as some of the teachers try to get the kids to applaud. She smiles, but I can tell she's sad but looks sad. I'm the only one paying her any attention – even the teachers look bored stiff.

"For a moment, I don't know whether she's going to burst into tears, or scream at the whole lot of us. For me at fifteen, this is pretty intense. I want to shove my way to the front, and wrap my arms around this little lady - give her a massive hug. But, of course, that's never gonna happen. She has no idea I'm alive, let alone the only kid there that gives a shit. She takes her reading glasses off, gathers her sheets of paper and moves to the side of the stage. I tell myself I would write her a letter when I got home. Because of what happens later, though, I never get round to it.

"There's this other guy: I haven't noticed him before - I've been too busy with my little Welsh lady – but he's this big, cross-looking bloke to the side. He's younger than her, and when it's his turn, he takes these long, slow strides up to the middle of the stage like he owns the place. As he crosses paths with her, he bends down and gives her a peck on the cheek, and I know I'm gonna like him.

"Getting to his place, he waits. He clears his throat. He waits some more. But no-one seems ready for him except me. He's starting to look pissed off now, and he moves the lectern to one side. He grabs this loose pile of notes he's brought with him, holds them up in the air and drops all his notes on the floor. They're scattered all over the place: some hit the ground at his feet, others float from side to side to side away from the platform. The girls are giggling, and the noise from them seems, for a moment, seems worse than ever. But he's got their attention. They want to see what he's gonna do next. So a quiet ripples back over the hall and this man, he stands there."

Oleg Kowalski had a twinkle in his eye. "Tell me what he is like, this man."

"Well…although he's well pissed-off, he exudes this air of , like, don't-give-a-shit. Baggy shirt, sleeves rolled up, heavy shoes – but it's not merely what he's wearing – it's the way he moves, the way he is. When he does get complete silence, he walks forward to the front of the platform, and sits down, his dirt-brown chinos riding up these thick, hairy ankles. He nods back to where the Welsh lady disappeared, and he tells us, in this strong Scottish accent, how long he's known her. He tells us that no-one alive writes finer poetry. He pauses. He adds – and excuse my French - 'But not one of you fuckers heard a bloody word, did you?' You can hear all the teachers do this giant, collective wince. There's giggling again, but more of the kids are shocked this time. I'm there not daring to breathe, but kind of thrilled at the same time.

"By now, of course, he has three hundred rowdy schoolkids in the palm of his hand. All the teachers looked scared shitless about what's gonna come from his mouth next.   I think it's pretty cool. With no introduction, he starts to read one of his poems out. It's another one of the ones we've been told might be in the exam - *Jane Air* it's called."

"As in Charlotte Bronte," Oleg Kowalski asked.

Hope nodded. "Kind of – but spelt A-I-R.   I know it off by heart - I've read it over and over since. I even got well into Bronte on the back of it. It's all about someone falling in love with a character from a book; how he kind of exhumes her from the pages to give her life. But he reads it brilliantly: you believe he loves her, and that he's making her real because as soon as you love anything or anyone that much, your love is the evidence of that object's existence."   Hope paused, recalling the moment with a quiet smile.   "So...right at the end of the poem, he turns the whole thing on its head. I tell you, man, he has the attention of every single soul in that hall. So the speaker in the poem is a child, watching his grandfather crying because he has just lost his wife. And that sheer, raw agony of grief turns into some kind of, like, epiphany, as he realises that the unbearable pain is evidence that love never dies; that *she* never dies. Grief is evidence of that." She stopped again, releasing a long, slow breath as a spike of pain ran through her torso. Her hand gripped the stand of the portable drip.

The old man held his breath, in awe of her resilience and emotion. He observed that the beauty of the poem she spoke of could never quite equal the raw vulnerability in her retelling of it. "You make it sound like a wonderful moment. Quite wonderful," he said.

"Yes. I s'pose it was." She added, "At least it might have been if it had come from some other bugger's lips...

"On the way home – in the coach - I plug my earphones in and watch the car headlights flash by in the opposite direction, kind of sad to leave it all, or his words, behind. I think of what waits at home. Mum. Her bloke -Spider. I want the coach journey to last forever."

She looked towards the window behind his bed, looking beyond, to where the sweeping headlights of a school coach, more than a decade distant, caught the shooting white lines of carriageway. "It doesn't, of course. The walk back to the boat is a good fifty minutes in the pitch black. My teacher offers to drop me off, but I'm too ashamed of where we live and, anyway, I want time to think. And all the way home, it feels like his poetry has been scribbled over the inside of my head."

"Walking along the river path, I feel the urge to talk – to hear my own voice reliving the events of the day. People say I'm a chatterbox, but Mum's always been the empty page I can write stuff on that I want no-one else to read: nothing you tell her will ever get any further. She doesn't process much outside of her own existence.

"Outside the houseboat, I can hear the telly blaring through the thin walls, the noise carrying across the water. As normal, I pray Spider's not back, and I go inside. When I first see her, she hasn't moved from the position I'd left her in that morning: comatose on the sofa, some crappy show on the telly making a noise. I can see Spider's been around – he's got bags of cash and some bags of gear on the sideboard; but he's gone out since. I turn the telly down a bit and start talking to Mum as I take my coat off.

"While I'm fixing something to eat, she comes out of it for a while, looks down the length of the boat and sees me for the first time since I got back. She asks me how my day's been, even though I've spent the past half hour telling her. I go back to the start and tell her about the kids playing up on the coach, the Welsh lady, and the Scottish dude with the beard who tells everyone to shut the fuck up. That bit makes her smile – the first I've seen for weeks, maybe months; and I'm reminded that there must have been a time when it wasn't all about scrabbling together a few quid for the next fix, or being Spider's punch bag – a time when she was a member of the human race. But there's a point in my story where her face changes. I think it's when I mention that poem – *Jane Air*.

She asks me if I can feed the dog for her. This is weird - I'd done it when I came in - that sort of day-to-day stuff is never on her radar. But I go through the motions to keep her happy and when I come back with my bowl of pasta, she's sat upright, biting her finger and looking dreadful. Over the years, I've learned to pick up on her moods quickly. She stares at me with these wild eyes, and says, 'You won't ever leave me, will you, Hopie? For anyone else?' I tell her no; course not. I can't stand these conversations, her neediness, the feeling of being tied to her for ever; so to throw her off the scent, I put the pasta to one side and I root through my schoolbag until I find the tatty old anthology, the one with my notes crawling all over it. It falls open at one of the little Welsh lady's poems, and it's one I love, so I start reading it. "NO," she snaps. "Don't read that one. Read the other one. The *Jane Air* one." Frankly, I'm surprised she even registered me talking about that part, but I find the poem, and read it. Listening, she eases her legs off the sofa, so that she's looking on the verge of getting up. You can see the outline of her legs under the tracky bottoms – so thin I wonder they don't snap in two. I move in next to her, the page still open on my lap. She's staring at the tiny profile pic at the top of the page: the big Scottish guy in black and white. No more than the size of a postage stamp.

"I come to the end of the poem. She moves her arm, and sends my bowl of pasta to the floor. The dog's in there hoovering up and I'm trying to pull him away. She's transfixed on the photograph, and she's shaking.

Hope's voice became more distant. "I have this awful memory from when I was a kid – being packed off to the countryside to a foster parent when Mum can't cope – and seeing, down some country lane, this awful shivering shell of a myxy rabbit. Sat there, rooted to the middle of a road, it's eyes bulging, mouth hanging wide open. That's how Mum looked at that moment.

" 'Mum?' I say. I have to grab her shoulder, because she's shaking so much. Normally, I'd put it down to her coming off something, but this time it's different.

"She's put her foot down on the floor, straight into some of the pasta tubes, but she doesn't notice. Instead, she's over to the sideboard, head inside one of the cupboards, scrabbling about for goodness knows what. 'Mum?', I say again, but she's not listening. Out come tatty Christmas decorations, coupons, art catalogues and unanswered private view invitations, newspaper clippings, letters, red-edged bills.

"She freezes. She's found what she was looking for.

"It's a little shoe box, and from it, she gets out this picture. I get up and move round behind the sofa, so I can see over her shoulder. There's Mum. And a man. They're both so young. It's looks like Summer and everywhere, there are flags and tents and young people in welly boots. 'Glasto?' I ask her. But she says nothing. I take a closer look. His arm is curled round her shoulder, his body tuning into hers. Close. Possessive. They've both got a fag on the go; he's also got a cider bottle dangling from his fingers. Mum's still frail but in a pretty way, her face animated, excited even. Almost unrecognisable. And him - he's without a beard, and carrying less weight. I look at his face. It's *my* face. Christ! This is him: the Scottish poet who mesmerised me earlier. And more than that." She gasped the final words as a whisper. "This man is my dad."

Oleg Kowalski spoke. "When I looked at the back cover of your little book there, I must say that I was struck by an uncanny resemblance." A tentative pause. "So who spoke of this first?"

"Neither of us said anything for a while. We stared at the photo. The thing is with Mum – you're handling a bone china ornament that you're terrified of breaking. As long as I can remember, it's been that way. So, although I had a million questions on my lips, there's the familar angel on the shoulder: *you're the one who's taking care of her – don't rock the boat.* And I figure I can wait. It's taken this long. I can sit there an hour, two hours, all bloody night if needs be.

"So the minutes tick by: her curled up on the sofa, staring at the photo, the shoe box still sitting on her lap; me, stood behind the sofa, leaning in, arm curled around her chest, staring down at the photo that's resting on top. She goes on to do this thing that she's always done: pats the seat of the cushion beside her, stretching her arm out, ready to envelop me in a kind of maternal hug. And I'm gonna slip round and nestle in – of course I am. Not because I want to; but because it's what she needs.

"She closes her eyes as she talks. She always does. Her voice drawls; her speech is slow and slurred. Bu this is a lucid moment for her. She bites again at her finger.

"It turns out that I was the product of a brief but passionate dalliance. She's told me this before – on more than one occasion, I reckon – but she takers the story further this time. She'd tried to carry their relationship through the pregnancy, she said. She put up with a lot - his drinking, the young girls - his disappearing for days on end on benders, throwing his weight around when came back...he knocked her about a bit. She tried so hard to keep them together, she said, but was left damaged." Hope stopped and frowned. "Yeah – that was the actual word she used. All I know is, that the description of my father doesn't sit well alongside the guy I saw on that day – the one defending the little old lady.

"She carries on: 'He left before you were even born ,' she says. She clutches the sides of my face and tries to focus. Hers is wet with tears. 'But we've done okay, you and me, haven't we? We've got along okay without him?' Course, I want to say: no we haven't done okay. Ever since I can remember, I've grown up terrified of hurting you. Ever since I can remember, I've lied in bed listening to you sobbing alone; and when you weren't alone, you were bringing back strangers to get wasted with. I've made my own packed lunches since I was seven, phoned for an ambulance more time than I can remember, been packed off to pretend mummies and daddies while you got better. But, of course, I stay quiet, like I always do. I allow her to think she's, like, comforting me, when it's always the other way around.

"So she presses her lips to the top of my head and she carries on. 'You have to shut it out now, Hopie, love,' she says. 'Forget him. He's no good.' She holds me tighter, hushing me over and over, rocking me back and forth like I'm four or five again - me the adolescent carer contained and silenced in her stick-thin arms.

"*It'll be alright.*" Hope shook her head, and laughed. "You know what? I can't even remember if those were her words or mine.

"Anyhow. Later on, I take the dog out for its last pee of the evening. Mum's words about him are going round and round my head. I've got the that poetry anthology with me, and I reach the footbridge. I have one last look at his poem under the streetlamp. My eye runs over my hand-written notes next to my father's printed words. 'Annotations', Mrs. Waller called them. I take one last look at that little thumbnail picture of him at the foot of the page as the dog shows me the whites of his eyes, and lifts it leg to piss against the post.

"Nearby, there's a litter bin. I fold the anthology in half, take a deep breath and force it through the slot. *Forget him. He's no good.*

"When I get back to the boat, the TV's back on. She's still up, still clutching the shoe box. She's been going through it. I make us both a hot drink, and sit at her feet, her shins pressing into my back. She puts her cup down and I feel her touch over my hair, her fingers working each strand, folding, braiding, finding her little girl again; and the time when it had become only me and her against the world. It's what we do. She is telling me, good and proper: subject closed."

Oleg Kowalski nodded. He bided his time before asking the next question. Pointing at the red and black book, he asked, "Until recently?"

Hope looked downwards. She lifted it as though it were a lead weight. "Yeah – this. These are his latest poems. I'd managed to go for years and years blocking him out, convincing myself that what Mum said was true. It had to be – she was my mum, right? And as time went by, it got easier: I was a gullible, romantic teenager when I saw him, ready to see the best in anyone who could get me out of the God-awful shit-hole I was in. You see, I've never been bothered about the internet and going online, never even owned a mobile, so that part was easy – but we never spoke about him after that night and I never made the effort to find out any more.

"This was until a few months ago. Spider – Mum's bloke - he comes up to me when Mum's out of it. Says he'd found the shoe box in the back of the sideboard. He's used what's there to trace my real dad. Turns out he's a famous writer, married to an even more famous lady who cooks on the telly. Katherine Kennedy." Here eyes widened. "Even I've heard of her."

Oleg Kowalski's looked surprised. "Goodness! Yes – I know of her too. Her book about kosher foods is excellent!"

Hope smiled. "I wouldn't know. So Spider reckons we should have it out with him. He says that it has to come from me, his daughter. I say, no way. Dredging it up again will do Mum's head in. But Spider's smelling big money, and when that happens, he's like a dog with a bone. While we're holed up in a shitty houseboat, he says, this bloke is lording it in a French castle with his loaded missus. How much damage did his buggering off do to Mum's career as an artist, what with her breakdown and stuff? How much maintenance has he got away without paying? Yep, says Spider, this guy owes us big time."

"And so you go along with the plan; you agreed to confront your father?"

Hope sighed. "Not straight away. But Spider's a bloody nightmare. I know that if I don't play bal, he'd get back at me by making Mum's life hell – it's happened before – either using her as a punchbag, or giving her bad doses of stuff. And besides, in a twisted way, I know part of what he was saying is right: this man my father has never bothered to find me and has never paid us a penny. Obviously, I say that I don't want Mum involved – she just too vulnerable."

"And what next?"

"So Spider says he's found out that the guy – my dad - is going to be doing some sort of gig – a book signing or reading – in London. He gives me the date. The place. The times. We need to be there, he says. It's our chance to finally have it out with him.

"I turn this over in my head. Maybe I go along. Maybe I just go to see what he's like after all these years - find out if he's Mum's misogynistic wife-beater, or my super-defender of Welsh old ladies. If it turns out to be the first, we go for him and get what Mum deserves. We could turn up and I could pick my moment. I don't often think about what I'm gonna do if that doesn't turn out to be the case…"

She stalled for a while, dropped her head, and ran her fingers over her cheeks, feeling for the scarred tissue. Her breath was broken with shivers.

Oleg Kowalski looked on with concern. "Perhaps your story should wait until a time when you feel stronger, my dear…"

She seemed determined to continue, and came up for air. "Wow," she breathed. "It comes in waves. To think that all of this was last Wednesday."

"So how did it go? When you both went to confront him?"

She allowed herself a tiny laugh, before clutching her stomach again. "Oh… about everything went tits up from the outset. I met Spider at Southbank, where it was all kicking off. By the time I got there, he'd already been X-in' and was as high as a kite. It was supposed to be about me; about the way I chose to cope. But I couldn't persuade him to stay away, and from the moment he got there, he wanted to run the show. He'd upset some posh woman, got into this ridiculous macho brawl with a security guard – pretty typical Spider – and ended up spilling a book display across the floor. But this other guy there – I think he was American - seemed to be able to calm him down – he slipped him some money to make him leave without a fuss – that works with Spider. Besides, Spider knew the last part was down to me. And I'd been drinking myself – Dutch courage and all that. I think it's the reason why I let Spider persuade me to go back in and have it out with him.

"So I found my way into this big hall and there he was - the great Jimmy Dunbar – my dad. He was talking to an audience. When he spoke, I was taken back fifteen years to the guy reading his poetry out. But, the thing is, I couldn't get Mum's version out of my head either. I sat there and listened for a while, but the more I thought about what I was doing, the more the place seemed to close in on me. His face was a blur, I could hear the breathing of every person near to me. I felt my chest constrict, and suddenly, I couldn't breathe and everything was feeling very distant. I don't think I'd ever had a panic attack before. I needed to get out.

"By the time it was over, and the crowd was coming back out of the hall, I'd recovered. The initial plan was to stand up and say something while he was talking, but that hadn't happened, Now, I found myself in the queue of people getting books signed. This, though, meant listening to people talking about him and his poems like he was some kind of god. I started to feel pissed off again. All these people buying books, lining his pockets. This stranger, my father, with his rich missus with her TV shows and royalties. And us, me and Mum, forced to live on some floating hovel. Spider was right about that part at least.

"By the time I was near the front of the queue, I felt ready to take him to account, and even to shame him in public.

"That was before I saw the kid with him.

"I remembered reading about a little boy, but now, here he was, in the flesh: my half-brother.

"I was like a rabbit in the headlights, staring at them both. I'd thought about what I was going to say while I was in that queue – pictured myself saying it like I was in the middle of a dramatic film. And this kid with his big brown eyes, blinking at me…" She shook her head. "I think all I achieved was to make a total bitch myself. I said what I had to say like some complete twat."

Oleg Kowalski could hear the melancholy in her voice. But he knew better than to ask her what it was that she said.

She continued: "The plan had been to, like, stand my ground; see what he had to say. But I bottled it - turned and ran. Before I got away, he'd managed to grab me and scribble down his number on my copy of the book. I should have thrown it at him, but I didn't – I found myself grabbing it and running. It was all I came out with, and Spider was as mad as hell. He tried to make me go back and finish the job, but it was too late. There was no way I was going back in there.

"Did you call his number?"

She turned the book over in her hands, and lowered her head. "Like I said, no mobile. And I didn't want to speak to him anyway."

"But you ended up seeing him again?"

Her face was close to the image on the back cover. She examined it, and sighed. "He turned up again that Friday at the boat – it was why I was such a mess when I saw you on the train. God knows how he found us. " She shook her head. "It was terrible timing. Seeing him had churned up all kinds of shit inside me. Just before he appeared, I'd been having it out with Mum about a letter I'd found – a letter he'd written to me about fifteen years after he'd disappeared. He'd left his details with it, said he would be back in touch if I felt the time was right. Mum had hidden it from me for well over a decade – it was only when I turned the place upside down that I found it."

Oleg Kowalski looked down at the little book resting on the bed. The small sheets of paper were visible. She followed his line of sight. "Yeah, that's the it." Her fingers moved to it. "I was, like at the end of my tether. What she'd told me – that he'd ran away, never been in touch since – wasn't the truth. Well, I'd stormed up and down that boat, having a bit of a rant. Took the dog out for a walk to calm myself. But as soon as I was back inside, we were back at it, hammer and tongs, again. By this time, I'd chucked some gear into my rucksack and was ready to leave her to stew in her own lies. It wasn't about going for good – I'd never do that to her – it was about getting some headspace.

"As I was leaving, there he was: waiting on the bank outside the houseboat. I tried to get rid of him before Mum clocked him or Spider came back, but she'd already heard his voice. I took him inside, mainly to avoid a scene. I reckoned I could have it out about the letter too. This wasn't to be my finest decision, as it turns out.

"Mum was just coming down off something when she saw him. Her reaction scared the shit out of me. Her face was as white as a sheet and she wouldn't say a word. And me – I didn't really feel mad at him any more: but seeing him there, and thinking what might have been and the mess Mum had made of her life without him made me feel... well.. kind of sad.

"We tried to have some kind of conversation at first. I'm not sure where it all went wrong - it's all a bit muddled up in my head – but I know that it kicked off after five or ten minutes in. He told Mum he was pissed off with her because she hid the letter. At some point, Mum drifted into the conversation. Then, without warning, she went ballistic. It's the way she deals with things, you know? It's like, you take your eye off the pan on the stove and, before you know it, everything's spilling over. There was a lot of yelling, and I was having to restrain her. I remember having this kind of out-of-body moment? Like you do in the eye of a storm? There they are, my parents: an overweight, washed-up poet and a paranoid junkie with me floundering between them. And that's when she lashed out at him – and I mean proper lasheing out.

"There was blood on his cheek - a lot of blood - and I was holding her back. But the sight of what she'd done alarmed her, and she laid off a bit. I remember this awful silence: him staring at her, not quite believing what she's become; her collapsing back into the state in which she often finds herself. I can remember the blood trickling over his fingers as he held his face, staring at her." Hope stopped for a moment, her head filled with the scene.

Oleg Kowalski gave her the space to continue. "Take your time, my dear. As I have said, any of this can wait."

She hadn't heard him. "You know...that houseboat can be a bloody place on a dark night. Voices can carry for miles over the water. You hear snippets of things that were never meant for other ears. And the shrieks in the middle of the night. I guess they must be birds, but I always fancied it was something far more sinister, like souls lost to the sea finding their way back inland. But for all that," she let out a long sigh, "it had never been more terrifying than that night. Silence. With the snow falling all around us."

She remembered that the old man was there. Looking up, she managed to smile through her trauma. Her eyes moved over the slight mounds of the bedclothes over his fragile, broken frame. "Anyhow. After that, I was more keen than ever to get away - for the time being at least. So I got my shit back together and... well, left them both to it. Headed for the station. I told him I had mates to go to, but there was no-one. On the train, headed Christ knows where."

"The evening of our meeting," Oleg Kowalski said.

"The evening of our meeting," she repeated after him. "That could have ended better!" She half-smiled, half-winced, and gripped her side. Somewhere beyond the hospital, the first grey yawns of daylight were met by the song a lonely blackbird. They both listened for a while, she still grasping her middle.

Oleg Kowalski tried to sound more stern. "You need your bed. You are very ill. I am no doctor, but I can see that much, my dear."

She raised herself with care, furrows of pain across her forehead. A soft smile. "I can't stay here," she said in a small voice. "Mum's bloke, Spider: he was here earlier. In the hospital."

Oleg Kowalski remembered the incident where the young policewoman dashing off earlier that day. "What did he want?"

"He was still mad that I messed up at the book-signing. Said h had a new plan and told me I was going to finish it right this time. He can be pretty convincing. And he wanted the book of poems that the phone number had been written in. I told him I'd lost it on the train, so he went ape-shit again. He didn't seem to notice I was lying there in bed with tubes going in and out.

"He was talking about the little kid. That's when I got scared."

Oleg Kowalski's face registered concern. "What would he want with the boy?"

"He didn't say. But Spider's capable of anything if he knows there's money at the end of it. This time he was desperate. He had one of the big shot suppliers on his tail for not paying, and he imagined he was so near to bagging what he said we were owed.

She paused, and toyed with the tube of her drip. "The thing is: I know he's going to do something stupid. And I know that it involves that little kid. But I need to get out of here and find out before he does anything bloody stupid."

Oleg Kowalski looked alarmed. "But... you can't leave my dear. Look at yourself. You are ill. You need to let the doctors treat you. It is too soon since the accident..." He took in the hunch of her shoulders, the curve of her spine and the dark patches beneath her eyes.

She shook her head and raised herself to her feet. "I have to go," she said. "Before it's too late." Finding the red and black again, she pushed it back towards him. "In the meantime, please keep this safe for me?"

He didn't answer. Nor did he take hold of the book. He watched her try to manoeuvre the wheelchair around as she gripped the drip stand, before wheeling herself towards the dark doors of the ward.

In his heart, Oleg Kowalski knew that this was the last he would see of this extraordinary young woman.

Ten – The South Coast - early morning Sun 4th Dec 2016

Jimmy Dunbar was wide awake. He was lying still in the darkness attempting to piece the hours together as one would attempt to reassemble a broken vase. He was turned on his side but he could hear the low, regular breathing of a woman beside him.

He touched his throbbing cheek, the pain returning with the abating of the effects of alcohol. Prodding the wound, he found that it had become congealed and encrusted. He wondered what had become of the dressing.

Sliding his right leg out from under the duvet, he found the floor. The air was cold, the skin over his calves puckering into goose bumps. Naked save his boxer shorts, he peered into the darkness for his clothes and his phone.

He had no idea had much time had passed since he had walked away from the houseboat, but he knew it to be more than a single evening.

His mind kept drifting back to the foot-bridge, staring into grey layers of falling snow, willing the young woman to reappear. Looking across the water to the sad silhouette of the houseboat, he had pictured Jasmine wasting in the dying light of the stove, cold, helpless and alone.

There, at the centre of the bridge, the ice-black water had been gaping like an open mouth beneath, a portal inviting oblivion. Holding his handkerchief to his bleeding cheek, he'd made a call to Hereward at that moment of his nadir. His initial enquiring after Alfie had been, at best, half-hearted. He'd asked Hereward for more time: it had become complicated - could they hold on to the wee lad for another day or two while he tried to find a way through it? But there had been no plan.

Hereward had been, as always, kind and obliging in response. "Take the time you need, mate." He had heard the sound of a kettle being filled from a tap. "Me and Cliff can find plenty of things to do to occupy the boy out here." He'd signed off with a tentative, "Keep in touch, yeah?" Jimmy had assured him that he would.

He'd looked back to the direction of the houseboat again. As the snow fell, he had no longer been sure which of the dark, innocuous shapes it had been. Looking to the opposite side, he'd followed the line of melancholic lights and low rooves until he'd located the public house he'd left behind half an hour or so before. He'd turned. Decision made. He would find a quiet table in the corner and think the situation through. He could make that plan over a half pint.

Siobhan O'Shea had begun the evening shift before Jimmy had left, that first time around. When she'd seen him return, she'd stepped from behind the bar.

"Goodness! What happened to your face?"

He'd looked down at the blood-covered handkerchief. "Got into an altercation," he'd said with as much humility as he could muster.

"Looks like a cat got ya. Or something bigger." She'd moved closer. "Let me have a look at it." She'd eased the handkerchief away to reveal three parallel gashes, angry and open, laced with fresh blood. "Ouch," she said. "You'll be needing something on that." She was younger, a dark-skinned girl with a kind expression and a soothing Southern Irish lilt. He recalled the smell of beer towels and bleach. "There's a first aid kit somewheres round here," she'd said. "Let's be sorting y'out, fella."

Pulling up a stool by the side of the bar, she'd patted it with a great deal of tenderness. "You know that bit in the fill-ums, where yer hero's been punching his way through a whole feckin' army, but flinches afterwards when his missus tends his wounds? " And she'd dabbed at his wounds with a cotton pad.

"This is your moment."

"I'm afraid that I'm no bloody hero." Jimmy had replied. "My assailant was in the singular. My ex. And she's got bloody sharp nails."

She'd winced as she'd applied the dressing. "I can see. And not very clean either, I'm thinking." She'd pulled herself from him, and stepped back, looking straight into his face. "I'm Siobhan, by the way."

"Nice to meet you, Siobhan," he'd said, trying hard not to recoil as she came near again. "My name's Jimmy." He'd nodded towards the optics. "Any chance of something medicinal? This is throbbing like a bastard."

Now, many hours later, shivering on the edge of the bed, he remembered random moments of subsequent events. He'd perched at the bar, working his way through a bottle of scotch while she divided her attentions between him and an assortment of raggle-taggled customers who passed through. He had some memory of finding a squalid guesthouse room in town, sleeping through till midday, before finding the pub again mid- afternoon, having found an off-licence on the way for a livener. Siobhan had been there again come early evening, this time entertaining a group of her uni friends. They'd made a noisy entrance and settling at a big table beneath the darts board. They were an irreverent, welcoming crowd and they reminded him of his old gang with Hereward: tight-knit, open, raucous. This lot were all mature students, though. Siobhan had introduced them with mock formality and Jimmy had opened his wallet - Jasmine would call him Charlie Free-Heart in those days before either of them had had any money. There was this moon-faced guy with a thatch of strawberry blond hair who told Jimmy that he'd recognised him – he'd studied his poems as an undergraduate. Jimmy had been left feeling flattered. He'd assumed that their neglecting to mention his recent infamy in the papers had been out of politeness on their part.

That second evening, it hadn't taken long for Jimmy bury such complications and allow those rough-hewn walls of the public house to become a temporary haven.

That moment had come – the moment that always comes at a certain point when you're drinking. The walls had fallen away and the pub had become this dark, muffled, little bubble of a universe, where all that matters were the faces around you and who was getting the next one in. Jimmy had some vague recollection of reciting some of his own works around this time.

Now, here in the darkness, he couldn't be sure whether he was still in the same building, or whether indiscretion had led him elsewhere. He crept forward, crouching as he felt for the edge of the bed, hoping that he might find a door.

There was a snap, and one corner of the room was filled with light. The woman beside him – he could see now that it was Siobhan – moved away from the bedside lamp and propped herself on an elbow, her face screwed up against the glare. She covered her face with her arm. She was pleasant-looking, her shaggy bob dyed a deep red. She spoke in a matter-of –fact manner.

"Hey. Are ya okay?"

Jimmy turned. His thrust his lower arms over the crotch of his shorts, in the hope that they would conceal the undignified mound of his paunch.

"Aye," he said, feeling awkward. "I didnae mean to wake you up." He scanned the floor for his things.

She pushed herself back, so that she was sitting more upright, and ran her fingers through her hair. "Epic fail, there, then," she said. "Guess you've fallen out of practice."

Jimmy spotted his clothes in a heap not far from the door. He moved back to the bed, and was pulling his trousers over his bare feet. "Look," he said, "I'm so sorry. It's all, well, a bit of a wee blur, as the cliché goes."

She looked at his wound again. "You're gonna need to get that dressed again, so y'are." She swivelled her body round until her feet found the floor. "Christ, my head! D'you want some tea? I could murther a cuppa tea." She was standing now, wearing a baggy 'Killers' t-shirt over her knickers. She yawned as she looked around the room, hoping to find something warmer to wear. "It's bloody freezing out here!" Settling for a duffle coat that was draped over the back of a chair, she hooked it over her shoulders.

Jimmy was fastening his belt. He found himself quickly checking the crumpled sheets, but she'd seen him. She said, "We didn't shag, if that's what you're worried about." She stopped in her tracks and frowned. "At least I don't think we did..."

Jimmy froze in alarm.

She laughed -a light, easy sound. "Look: what you would have been lacking in aptitude, I was lacking in inclination. Besides..." she nodded towards his wedding band and held up her own unadorned fingers. "I would need to be pretty far gone to get past your magic circle there, so I would. Fingers well-and-truly burned on that front many-a-time, I can tell ya." She moved towards the door. "Perhaps your saving grace is that I can't remember anything much past about ten o'clock either."

With a sheepish smile, Jimmy buttoned up his shirt and looked about the room.

She laughed again. "You're not so sure where you are, are yous? A few of the fellas helped you up the stairs. We're in the room above the bar. This here is my Da's place. And this here is the only bed in my Da's place. He's off to Seville for the Winter. I always look after."

"Ah," said Jimmy.

She moved towards the door. "Give me a minute, will ya?

I'm going down for supplies. Tea to be precise. And I'll find something to patch that face of yours back up again." She pointed at him. "Don't you go running off on me, ya hear?"

While she was gone, Jimmy found his jacket, and retrieved the phone from the pocket. He jabbed at the side buttons. Dead battery. Returning with two mugs of tea, Siobhan padded across the room and placed hers on a spent upturned beer keg by the side of the bed. She passed Jimmy's his. Like a cat, she slid back between the sheets and closed her eyes. After a while, she opened them again. Pulling the covers up over her chest folded hers arms across the outside and contemplated Jimmy for a moment. "Well?"

Jimmy gripped the mug. "Well what?" he said.

Wiggling her head from side to side, she sang, "Watch ya gonna dooo..?"

A lot was becoming more familiar about her. Jimmy was taken to a time earlier when he had been leaning across the bar in the wee hours; she, leaning across from the other side. They had broken away from the others while she was fetching him another drink. The main crowd were caught up in a game of *Cards Against Humanity.* He had begun opening up about his old life with Jasmine, and it hadn't taken long to move on to Hope.

She'd stopped in her tracks. Hope? she'd asked. She knew a Hope. "Ah, she's a lovely girl, so she is. Comes in here quite often. There are those people that, like, walk into a room and the whole place feels warmer. You know: the party has started. And she's a heart o'gold as well– everybody loves Hope. Mind you, got a tough craic with that mother and that Spider idjitt." She'd looked straight at Jimmy, eyes wide. "So you're really Hope Kelly's old man? Wow." She'd shrugged. "She's never mentioned you."

Now, as morning came, he felt the need to backtrack. "Umm... the stuff I was telling you last night? Sorry about boring you to death with it all. Truth is, I don't *know* what I'm gonnae do about it."

Siobhan stared into her tea. "It's a cliché, but Time is a healer. This time last week, that girl had no idea that you, her da, would come crashing back into her life. She'll be needing to process it – I expect that's why she wants to skedaddle for a while." Her voice drifted away, and she was somewhere else for a moment. "You wanna know something?"

Jimmy sat back down on the bed. He placed his hands on his knees. "Aye. Go on."

"About five years ago, I went for fourteen months without speaking to my old man. Me ma had been diagnosed with breast cancer. I found out that, a mere two weeks after she'd got the news, the bastard had an affair with one of her best mates. When Ma told me, I went psycho. Did the whole chucking-his-clothes-out-on-the lawn thing like you do - a-hollering like a bloody banshee from the upstairs winder on the Old Girl's behalf. I tore up the family photies, so I did; got rid of every trace of the bastard that I could find. Never once consulted Ma over it, of course – didn't even stop to ask her how she felt. Ma said nothing at first. There was the chemo, an operation – but she got the all-clear in the end. It was only at that moment that she sat me down during all that, that we could talk it through. Told me that, eight years back, she'd had a fling as well – not, she said, that that fact alone made his actions or piss-awful timing any more excusable. Shit happens, she said. But it was their shit. For husband and wife to deal with. I didn't need to get involved. In the meantime, she said, Da was still my da.

Her smile was melancholic. "Of course, the marriage was long dead in the water. But if she could forgive the old bastard, so could I. In the end, that's what I did." She winked at Jimmy. "We're all in a good place now, so we are. That's why the old bastard trusts me to look after this drinking-hole." She sat there for a moment, smiling, before reaching over to touch Jimmy's knee. "You're a decent enough bloke, from what I've seen." she said. "I hope, despite the rawness of it all, your girl will have seen a glimpse of that too."

Jimmy sighed. "Maybe you're right." He looked at her soft, round, open face and blew out through his cheeks. "I really need to get my shit back together. How long has it been since I first came here?"

Her brow furrowed. "You came in the night before last. You were in again yesterday lunchtime – right the way through to last orders last night. I think it's what we in the trade call a bender."

Jimmy ran his hand over the back of his neck. "Jesus. And there I was thinking I was past all that. What a gallus." He shook himself and looked at her with a grim smile. "Maybe it's the case that you've facilitated a Damascene moment in me. It's a shame I havnae got the greatest record where redemption is concerned." He straightened his frame, as if to move away. "Anyhoo," he said, "I should be getting back to the lad."

"There you go," said Siobhan. "You do that. And I'm sure that Hope'll be back in your life at some point. If there was ever a girl wid a sensible head on her shoulders, she'd be the one. Give her some time and space, won't ya?"

***

Later that morning, as Jimmy climbed into the passenger seat of the Land Rover, a muted Hereward peered through the fog at what he could see of the road ahead.

Jimmy eyed the other man. "Sorry I've been out of touch for so long, pal. My phone ran out o' juice." He added by way of an excuse, "I had to use the payphone in the pub." He was conscious of the alcohol lifting from his skin with each movement.

Hereward didn't take his eyes off the road. "There was this other writer guy called Aldous Huxley," he said. "He once said that several excuses are less convincing then one. Besides," he glanced Jimmy's way, "I can smell it on you."

Arching his back, Jimmy lifted his arse cheek in an attempt to fart with some discretion, but his body and the leather interior combined had other ideas. It came rasping through the cabin of the Land Rover like tearing fabric. "Christ," said Jimmy. "I'm sorry about that."

Hereward pursed his lips and wound his window down. The sounds of the morning invaded the car: the dripping of the thaw, car tyres cutting through sludge. A thick grey fog muted the morning: the world rendered to flat, indefinable shades of grey.

Hereward now remained very quiet. Jimmy noted how his friend's knuckles reddened as his grip on the wheel tightened. He turned over the ignition and swung the vehicle out of the pub car park, until it faced the thick grey blanket beyond. The Land Rover growled as it pushed forwards over the snow-covered carriageway.

After a few minutes, Jimmy, again, tried a more conciliatory tone. "Everything okay with Alfie?"

"Alfie's chipper. He's had a blast." Hereward shot him a look, taking in the rumpled clothing, the patched up cheek. "Looks like his old man has too..." He looked back to the road.

Jimmy slouched down in his seat. "It didnae go to plan. I should've called earlier. I'm sorry."

Hereward's mouth settled into a grim line, and they fell into silence again. All Jimmy could think about was that he needed more sleep. And after that, he needed another drink.

After a while, Hereward spoke. "You ought to know: your missus phoned."

Jimmy eyes flickered open. He blinked twice. "What? Kat?"

"She wanted to know how the boy is."

Jimmy shifted in his seat. "How in the hell did she know where we are?"

"Don't ask me. Of course, I covered your arse. Like I always done. Told her that you'd popped out and would call her back."

"Thanks." He frowned and added, "I think." He removed his glasses and wiped them on his jumper, before looking across to Hereward. "How long ago was this?"

"Yesterday night. About ten-ish. And again an hour or so later. Have to admit, we let the second one run to answerphone. And the third."

"Aye, that's Kat for you. What did she say? On the message, like?"

"She said she was on her way over to England to fetch your lad back." He cast a queer, sidelong look at Jimmy. "Trust you're okay with that?"

Jimmy breathed deeply. "Shee-ite. Kat. All I fucking need. Maybe the weather'll delay her a wee while."

"I've never met your missus mate. But I've seen and heard enough to know she's to let a touch of fog or a few flakes of snow stand in her way." Pulling onto the dual carriageway, the fog had cleared a little, and Hereward lurched up a gear. "I wouldn't pick a bloody fight with her, either."

Jimmy groaned. A wave of nausea subsumed him and he rested a hand on his stomach. "D'you mind slowing down, H? I'm not feeling too clever."

Hereward fixed his eye on the other man for a moment. He let his window down an inch or so, and the cool air whistled through. Some two or three minutes passed, and Jimmy felt his eyelids becoming heavy. They both drifted into their own worlds for a time, one punctuated by the mesmerising rhythms of the windscreen wipers and tires burring over icy roads. Blurred circles of headlights caught sporadic shards of sleet as the Land Rover cut through the slushy roads. Without warning, Hereward jerked down on the wheel and turned a sharp left onto a carriageway. Startled, Jimmy shot upright.

Hereward cleared his throat. "So how was Jas?"

Jimmy rubbed his eyes. "You were right about her not looking too clever. Whatever shit she's been doin' has taken its toll. She could be sixty if she's a day."

Hereward didn't comment. "And the gal? She was there?"

"Aye. she was there." Jimmy shifted in his seat. He carried on. "That letter I told you about? The one I'd written all that time back and popped through Jas's door? It only turns out that Jas had hidden it from the girl all this time."

Hereward was nodding. "And does that ease your conscience?"

Jimmy looked at the other man. Back in the day, Hereward had always been the weaker one, the foil. He felt irked by his reticence. "Give me a wee break, H, will ye? Aye, it's a given that I was an self-centred shite in those days. I did stuff that I'm not proud of, but who doesn't? But I was never... well... bloody *abusive* or anything like that, was I? And this was what she's been making out about me. Abusive! That's a big bloody word to bandy around, huh?" He felt for the dressing on his cheek. "The bloody irony..."

Hereward glanced at it, but didn't comment. He indicated right and turned off the dual carriageway.

Jimmy continued, regardless. "God only knows what kind of crap that woman has peddled the lass." He turned away, feeling the need to give her name a voice. "She took off afterwards. Never said where she was going. Doesnae even carry a phone."

Hereward said, "That's unusual in this day and age. Maybe you should give her a break for a while. After that, you can talk properly, without Jas being around. And she can get to make her own mind up."

Rubbing his face with his palms in a series of slow, deliberate movements, Jimmy tried to make sense of it all. "Maybe." His voice was strained and his throat dry. "Christ, H, I could do with a drink to take the edge off the bloody hangover." He saw Hereward's wordless reaction and changed tack again. "Oh. And I forgot tae say: thanks for taking care of the boy."

"Cliff's the one you wanna thank, " said Hereward. He smiled to himself as a private thought crossed his mind, and the Land Rover swung left towards the narrow, dark track heading towards to the Old Schoolhouse. It battled against the ridges of slush, the snow piled high either side. "You now have a son who knows how to play chess."

"Chess? Jesus. The lad's only five." Jimmy pulled his collar up around his neck and cheeks, and folded his arms.

Hereward said, pointedly, "Alfie's a great kid. Dunno if the fostering thing'll work out; but if it does, we'd be happy with a nipper who turned out the way he has."

After a while, the Land Rover skidded into the drive alongside the solid walls of Hereward's hostel. Beyond, towards the Downs, lay a suffocating blanket of fog. The engine cut out and Hereward kept his hand on the ignition. As he looked across to the building, his frame stiffened. "That's not right", he said, more to himself than to Jimmy.

Jimmy followed his gaze. The door to the hostel was wide open: a shocked gasp of white-yellow light with a thin carpet of grey-white sludge creeping over the threshold. Without closing the driver's door, Hereward was out of his seat, fumbling towards it with his walking stick. A few metres short of the building, he planted the foot of the stick in the ground and stopped. "Cliff?" He waited for a response.

Jimmy was out of the Land Rover now, and had caught up with him. "What's happening?"

Hereward held a finger to his lips. As still as dead men, they listened. He gestured towards the building "The door." He said again, "Something's not right."

From somewhere through the fog, way beyond the building, came the distant shout of another man.

Jimmy turned his face towards sound. "Who in the hell was that?"

Hereward was hobbling away from Jimmy, reaching the North face of the building to move along a slippery concrete path that gave way to a lattice of ancient paths and heathland. Letting his stick drop to the snowy ground, he moved on, unsupported.

At the bottom of the first field, there was a stile. As Hereward fumbled his way over, the bigger man gained some ground. Heaving his limbs over the rickety wooden structure, a small chink in the fog revealed the vast stretch of the Downs falling away before them.

The path ahead had been smothered by snowfall, but beyond lay a low, huddled line of naked, shrubs. Heavy breathing and branches cracking underfoot could be heard ahead.

Hereward pointed in the direction of the sound. "Over there…"

The cry was new. The words of the voice were now discernible: "Alfie?"

Hereward had reached a thin line of tall bushes. His jacket caught on the thorns as he moved through. Jimmy followed, the burrs tearing through his skin on the backs of his hands. Out of nowhere, a stumbling figure and a feeble beam of torchlight appeared.

"Shit!" Hereward cried. "What's happened?" The other figure looked about himself in a state of abject despair.

Now, Jimmy had reached the two of them. He could see now that the man was Cliff.

Cliff had dropped down to all fours. His body heaved as he gasped for breath, and his coughing became an agonised retching. Hereward dropped to his knees beside him, placing a hand on the other man's back. "Cliff?" Cliff looked up for a moment, with wide, watery eyes. He faced the ground again, and a splatter of vomit hit the earth.

"Cliff? What's happening, man? Where's Alfie?"

Cliff had no words. He stared at Hereward, open-mouth, shaking his head.

Jimmy watched aghast for a second. Without warning, he was upon Cliff, grabbing him beaneath each arm, and hauling him to his feet. He held the man by the lapels of his jacket and yelled into his face: "Where's my boy? Where's Alfie?" Cliff tottered on his tiptoes, eyes bulging as Hereward looked up from the ground.

Behind them, a small group from the hostel that had heard the alarm raised were approaching. One of the crowd was the man who'd passed Jimmy on the stairs a few days earlier. They stood, helplessly about the two men. "D'you need help?" the first man panted. "We heard calling out?" Should we call the police?"

Cliff still dangled like a speechless marionette, shoulders around his ears, mouth gaping open. Small beads of spittle were forming at the corners of his mouth. Hereward came behind Jimmy and lay a grip on his shoulders. "Dunny! Please! Let him go! You'll get nothing out of him this way…"

Cliff's lips writhed around his large yellow teeth, missiles of saliva splattering Jimmy's beard as he tried to find words.

Hereward hissed into Jimmy's ear "Dunny!"

Jimmy was losing the strength in his shoulders, his grip on Cliff weakening until the other man's feet found the earth once more. But finding the ground empowered the younger man: the helplessness on his face had gone, and it began to contort with retaliation and rage. He slipped away from Jimmy's weakening grasp, took a grip of Jimmy's upper arms, and kneed him hard in the groin.

Jimmy doubled in agony and dropped, sack-like, to the ground, pulling his legs to his chest, writhing in agony. Cliff was on him, turning his body over and thrusting the small of Jimmy's back, wrenching the big man back into a head-lock. He forced Jimmy onto his knees arm tightened around his neck. Cliff's face worked with turmoil. Some of the crowd from the hostel had moved in, trying to wrench Cliff away, but his grip only tightened.

Jimmy could manage no more than a strangled gasp: "What have you done to Alfie, you bastard?" he rasped.

Hereward dropped to his knees beside them, moving his lips close to Cliff's ear. "Cliff! Listen to me: it's Hereward. Let him go, for Fuck's sake! This won't help. Tell us what happened. Please, Cliff..."

Jimmy was weakening, his eyelids closing. But Hereward had penetrated Cliff's rage. Piece by piece, the agony and ferocity dropped away to reveal naked terror.

Cliff's arms became limp. He staggered back into the snow, exhausted. Jimmy fell forwards in a heap, gripping his own his neck, coughing and spitting into the dirty snow.

Hereward's voice was gentle now. "Cliff," he said. "We need you to tell us what's happened. We need to know where the boy is."

Cliff lifted his head and stared. Jimmy still regaining his breath, watched them both. The others from the hostel crowded around. "I can't get a signal out here," said one of them. "I'll have to go back if we want to call the police..."

Cliff whispered, his breath a dissipating cloud in the morning air. "He said... he said was hungry. I went to make breakfast. When I got back... he'd gone..."

"What if the bastard's lying?" coughed Jimmy.

Hereward ignored him and held Cliff's shoulders. "But he can't have gone far? Why were you looking out here? Didn't you check inside first?"

Cliff shook his head, his chest rising and falling. His face crumpled in despair. "The front door was open. I saw his prints in the snow. But I lost the trail..."

Jimmy was back on his feet. He staggered forward and leant over Cliff. Hereward tried to fend him off. "When?" Jimmy thundered. "How long ago?"

Cliff closed his eyes, still gasping for breath. "Five, maybe ten minutes,"

Jimmy turned and stared towards the Downs. It was a blank void. He took a few uncertain steps into the mist, looking like about him as a madman searching for his wits. Cupping his fingers around his mouth, he yelled his son's name again and again.

From the distance, only the disparate echo of his own voice came back to him.

Hereward persevered with Cliff. "Didn't you hear nothing? A car engine? Voices?"

Cliff shook his head. "I looked up and down the road. Nothing. So I came out here."

Hereward stood again, and looked across to where Jimmy stood. He glanced up at the crowd of onlookers. "Any of you lot seen or heard anything?"

The man with the mobile shrugged and looked to the others. "Nothing. I'll get back to the hostel and call the police, yeah?"

Jimmy brushed the snow off the front of his coat. He spat into the ground. With his hands on his hips, he looked to Hereward. "Actually - I know who it is. It may be okay. It'll be Kat. That message she left at yours. All those missed calls." He still spoke through heavy breaths. "She'd take him without saying a bloody word, I know she would. Or she'd send someone else to do it for her..."

Hereward looked less certain. "I guess if at least we knew if it was her, he'd be safe, yeah?"

The man with the phone and a couple of the others headed back to the Old Schoolhouse, as a sound cut in through the fog from a distance It was the high revving of the engine of a car, its tyres skidding in the snow. They raised their heads in the direction of the noise. Where the main road lie, a set of car headlights breached the brow of the hill.

"Come on!" yelled Jimmy. He staggered back in the direction of the hostel, one foot planted ahead of the other through the sludge and mud of the narrow track. Some of the younger men who'd stayed behind were overtaking him, leaping over the stile to disappear at the top of the field where the path curved back towards the building.

By the time Jimmy had reached the area to the front of the The Old Schoolhouse, he found them stood around a sleek, black hire car. The engine was still running. It had reversed into the drive, its headlights still on main beam, and was facing the road. No-one could see through the tinted windows of the vehicle. Jimmy stepped forwards in front of the others. The car engine stopped.

Both driver and passenger door opened. From one side, emerged a man; from the other, a woman. The latter was dressed in dark layers and wore a scarf around her head.

The trees around them shivered, and thin gust of air lifted the last layer of snow in a thin upward drift, bringing with it the first familiar hint of the woman's fragrance. Her glove rested on the passenger door, and she turned her head.

Jimmy staggered towards her. "Kat."

Unusually for her, her face was not made up. When she looked at him, her expression was cold. "I'm here for Alfie."

Jimmy held her gaze before moving towards the car. Crouching beside the rear passenger window, he held his face to the glass, shielding his face from any glare. Seeing nothing, he groped for the handle. In an instant, there was a beep, a double click of the central locks, and he felt himself tugging at the door in vain.

He rose to stare at the male driver, who had remained by the driver's door. The man removed a pair of aviator sunglasses. It was Lefevre.

Jimmy made for the front passenger's door, forcing Kat to step back in haste.

"What in God's name are you doing?" said Kat. She recoiled, smelling the alcohol on him. She straightened up with a look of horror and stepped away from him. "Christ, have you been drinking?" she gasped. "Take me to Alfie right now."

Jimmy continued to work the door handle with increasing panic. "What are you talking about, woman? You bloody have him! Open the doors of this bloody car!"

Lefevre stepped around the front of the vehicle as Jimmy pulled and tugged some more. "James – will you give over? Katherine asked me to bring her here to fetch the boy." He raised his voice. "James?" He held onto Jimmy's arm.

Jimmy shook it off with a violent gesture.

The two men stared at one another for a moment. Lefevre clicked on his key fob again, and opened the car door. "Look for yourself. There's no-one in there." Jimmy stared at Lefevre. The others, Hereward and Cliff among them, looked on.

Lefevre spoke with deliberation. "Look James: "Why don't you go and fetch the kid and his stuff and make everybody's life easier? Alfie gets back with his mom, you get to clear up whatever shit you're in at this end and we all die happy, huh?"

Hereward was with the others. He leant on the stick, the events having taken their toll. "We've called the police," he shouted over. "They're on their way." He looked down on Cliff, who had sat down on the ground and tucked his head between his knees. Impervious to developing events, he rocked his body, forwards and back.

Jimmy's arms dropped to his sides. Staring into Kat's widening eyes with impending horror, the penny had finally dropped.

Neither had the boy. The boy was missing.

They both turned to stare at the unyielding world beyond - a diaphanous veil that shifted about them, masking the Earth in deceit and pale subterfuge.

Kat moved forwards, her elbows bent, her fingers stretched and ramrod straight. She craned her head forwards and, with no warning, screamed her son's name into the void.

"Alfie!" She shouted again and again until her voice became hoarse.

Her cries died away. The silence swelled around them all.

From nowhere, something tiny and plaintive in the distance. A cry – whether an animal's or a child's, it was impossible for Jimmy to tell.

Kat turned. She whispered, "You heard that, right?"

Jimmy craned his neck forward into the thick, stagnant air. The fog was all-consuming. "I...I think so."

Behind them, feet scraped through the snow and gravel, accompanied by the sound of panting. They turned to see Cliff. Strings of snot and tears sullied his face as he staggered up to Kat, almost bent double with torment. He wiped his face with his sleeve, pointing through his tearful despair, toward the main road.

Horrified, Kat went to move back to the car, but Cliff had grabbed a hold of her wrist. She stared at him, appalled, not knowing who he was or what part he had to play in the awful events that were unravelling. "Please," he said. "You're his mum, yeah? It was me. My fault. I was supposed to be looking after him. He disappeared on my watch."

She stared at him with a blank expression. From the same direction, as far as half a mile distant, came the distant choke of an engine turning over.

Lefevre called to Kat: "If it's him, we'll never catch them. Whoever it is must be almost mile away. They could go anywhere from here..."

Jimmy moved in closer, until his face was almost touching Lefevre's. "Get in and fucking drive to the main road, Lefevre."

Jimmy slid into the back seat; Kat was already inside. Lefevre paused. Whatever audible traces of a car they had heard - whatever car that happened to be – had long since faded. "This is insanity." He bent down and addressed Kat and Jimmy. "The car might be anyone's. The guy there says he's called the cops. I say we sit tight and wait..."

"Just drive!" screamed Kat and Jimmy simultaneously.

***

As the car tires skidded through the slush and pulled them away from the building, Jimmy watched the crowd of figures move back into the building, Hereward and Cliff bringing up the rear. Jimmy wound the window down so that he could hear what they were saying. Despite his fragile state, Hereward had both arms wrapped around his friend, desperate to console him. "Don't give up hope," Hereward was saying. "We still got a chance, mate. They don't need to know about this." The door of the Old

Schoolhouse closed behind them.

In the car, Lefevre wiped some condensation off the inside of the windscreen with a handkerchief. "Maybe the kid wasn't taken? Maybe he's wandering about outside somewhere? Hell, isn't that what kids do?"

Kat refused to take her eyes off the road. "Not Alfie. My Alfie wouldn't do that. And anyway: that was his voice," she whispered. "I know it was. I'd know it anywhere."

The car bumped across the winding track for two or three minutes, its cargo mute. It jolted and skidded into ruts of ice, Lefevre almost coming to a complete halt once or twice. Jimmy leant forwards. "For Christ's sake, Lefevre. This is a four-wheel drive! Can't you keep the bloody thing on the road and make it go faster?"

Kat was biting her nails, still staring ahead. "Shit, shit, shit," she murmured under her breath. No other vehicle had either passed them or could be seen ahead of them.

The track became a B-road, the ragged dense bushes and hedgerows falling away, the fog clearing a little as they slowed into a narrow junction that opened onto the main artery. Here, out of nowhere, thick rush hour traffic traversed from either direction.

The three of them watched as lorry, car, van blurred through from both directions. Lefevre let his grip slip from the steering wheel to drop onto the handbrake. "Okay. What now?"

Jimmy felt a wave of nausea swelled from the pit of his stomach, up through his chest and sucked the blood from his face. He was overwhelmed by the realisation that his son could be in any one of those vehicles, or one of many more that, with every second, buried further and further into oblivion.

Kat turned in her seat to face Jimmy once more. Her expression was as startling as it was unfamiliar, her voice the low hiss of gas, leaking from an ice-cold cylinder. "I don't give a shit what that man said back there, Jimmy. Whatever happens to Alfie, I hold you personally responsible. Understand that much."

Eleven – the afternoon of Monday 5th December

It was the morning after. In the spinal ward of the hospital, the frail old man was woken by a voice. "Mr. Kowalski? Are you awake?"

He opened an eye, struggling to move his lips and find a voice. A whole day and night had passed since the visit of the girl with whom he had shared that fateful train carriage. "I am now. You have asked what they call a self-fulfilling question, young man." He smiled. "Hospitals do not encourage sleep. Too much business all through the night." He sighed. "And too many thoughts galloping through an old man's head."

Simon, the nurse on duty, took a step closer to his bedside. "We can give you something else to help with your sleeping, if you'd like?" He went to the curtains near the bedside and gently drew them back. "I've brought you a cup of tea..." He placed the mug on the surface of the bedside cabinet.

"The answer to every all ills."

Simon smiled. "And I have a question about something that happened the night before last? Saturday?" He paused. "You had a visitor, I believe?"

Oleg Kowalski raised his eyebrows in response. It was not something he had spoken to another soul about, and he worried that it would bring her trouble.

"The other passenger who was pulled from the train carriage with you? Her name was Hope Kelly?"

The old man's mouth formed a grim line. "Yes, yes. She came to speak with me. What of it?"

Simon unhooked the clipboard from the end of the bed and read through it. "Well, it's an odd thing: someone working on her ward has spoken to me about it. That night, after visiting you, she took off. Discharged herself. Bed empty, all her stuff gone before they began the morning rounds."

Oleg Kowalski was disturbed by this. "I am sad to say that this does not surprise me. A lovely young lady, but a restless soul. My guess is that she has had much to contend with." He looked to the nurse. "Do you know what injuries she had sustained?"

Simon shook his head. "We hadn't got to the bottom of it. But they were suspecting something internal, a chance of blunt abdominal trauma. She was on a drip. She's put herself in great danger by leaving."

Oleg Kowalski nodded slowly. "I suggested to her that it was not the best idea. But this one is headstrong. Was there nothing you could have done to prevent her leaving until she was well enough?"

Simon rubbed the back of his neck. "Well, no – I'm afraid it doesn't work like that. When she arrived, we wanted to keep her under observation overnight following concussion. She was also showing obvious signs of something more serious causing pain. But they weren't on top of it, because she was refusing pain relief, and A and E were very busy, it being the weekend. She was booked in for a laparotomy the evening before she left, but it was put back to the following morning."

"And after that? No-one saw her leave?"

Simon shook his head. "She slipped out sometime after she'd been in here with you. Would you think me rude to ask what you talked about?"

The old man shrugged. "Nothing was said in confidence

Initially, she came to find out how I was doing; evidently a young lady with a most kind disposition. After that, she opened up a little more. Perhaps talking to me took her mind off the pain. She told me that, even before the train accident, it had been a difficult time: recently, she had come face to face with her father for the second time in her life, not having been aware of his existence throughout her childhood."

"I see," said Simon. "So would this have been the guy who gate-crashed the ward? The one who I took the policewoman to?"

Oleg Kowalski shook his head. "She was talking to me also about this. No. The man of whom you speak is not her father. This is her mother's partner, a man who calls himself Spider - not a pleasant individual, by all accounts. She alluded to him visiting, but was reluctant to elaborate. Before I continue, perhaps you can tell me more of what happened there?"

Simon returned the clipboard, pulled up a chair and sat beside the old man's bed. "I'll tell you the part I know about. By the time we arrived on the ward, this guy was kicking off. Security was already there, plus the staff on duty. She was sat on the edge of her bed in her hospital gown; this guy was up close, eyeballing her. All the time, he was shouting in her face, but she was looking down at the ground, shaking her head – not wanting to look at him. She kept saying, 'No… no way', like he was asking her to do something, and she didn't want to go along with it. When he got more aggressive, the policewoman tried to get him away – politely at first. I chipped in at this point – told him he was causing the patient distress. This made him worse – he was gripping the girl's arms, shaking her. I'd say he was under the influence. A substance abuser. The young woman looked ill and frightened. So the security guard and the policewoman had to step things up until they were trying to pull him away from her, like physically."

Oleg Kowalski's brow furrowed, and he wrung his fragile fingers over one another. "Goodness me. The poor child."

Simon nodded. "But by the time a couple of other police officers had arrived, he seemed to see sense and back off. But he kept his eyes on the young woman, pointing at her as they led him out. You could still hear him swearing when he'd got past the end of the first corridor. The young woman was crying and trying to get out of the ward – but one of the nurses persuaded her to get back into the bed. She slept after that. I'm guessing her visit to you was a few hours afterwards. I never found out what the bloke was after. I'd always assumed they were related."

Oleg Kowalski was quiet for a moment. The nurse's face was a rounded one with plain, open features. It was an earnest, open-book waiting to be written: one that invited trust. The old man's mouth formed into a grim, yet decisive line. He pointed towards the bedside cabinet. "Something I need to show you is in there," he said, "A slim red book in a plastic wallet. Would you be kind enough to fetch it out for me?"

Simon found the book.

"Look at the back cover," said Oleg Kowalski. "You see the gentleman in the picture? The author?" Simon nodded. "He is the father. A writer of verse."

"Ah." Simon looked at the picture carefully. "She looks like him." His face was pinched in thought. He frowned, and then his face sprang into surprise. "Bloody hell! Hang on - I'll be right back!" He dropped the book down on the bed and disappeared through the entrance to the Unit.

Oleg Kowalski groaned with the effort of reaching forwards for the book. He slid it across the sheets toward himself and thumbed through until he found the two sheets of notepaper and, with a swift motion, tucked them under the fold of his bedsheets.

Within the space of minutes, the nurse had returned, out of breath. He carried a folded newspaper under his arm, one recently purchased from the news stand a few corridors down. He laid the edition on the old man's bed and pointed to the front pages. "Look!"

Oleg Kowalski's eye followed the younger man's finger. He frowned and looked up. "My glasses, please? Also in the cupboard."

Simon passed the case over. The old man pushed his spectacles up his nose and peered again. There, on the front page and within the frame of the picture, a large, bearded man had his arm around glamorous-looking woman. She kept her head, which was wrapped in a dark headscarf, down. Her eyes were shielded by large, round sunglasses and she clutched a large bag to her front. A third figure was to their left – younger, smartly dressed, closed-faced. Amongst a dense jungle of boom mics, the press and other members of the public crowded in on them. The old man scanned the headline:

Kat's Twelve Hours of Hell: Nationwide hunt for TV Chef's missing boy, 5

He lowered the paper. "He has a younger son also? And he has gone missing? My goodness. Unimaginable." His eye drifted into the mid-distance for a moment in thought, before returning to Simon. He nodded and pointed to the bearded man in the picture. "Yes, yes - this indeed the writer: the young lady's father."

"So the older daughter takes off, the younger son goes missing – is there some connection, d'you think?"

Oleg Kowalski looked over the article with concentration. "The thought of her being responsible for any such thing..." He shook his head. "Such a sweet girl. And besides," he murmured as he read, his finger drifting over the page, "was she not here in the hospital while the boy was said to have gone missing?"

Simon leant forwards, so that he could see the article again. "She would have left between, say, late Saturday night and Sunday morning. The boy went missing, what, Sunday morning? Who knows? Not sure she would have been up to that sort of thing in her condition, though."

The old man shook his head and spoke more to himself than the other man. "I will not believe that she is capable of such a thing. Not my Good Morning Girl." He removed his glasses and reached out. "Would you be so kind as to pass the book again?" He took it from Simon. "The man who wrote these poems – the father. I wonder what he knows of his daughter's fate. Of the train. Or her time in hospital..."

Simon looked concerned. "I don't think that's for you to worry about, Mr. Kowalski. You have enough on your plate as it is."

Oleg Kowalski removed his spectacles. "This man – he needs to be aware of what has happened. From the way that she spoke about him, she will not have told him for sure. He has a missing child. But he also has a sick daughter. " His mouth contracted, again, into that thin, determined line. "My meeting with Hope Kelly, what happened on the train, and now news of this little boy missing. We...I... have a responsibility. " He paused and looked towards the window, the furrows on his face creasing with each depending thought. He took one deep breath. "I would like a telephone please. I should call this man now."

Simon looked anxious. Seeing strength of will in the old man's stern blue gaze to which any challenge was inappropriate, he capitulated. "I'll go and fetch my phone from my locker." As he walked away, he looked over his shoulder. "I'm not sure what good it can do, though."

Oleg Kowalski watched him walk out of the ward before retrieving the papers from their hiding place. They had been folded and unfolded many times until they had the feel of delicate fabric rather than paper. He examined the writing: plain, cursive, right-slanting.

The old man slid his glasses back onto the end of his nose, and read.

January 2000

Dear Hope,

I've thought long and hard about writing. Getting a letter from a dad you've never met won't be an easy thing. But here it is.

I don't know how much your mum has told you about me, and why I left. Neither do I know what she's decided to leave out - but I'd imagine that whatever pieces of the jigsaw you have, your overall picture of me isn't great. Despite this, I figured that, now that you're no longer a kid, it might be a good time for me to introduce myself from a distance. That gives you the choice to look for those missing pieces, or to put the puzzle back into the box for a few years more - if that's what you want.

So to the heart of it. When your mum and I were together, we were very young. We loved each other – but in the way that two young people with their lives ahead of them do - too young to know each other well, and too young to start making plans. At least, that's how it felt for me. I was neither the kind of person who wanted to make plans, nor, I imagine, the kind of person that another might want to share plans with.

I wasn't, in short, the kind of guy a girl could rely on.

Mum must have been pretty scared when she found out that she was expecting you. We didn't have a place of our own – she was living at her parents' place. I was in digs. We were both artist-types: we weren't saving up for anything in particular, and whatever money we had was spent on a selfish and sometimes lavish lifestyle. From the outset, I suspect that she knew she could never count on me.

Now the hard part.

Your mum never told me that she was expecting a baby because I never gave her the chance. There was this one night when I came back to her parents' place, and I overheard her tell a friend. They never knew I was there, listening in.

When I heard, I was filled with too many selfish thoughts: horror, entrapment, standing in rainy playgrounds on Saturday afternoons pushing swings in the park. That wasn't for me. So, instead of talking to her and entertaining the slightest thought of entering that stage in my life prematurely, I did the worst thing. I ran away. I told myself that if you wanted me, you could find me; maybe I would try to step up the mark and give it a go.

I don't need to tell you what happened to me after that – none of it is that important. You can choose whether you want to believe me when I say that I thought – think - about you a lot, but that is the truth. I never hid away, neither did I make myself visible. Every few months, I checked up on you without you knowing but, as weeks drifted into months and into years, less so.

But, you see, the thing is: my whole life, I've felt guilty. Since I was a wee lad, I've gone through life feeling that I've done bad things, and let people down. Perhaps it was the Catholic upbringing; but, more likely, I'd done plenty to feel guilty about. I still feel as guilty now as I've ever felt. I suppose that this letter, then, is my confession.

So you must be, what, thirteen now? Old enough to think for yourself, and to make your own mind up. Therefore, I want to tell you that I'm here if you'd like to meet up or call. Maybe you can keep the letter and choose your time when you feel ready. I've addressed the letter to your mum, as I know it's important that she knows that I've sent it too. Keeping secrets never comes to much good. I've learnt this the hard way.

If and when you meet me, you'll find out that I'm never going to win 'Dad of the Year' - I'm way too selfish-centred. But I can be more than a name or a character in your history that you've never met, and I'd like to be so when you feel ready to have another parent in your life. We can take as much time as you need to get to know each other. If you choose to ignore all of this, that's entirely your right.

I'm leaving you a PO Box number. I move between places quite a lot at the moment, so it's the most sensible thing to do.

Hope to hear from you soon. All the best for now,

Jimmy

Twelve– Monday 5th December 2016

Jimmy Dunbar stared through the glass walls of the foyer. Beyond the reflection of a haggard and lost middle-aged man who'd neither eaten nor slept for twenty-four hours, the world still turned.

In the car-park opposite, a young couple fussed like sparrows by their car. There was the pulling on of wellies, coats, hats and scarves, the commotion of extracting a folded buggy from the boot. The woman moved back to the rear seats and handed a long succession of baby paraphernalia to her husband – changing bags, coats, toys and such like. As was his duty, he hung them over various knobs and hooks attached to the buggy – a practised ritual. At last, the mother emerged, triumphant yet terrified, with the child itself – an almost spherical bundles of preciousness wrapped up in coats and booties and mittens, its little limbs jutting out like a starfish. Once placing the child within, they both bowed over the tiny deity, ensuring that every risk had been assessed, no matter how sleight. The father came up first, rubbing his partner's back with tenderness and affection. She shortly followed, stood on her tiptoes, and kissed her partner on the cheek.

It had been like that for Jimmy and Kat some five years ago. He remembered that innate fear of handling something so precious and vulnerable that you could barely bring yourself to touch it.

His gaze moved beyond them, to the traffic that flowed beyond. The very fact that the world was still allowed to keep turning seemed, to him, unfathomable. When a child, *your* child, went missing, every flight had to be delayed, every port shut, every road blocked, every house visited and bag check, didn't it? They were looking into an abyss, around the walls of which his imagination had scrawled the vilest and most obscene reasons for Alfie's disappearance.

Jimmy touched the breast pocket of his jacket. There, his fingers felt the shoulders of a half bottle of bourbon tucked inside. His made a tight fist as dark thoughts crowded into his head. Fighting them, he turned back towards the reception desk, across the way. The receptionist was in her early thirties – perhaps a mother herself. "D.S.I. Bridger shouldn't be long now," she said. "Are you sure I can't get fetch either of you anything, sir? Tea? Coffee?" She spoke in a funeral voice and was almost tearful in her desire to oblige.

Jimmy looked to his wife. Perching on the edge of a seat, her body was held tight and hunched over. Her elbows rested on her knees, her long fingers pointed upwards, held across her lips in intense concentration. He said to the receptionist, "Not for the moment, thank you." She smiled again, and disappeared through a door with a bundle of files.

Kat addressed Jimmy. "Could you please stop pacing around? For a second?"

Jimmy thrust his hands in his pockets, before easing himself into the seat beside her.

Taking the weight off her elbows, Kat leant back against the rest and drew her arm across her stomach. Her face was pale, her hair tied back in a high ponytail. "God." She closed her eyes. "I keep thinking I'm going to throw up."

Jimmy shifted in his seat. "Aye. Me too." He didn't know what else he could say. Seconds turned into minutes. Jimmy decided that he should break the silence. "Hey - I saw Lefevre dropping you off outside earlier, getting you through the bastard press. Where are you staying tae?"

She looked over to the posters covering the far wall. "Does it matter?"

He shrugged. "Guess not. Just wondering, like."

A door opened behind the reception area, and they both looked up. A cleaner rattled through, mop and bucket clattering against the door frame. Straight away, he was alert to Kat, his recognition of her apparent. His lips pursed into a question, but he thought better of giving it voice.

Kat's lips parted and her breathing quickened, becoming more irregular. On her lap, her fingers worked against the pad of her thumbs with a furious intensity.

Desperate to fight the agonising silence, Jimmy threw down a card from his previous hand. "I've known Lefevre now for, what, nine, ten years? And dy'e know what? Not once has the bastard invited me round his place. What's it like?"

She stopped breathing for a moment, every inch of her still. With no warning, she turned to face him, full on. "What did you say?"

Jimmy shook his head. "I was only wondering..."

She searched his face for a moment, and turned away again. She had covered her mouth, and a series of tiny, aching breaths passing through her body.

Jimmy watched her aghast. Hopelessly, he went to touch her back.

She flinched. "Just piss off." Reaching for her handbag, she began sifting through its contents with a quiet mania before extracting a small pack of tissues and some ibuprofen.

The water cooler was beneath the posters on the far wall of the foyer. She moved to it quickly, and filled a plastic cup whilst pressing a tissue to the corners of her eyes.

Jimmy stood up. "Kat! Please? I only meant..."

She was looking down at the mascara-stained tissue. "You're bloody unbelievable," she sniffed.

Jimmy stood. "I didnae mean anything by it. I thought..."

"Just don't." She cracked the pills from their packet and, one by one, placed them on her tongue. Throwing her head back, she chased them down with water. "Our little boy has been missing for two days and all you can think about is whether I'm shagging Lefevre." She turned to face him. "I can tell you one bloody thing: Lefevre is being so kind and supportive through all of this. And, for your information, I am not staying at his place - he's being harangued by the press as well. He's put me up in a hotel room..." She stopped as he came nearer. He knew now that, for the first time, she could smell the alcohol on his breath. "Perhaps you might stop, for a tiny moment, to think how you are measuring up, as our missing son's father."

Jimmy frowned and looked down at his shoes. Without speaking again, he turned away and walked back towards the seats. He felt the weight of the bottle shift with his motion. He growled into his beard. "'Kind' and 'Lefevre': two words rarely found in the same sentence." He looked back towards her. "Lefevre is a man interested in one person only – his bloody self." He sat down again.

Kat spoke under her breath. "God, the irony."

Caught between a rock and a hard place, JImmy knew it was wrong to be talking about this now; but to him it seemed strange but relevant. An earlier conversation with Hereward entered his head – the incongruence of Lefevre with the tall, ungainly intruder, together in a café at some point in the recent past. How could that ever have been?

Kat was pulling herself together, resting her arm on the water machine. It was not a good time to raise such doubts. And besides, Hereward was not the most reliable of narrators.

The receptionist returned. She attempted to ignore their exchange. Kat was sitting near to him again, this time with a spare seat between them. She placed her bag on it and sighed. "You know what I keep wondering? Why didn't you bring him back when I asked you? You've always been so keen to get rid of him at the first opportunity."

Jimmy bridled, his lips pursing beneath his beard. "That isnae fair, Kat. We've been over this. Alfie was with me in the first place because you said you were busy. What if Alfie had stayed in France with yous, like I wanted him tae? What if Lefevre had never lined up the do at Southbank? Anyone could go on like that for ever – what if..? – what if..? You could blame any bastard for anything." He softened his voice. "It's bloody futile going down that road, love. No one is tae blame but the bastard who took him away from us. Let's focus on that..."

Her eyelids were heavy, her whole demeanour one of aching despair. She spoke again. "All my life, I've been lucky. I've never lost anyone." She caught her breath. "It hurts so much." She looked at him, her eyes wide and brimming with tears. "Is this what grief feels like?"

Jimmy's face crumpled in misery. He took her bag off the seat between them and went to take its place.

"Don't," she said. "I don't want you near me right now, Jimmy."

The sound of a door brushing against carpet interrupted them. The receptionist was on her feet now, and a younger man with dark brown, slicked-back hair moved past her, placing a file on her desk.

He stood before Jimmy and Kat with some awkwardness, and they both got to their feet.

The man noticed that Kat was clutching balls of scrunched-up tissues. "Would you like some more time before we begin, madam?" he asked. "I can always come back in a minute or two..."

"No, no," said Kat. She stood up and extended a hand. "Kat Kennedy." They shook hands. "This is James Dunbar, Alfie's father."

"Ms. Kennedy, Mr. Dunbar." His grip was strong and cool. "I'm Detective Inspector Bridger. I'll be taking over from this point."

Jimmy's eyes ran over him. He seemed very young. Fast-tracked. "Our Acting Chief Constable is also keeping a close eye on the case, obviously." He gestured towards a side door. "Would you like to come through?" He spoke as they walked. "As you know, we've stepped up considerably since the first Missing report."

He stopped talking as the ringtone of Jimmy's phone sounded in his pocket.

Jimmy went to clutch the vibrating object. Kat and D.I Bridger turned towards the noise. Jimmy slid it out and looked at the screen. "It's an unknown number." Despite everything that had happened, it wondered if it might be Hope calling him.

The D.S.I. watched him, impervious. "I suggest you take the call," he said.

Jimmy clasped the phone to his ear, covering the mouthpiece. He looked at his wife and the policeman with increasing unease and stepped away, turning his back to them.

"Hullo?" He listened for a moment, cupping the microphone. He looked back to Bridger. "It's some crazy fella with a Russian accent." He returned to the phone once more. "What do you know about her?" He cast a furtive look towards Kat. "An accident? What sort of accident? D'you know if she's okay?" He took a step away from Kat and Bridger, his shoulders hunched against them both. "Disappeared? How d'ya mean? And how did yous get my number?" He listened to the reply, and his face fell. "Oh. I see." He cast an anxious look round at the police inspector, who was frowning.

Kat took a step towards him. "Jimmy – for God's sake! Can't this wait?"

Jimmy spoke into the phone again. "Look – can I call you back? I've got stuff going on…"

When Jimmy ended the call, he stood still for a while, feeling like a man whose sanity was running, like sand, through his fingers. Bridger's voice drifted through the fog: "Mr. Dunbar? Is there something relevant here that we need to know about?"

Jimmy tucked his phone away and rubbed the back of his neck. "Well, no. " He stared across the foyer into the distance. "At least I don't think so." Bridger remained silent, waiting for more.

Jimmy spoke without knowing where he was any more. "It's my daughter." As the word came out of his mouth, he felt its resonance smack Kat in the face. He could bare bring himself to look at her. "You see… before all this… we'd met for the first time." His speech faltered. "But… turns out she's he's been involved in some sort of accident. On a train. The guy who phoned – A Mr. Kowalski? – he was in the same carriage as her when it happened. They ended up in the same hospital…" On impulse, his fingers moved to the healing wound on his cheek. "When she was on that train, she was running away from me. It was my fault that she was there."

Kat rolled her eyes and turned away, her arms folded across her chest.

Pushing the next door open, Bridger gestured for them to move through. "I can understand that this must be upsetting news on top of everything else, Mr. Dunbar." He looked from Kat's face to Jimmy's. "Look – if it's the incident I think it is, I can make some enquiries with my colleagues from the Hampshire force."

Kat rounded on Jimmy. "Christ, Jimmy. Whoever this person is, she is an adult. Alfie – your child who is fucking missing, is five years of age…"

Bridger stopped him. "Ms. Kennedy is right. We need to focus on the child." He gestured towards the doorway. "Shall we go through?"

Jimmy nodded, feeling foolish. He followed Kat and D.S.I. Bridger through a set of glass doors, into a sterile interview room.

Thirteen

An hour later, Oleg Kowalski had tried to call Jimmy Dunbar for a second time from his hospital bed.

He stared at the blank screen, before returning to Simon, the nurse on duty. "Again, I leave a message." He sighed. "Perhaps you were right. Perhaps I should never have called him. This man has much to contend with, after all."

Simon took the phone from the old man and tucked it back into the pocket of his tunic. "You tried..."

Oleg Kowalski was not content with this. "Here is a man whose five-year-old child has either gone missing or has been taken - most probably the latter – and now he is also finding out that his daughter has been involved in a serious accident. Now, she too has gone missing. The police should be informed, should they not?"

Simon shrugged. "I don't know whether they'd be interested. Although the self-discharge was AMA, it was her prerogative, Mr. K. And she's been gone for, what, twelve hours or so? The father could make out a Missing Persons report, I suppose, but, as you say, it sounds like he's got much more on his plate..."

Oleg Kowalski pinched his bottom lip. "Perhaps they might be more interested if they felt that there was any connection between her absconding and the disappearance of the boy."

"Wasn't it you who said, though, that she wasn't the sort of person who could do such a thing?"

The old man's mind drifted back to the train, her tears, their conversation, the kindness in her face, the broadness of her smile. His brow furrowed. "She is not. We had not known each other for long, but I recognise a good soul when I see one." With as much mental energy as he could muster, he shook the last vestiges of reverie from his brain. "What is a foolish old man to know? We all, at different times in our lives, make poor judgements of character. But these are the facts: this young woman, Hope Kelly, arrives at this hospital and, afterwards, an unwelcome visitor finds her and causes a commotion. That night, she visits me and asks me to take care of the book of poetry written by her father. His number, and a letter that he wrote many years ago are contained inside. She tells me of matters she needs to see to, despite her obvious distress: matters relating to the rather rude visitor of whom you have spoken. At an uncertain time, some hours after, this young lady vanishes off the face of the Earth. Shortly after this, the news breaks of the disappearance of the young boy."

Simon watched the old man, taking in his wistful, ethereal face, the gentle tremor in his fingers. He sat down. "Want to hear something? When I was a kid, I wondered off on a beach during a family holiday in Majorca. It took the Spanish police about three hours to find me. All the time, I'd been as happy as Larry, digging a hole in the sand, a few hundred yards from where Mum and Dad had been. Mum was so traumatised, she spent the rest of the holiday in bed. Seeing her like that made me understand what she felt about losing me."

Oleg Kowalski smiled his kind smile. "So you don't have children, Simon?" Simon shook his head. The old man spoke in a wistful voice. "I came close to being a father." His tone invited confidence. "My wife, Nancy, and I lived in a small basement flat in the centre of Bristol. We were eighteen months into our marriage, poor but very happy. One morning, I woke up to see a change in her: a knowing glint in her eye, a glow to her cheeks. At that specific moment, we both knew our lives were about to change forever. I had selfish thoughts of my own that many men have: I would have to share her with another; I would no longer be the centre to her universe." He continued to stare ahead. "Sadly, it wasn't to be. We lost the child at fourteen weeks into the pregnancy."

"Oh. I'm so sorry,"

Oleg Kowalski held up a hand. "I wondered: if I had wanted the child as much as she did, if I had put my every hope and thought into it as she did; could I have willed the unborn child into fighting its way further into our world?"

Concern passed over Simon's face. "You don't need to be telling me about this, Mr. K."

He concentrated. "I have heard it said that when a woman loses a child before it is born, she loses more than the child. She loses the part of herself that she had already given the child." He fixed the nurse with a determined stare. "I lived with her grief for many years. It was a terrible, terrible thing. Perhaps, for the parents of the missing boy, the not knowing is even worse - as with the not knowing your own mother had, albeit for those long hours..."

The two men went their own separate ways for a moment, the elder sitting on the edge of a bed holding his distant young wife's cold wrist; the younger listening to his mother sobbing in a beige hotel room on a Spanish holiday island. "Wretched hospitals!" Oleg Kowalski said, making Simon start. "The things you think of when you have so much time to kill!"

Simon looked at the frail little old man in the bed, with his wise, delicate face. He looked so alone. "Do you mind me asking when your wife passed away?" he asked.

Oleg Kowalski fought to bring himself back from the past. He blinked and blinked again, as if roused from sleep by a gentle voice. Confusion haunted his features, as light, diaphanous clouds across a moon. "Passed away? Nancy?" he shook his head. "Oh no: Nancy is still very much alive."

Simon raised his eyebrows and sat forwards. "Oh? I'm sorry. I assumed..."

Oleg Kowalski shook his head. "I know. You are wondering where she has been - why she has not come to the hospital to visit me. " He sighed. "The sad truth of it is that it is I who no longer visits her..."

"To explain, I will need to take you back to the day after we lost the child." His brow furrowed with concentration. "It was a bitter January morning –shortly, I recall, before lunchtime. I drove her back from the hospital and remember carrying her little pale blue vanity case down to our basement flat, before returning to the car, where I opened the passenger door to help her out. I remember reaching out for her, but she brushed me aside and clung to the iron railings. Never had she done anything like this to me before. A small gesture, but one that foreshadowed subsequent events. Inside our home, I had been hard at work: arranging her chair by the fire; a glass, a jug on the little table, with some of her favourite books and magazines. But, as she stepped inside, closing the door behind her, I could see that all was not right. I wanted to make everything comfortable for her. Would she like the radio on? No, she didn't noise. Should I make lunch? No, she had no appetite. Myself, I needed to keep busy, so I went into the kitchen to make a plate of sandwiches – she could help herself to some later, should her appetite recover.

"When I returned to our drawing room with the sandwiches, her chair had been vacated. I heard movements nearby and when I looked across the hall, I saw her standing at the doorway of the room that would have been our child's nursery. She spoke to me as if I were a stranger. Where, she asked, had everything gone?

You see, I had spent the two previous nights dissembling and moving anything that would remind her of the lost child: a cot-bed, blankets, a hanging mobile, some toys our kind neighbours had passed on to us. I spoke to her gently: things had been put away. For the time being. It was for the best while we were getting over the shock. I reminded her about the sandwiches..."

Oleg Kowalski paused. His fingers moved through the air in a delicate motion, as if stroking her cheek. "Her face at the time... I see her so well, as she turns from the room, back towards me, her eyes colder than that January afternoon."

"For many days, she stayed that way: silent, cold. Each night, she lay in our bed, her back towards me. I knew that she never slept. A week or more passed. Waking one night, I found only a space beside me. I remember turning on my bedside light and seeing her clothes scattered where she had dropped them on the bedroom floor. You see, before this, she had always been so fastidious in folding them over her chair. Seeing a thin strip of light beyond the door of the room and feeling the chill of the outside air, I realised that the door to our flat must be ajar. I put on my dressing gown and went into the night.

"It was so bitterly cold: the steps leading up from the basement were already coved with ice. As I reached the top, I could see my wife. She was half way down the street, barefoot in her nightgown, stood as still as a statue, her back to me. She was looking, I remember, through the railings and into the darkness of the park that was opposite our terrace. I rushed towards her. 'Dear God, my love!' I was saying. 'What are you thinking? You will catch your death of cold. Come inside!'

"She allowed me to place my dressing gown over her shoulders, but there remained this feeling that, for her, I was no longer there. I tried to coax her back towards our flat – perhaps I was more firm than I care to recall - but she refused to move. Her eyes! They were fixed to this one spot in the darkness of the park. And she found her voice. 'She brought me here...' she said. "

Oleg Kowalski shook his head. He looked ahead, his body still. "I cannot tell you how frightened I was. This sense of the woman who was captain of our little ship looking so bewildered and distant. I wondered – was she sleepwalking? I tried to move her towards our home once again, my arms either side of her, but she spoke once more. 'My baby brought me here and now I'm waiting for her.' Those words. *My baby.*

"It is at this time, that she begins to cry out – quiet at first, but it becomes much louder. I am not a violent man, but... the need to get her inside in the warm... away from the prying neighbours in the street.

"I knew I could overpower her. I had her by the waist, half lifting, half dragging her little frame back towards out door. I remember the curtains of the terrace twitching, lights clicking on. All along the row.

"Her cries become yells; her yells turned to screams. A door opened, an old man – a neighbour of ours - stood staring in his doorway, tying the chord of his dressing gown. Should he call the police, he was asking. Dogs were barking, children crying. I covered her mouth as we got as far as the door, and she clung to the frame, fighting against me."

Oleg Kowalski stopped and swallowed. "As the door closed behind us, I became so very aware of how we were: me, restraining her. That sensation of her tongue against my palm, teeth sinking into the flesh..."

Oleg Kowalski faltered. He lifted his arm from the bed, and held up his hand, palm towards him, fingers spread. His sad gaze trawled the patched surface of tissue, as raw and angry as it had been all those years ago. He showed Simon, and the nurse winced.

He acknowledged the younger man's surprise with a smile. "It looks a lot worse than it is. It stopped hurting many years ago." He tapped his head. "Up here. Now that took a lot longer to heal."

With horror, Simon peered at the scarred flesh. "After that?"

"Back in the flat, she became more disturbed still. My blood was on her lips, her teeth; it dripped down her chin. Once free of me, she ripped through our flat, grasping every object that could be thrown in my direction, while I curled up in the corner of the kitchen, my arms over my head.

"After a while, collapsed in a heap, exhausted. I carried her to our bed, where she would stay sleeping for two whole days. In the meantime, I sat at the kitchen table through each night, terrified of her waking and finding me asleep. You see, thought she might kill me. But, I told myself that she would mend; everything would be as it was. I was wrong." He looked up. "You ask me when my wife passed away? I suppose, in many ways, it was that night."

Fourteen – Tuesday 6th December 2016

The next day, Jimmy Dunbar and Kat were recalled to the police station.

The escalation of the operation had been exponential: statements, press appointments, line taps, nationwide searches. As someone who had spent a significant part of his professional life envying his wife's fame, Jimmy enough humility to thank her for it in this respect. As well as this, it also went the way that the crap in your past that brought you down could also give you a leg up. Unfortunately, when and where those moments came in your life appeared to be unfathomable.

Jimmy had found his way to the loos in the station. Clicking the lock of the cubicle door behind him, he pulled the toilet seat down, and sat, resting the back of his head against the wall. Being loose, it slid against his weight.

He felt his own weight. Sitting forward, he rested his elbows on his knees, and pressed his fingers against his lips. The shift of the half bottle of bourbon in his inside pocket made him imagine its redolence once the cap was unscrewed – he could see and taste the viscous coffee liquid rolling against the round glass shoulders.

He held his breath as he slid it from within. Every ritual foreshadowed both the pleasure and subsequent guilt. Tip. Swallow. Sure enough, the fire scorched his throat, caught in his chest, found the twitching tips of his fingers. He drew his lips back from his teeth with a grimace, and wiped his beard with his forefinger.

Positioned the bottle on the ceramic tiles of the floor with a conspicuous clink, he went to check his phone. One missed call and a new message. The former was from the old man in the hospital. The man had passed on information, and Jimmy had thanked him and taken note. What more could he have to say? The old, Jimmy knew, collected and clung to conversations like squirrels do nuts. Or perhaps he was after a reward?

Jimmy ran his fingers through his hair, and over the flesh of his face. He leaned to one side for his bourbon again before glancing at the phone once more. He flicked through his social media apps. Six thousand new followers that morning; one thousand new readers of last year's inaugural blog. Messages of support. Hashtag, 'FindAlfieKennedy.'

Jimmy scowled. "Dunbar," he mumbled under his breath. "It's Alfie fucking Dunbar." He jabbed the screen, finding Kat's account. Her huge fan base was haemorrhaging more empathy and support than she would ever see or be interested in. For her, fame was a bi-product of success, never the ultimate goal.

His thumb swiped across the surface of his smart phone. The story of Alfie's disappearance was everywhere: appeals, Facebook support groups, volunteer search parties. And there was the inevitable dark side of social media: hate-filled trolls and a plethora of conspiracy theorists, some of which even pointed the finger of blame at him.

One picture, one that kept cropping up, caught his attention. It must have been taken the previous afternoon when they were first at the station. Jimmy had left before Kat, in an attempt to throw the press off the scent. They were not to be fooled, and had circled, scavenger-like, for the main event.

In the image, Kat's entourage were attempting to breach front doors of the police station, subsumed by a circus-like media scrum. Her head was wrapped in a scarf and held down, her angst hidden by sunglasses.

Jimmy shifted his spectacles to the top of his head. Flicking his thumb and forefinger apart, he closed in on the image. There was an arm curling around her back – and a large signet ring he immediately recognised: Lefevre's.

The phone's shrill ringtone made him start. His reaction sent the bottle at his feet skittering over, a brook of coffee-coloured liquor trickling like ants on track along the grouting to breach the confines of his cubicle before there was anything he could do to stem the flow.

"Shit." He made a grab for the bottle.

He heard, from beyond, the sounds of someone's flies zipping, a cough and piss hitting porcelain.

The phone was still ringing. Placing the bottle on the cistern, he pinned his phone to his ear with his shoulder as he grappled with his trousers and tugged at his belt buckle.

Kat's voice was a fierce hiss at the other end. "For Christ's sake – what are you doing in there? You need to get out here. They've got some news…"

"Aye, I'm there, I'm there." He screwed the cap back on, crouched on his haunches and mopped up the bourbon within the cubicle with fistfuls of toilet paper. The dark, musky scent hit his nostrils and he shoved the pulpy mass into his mouth and sucked like a greedy infant at the breast. He savoured the burn until, disorientated, he fell into the door of the cubicle, his knee and shin resting in the remains of the pool.

Outside the cubicle, the rush of taps; the whirr of the hand-dryer.

Jimmy held his breath waiting for the intruder to leave. There were no further sounds. He fumbled with the catch and stepped outside.

Bridger was stood with his back to him, adjusting his tie in the mirror. They caught sight of one another in the mirror, the policeman pausing over the knot. Bridger gave a curt nod.

Jimmy took in the straightness of his back; the well-pressed, shiny suit trousers.

The policeman tracked his movements in the mirror. He waited a while until,, half turning, his eyes rested on the damp patch on the knee of Jimmy's slacks.

Jimmy turned away, and walked towards a basin. He turned on the taps. "I hear there's some news?"

Bridger considered his answer for a time. "Indeed. Significant news." His walked towards the outer door, before glancing once more at the trail of brown liquid that continued to trickle across the floor tiles. "I'll see you back in there." There was a pause before he added, "Sir."

By the time Jimmy had returned to the interview room, another two uniformed officers had joined Kat and Bridger. Still standing, the police inspector started by sliding a large printout of an image across the table. Jimmy felt the blood drain from his face.

The image revealed two figures from behind: a boy holding the hand of a much taller man, whose face was shaded beneath a shop sign, but turned sideways on. The two of them were crossing a nondescript stretch of some shopping mall or walkway.

Kat looked from the picture to Bridger. "Oh my God! That's him! That's Alfie!" Her fingers passed over the grainy image as she stared at it. "Shit," she whispered.

Jimmy leaned in. "Och, that'll the wee hoody he had wi' him." He looked up at Bridger. "Where is this?"

"Speyfields Shopping Mall. Fourteen-hundred hours yesterday afternoon. We've poured over film from every other camera in the vicinity, but this is the only one we have. It's almost like the assailant wanted to us to see them." He leaned in, and turned the image away from Kat and towards Jimmy. He tapped the taller figure with his forefinger. "The adult male: you recognise him, sir?"

The long gait, the dreadlocks, a shiftiness of poise. Jimmy didn't know how he hadn't recognised him sooner. "Hell, yes! This jakey was at my book launch last week!"

Incredulous, Kat stared at him. "You know this man? For the love of Christ, Jimmy - who is he?"

"He was there with the girl who said she was my daughter – the one who was in the train accident. Maybe it was all a ruse and she isnae who she says she is after all…" His words tailed off – as soon as it had come out of his mouth, he knew it not to be true. The picture he had been shown didn't seem to make any sense.

Bridger nodded to one of the uniformed officers, who had removed a notebook from his inside pocket. "Names?"

Jimmy shook his head. He knew Kat would be seething. "The fella in the picture, they call him 'Spider' - I dinnae know his real name. The name of the girl - my daughter - is called Hope Kelly." He paused, feeling some sense of betrayal "She's taken her mother's name."

Kat got to her feet, the legs of her chair scratching the floor. Her voice was low and cold. "What the fuck is going on here, Jimmy?"

Bridger spoke with a calm authority. "Okay, Mr. Dunbar. So

we've established that you met this man recently..."

"Not met as such – he was just there. He caused some trouble. I didnae speak wi' him..."

"And you've never met him before, then?"

Jimmy bristled. "No, man. I told you that."

"And the young woman?"

"Aye. This was the first time I saw her too..."

Bridger was taking notes. "And have you seen either of them since – I mean since the book signing event in London, but before the disappearance of your son?"

Jimmy hesitated. "Well, aye, I did that." He tried to avoid Kat's eye. "After she'd said she was my daughter an' all, I thought it was the decent thing tae try and find her. I'd written my number down for her, you see? But she never got back tae me. My pal Hereward knew where she lived with her mother, so I went tae visit. That was on the Friday."

Bridger looked at the other policeman again. "We'll need the address." His finger jabbed the CCTV image again. "Plus details of how we can contact your friend. And he was there on Friday evening as well? This 'Spider'?"

Jimmy shook his head. "Only her – Hope - and her mam. The mam's name is Jasmine Kelly. I cannae give you an address, but it's in Shoreham - one of the houseboats near the new footbridge."

"We'll find them." Bridger glanced towards an officer who was already unclipping her radio and making to leave the room. "Confirm the location and check the it out, Colesey, will you?" He turned back to Jimmy. "Look. Mr. Dunbar: this CCTV places your boy and this man in a specific location at a specific time. Additionally, we now have the information that you have given us about this man. This will bring us a lot closer." He leant forward, and looked, hawk-like, at JImmy. "But is there anything else – anything at all - relating to this man and the young woman that you can tell us that will help us find your son any more quickly?"

Jimmy shrugged his shoulders. "Nothing I can think of."

Kat's voice cut through like a blade. "Jesus, Jimmy. If any crap that you've mixed yourself up in has led to the disappearance of my boy, I swear to God…"

Jimmy felt Bridger's curiosity burning into him. The policeman persisted.   "Anything further that can help us with our enquiries, Mr. Dunbar?" He pushed the picture closer still. "You need to think carefully. If there's anything you're holding back?"

Jimmy looked from the policeman to his wife.   Without blinking, she stared through him. He had a sudden feeling that their world was unreeling. He felt the unbearable pressure of scrutiny. His voice was higher than normal.   "Holding back? Christ, what's happening here? Why am I expected to be the one who has all the answers? This is my son who's gone missing too, you know…" Everyone else in the room remained silent. He half stood, his mouth hung open. He pummelled his chest. "D'yous all actually think I'm deliberately withholding information, when it's my boy's life at stake out there? Honestly?"   He slumped back in his chair and stared from one corner of the room to the other. "For fuck's sake…" Jimmy focussed in on Bridger. The bourbon, he knew, was hitting the spot, with that accompanying sensation of losing control and not not giving a shit. He spoke loud, to ride over the slurring of his words. "What next? Is this the moment when you advise me to call my solicitor?" he asked.

Bridger remained calm. He sat down. "Mr. Dunbar, as I'm sure you can appreciate, we have to pursue every line of enquiry. While what you've suggested is not necessary right now, you are free to make a phone call if it would make you comfortable. Of course, I'm sure I do not need to add that, should it transpire that you're withholding anything that could move us forwards, that might become a necessity." Resting his elbows on the arms of the chair, he leaned back and pressed the tips of his fingers together.

Jimmy folded his arms and drew breath. "Okay. So it's that way. I get it." He narrowed his eyes, remembering that he had another card to play. "Well try pursuing this," He leaned forward across the desk, resting his weight on his elbows. He heard the slur in his breathy voice as the word escaped his lips. "Lefevre." He gestured between himself and Kat. "You 'pursue' that slimy get." He tapped the CCTV image again.

Bridger looked perplexed. "And Lefevre is who?"

Kat cut across them. "Lefevre? What are you talking about?"

He was aware that Kat was watching him carefully as she spoke. "Lefevre owns a PR company. We've worked together for ten years or so. He's represented Jimmy for the last three." She arched an eyebrow, and said, "He's dropped Jimmy from his clientele. Beyond that, I have no idea what my husband is talking about."

Jimmy held his hands aloft, palms exposed. "Okay. The mate I was talking about , His name is Hereward." He focused on Bridger's face, but it was starting to diverge into two Bridgers. "He was there at Southbank too, and he recognised this bloke, right?" He jabbed at the CCTV image with more conviction than he felt, "He says he saw him in a café – with Lefevre. Och, it was months and months and months before…"

Kat's lip curled with disgust. Jimmy knew from experience that she would have smelled the alcohol on him a long time since. "Is this going anywhere, Jimmy? Because I, for one, am finding the thread very hard to follow."

Jimmy's fist connected with the surface of the table. "It's not bloody rocket science: Hereward was at the bookstore last Wednesday. His recognised the fucker in the picture as someone he'd seen in a café on Shoreham High Street. And Lefevre had been with him – in the bloody café." He jabbed a finger at the picture. "Before that, I'd assumed that the signing was the first time that Lefevre had ever seen this guy in the picture."

Kat turned to Bridger. She appeared calm. "If you knew Lefevre, you'd realise how absurd all of this sounds." She cast a disparaging look his way. "We're all tired. And some of us are more than a little raddled."

Bridger got to his feet and swept the CCTV image off the table. "With respect, this is starting to feel cluttered," he said. "I don't like to work with clutter," he said. Reaching down to a drawer beneath the desk, he extracted a clean pad of paper and a pen and, with a sharp movement, turned them on the table, pushing them Jimmy's way. "We'll need some contact details for Mr. Lefevre," he said. "And your friend Hereward also."

"Aye, of course." Jimmy reached for his phone from his inside pocket, and caught Kat's eye as he did so. Evidently, she'd already seen the navy blue cap of the half-bottle sat squat inside . Leaning across, she took the pad from him. Her tone was matter-of fact. "I've got his details in my bag. Lefevre is coming to pick me up when we're done. If you'd like me to ask him to come into the station to speak with you, that can be arranged."

Jimmy sat back in his seat. "I'll bloody speak him, if he's got anything to do w'it."

Bridger took the pad back from Kat. "With respect, sir, you need to leave the questioning to us. Any more altercations could well jeopardise the safe return of your son."

Outside the station, an afternoon sun cast long, low shadows across the yard. Squinting into the light, Jimmy Dunbar used his teeth to tug a cigarette from its packet.

Kat caught up with him . "What the hell was going on in there? Do you realise how little sense you were making? There is nothing..." Her eyes were flashing, her head held forward "...*nothing* that could be worse than the situation that we, as parents, are in. Yet you choose this bloody moment to fall off the bloody wagon." Her dark eyes flashed. She looked, for all the world, like she could kill him. "For fuck's sake, Jimmy... we have a press conference tomorrow, and God knows how many interviews lined up after that. Do you comprehend what this will look like?" She drew in her lips. " I mean, even how...?" She covered her mouth, and looked away, her eyelids slamming shut.

Jimmy struck a match and bent down to light his cigarette, shielding the flame.

He looked beyond her, where the barriers of the carpark lifted to admit a sleek black Jag. It was Lefevre.

Kat glanced at her watch. Without comment, Jimmy watched as she walked past him, in the direction of the parked car.

"There's your man," Jimmy called after her. He was shouting now. "I'll be bloody interested to hear what that slippery cunt's got tae say."

Kat walked on. As she reached the driver's side, the window lowered.

Jimmy threw his cigarette to the ground and ground it into the concrete with the toe of his boot.

Kat glanced back in his direction. Lowering herself to the level of the driver's window, she spoke with Lefevre. Jimmy saw the glint of his sunglasses in the side mirror. Kat straightened up and turned back towards Jimmy. She took a step forward and folded her arms in a provocative gesture, head to one side.

Jimmy held out his arms and staggered slightly. "Okay, okay. I'm gone," he shouted. He turned on his heels with a slight stumble, and headed for the side of the building, where a narrow path lead to an outdoor smoking zone.

Once around the corner, he stopped and tucked himself against the wall. Not before long, he heard the tapping of Kat's court shoes as she came approached the building for a second time, now accompanied by Lefevre. The Canadian sounded rattled, his smooth accent edgier than normal. "I'll look at the picture, okay? If I know the guy, I will tell this Bridger dude that I know the guy. But I can tell you this for a fact: that signing in London was the first time I'd ever set eyes on the guy."

Kat sounded tired. "Okay –don't shoot the messenger. I'm only repeating what this friend of Jimmy's said." Her voice softened. "Hey."

"Yeah?"

"I need someone to lean on through this."

"I'm here, babe."

She paused. "Jimmy's drinking again. He's falling apart. I mean, of all times... our little boy..." Her voice cracked.

With his back against the wall, and his fingers splayed over the brickwork, Jimmy held his breath. He pictured Lefevre's arms around his wife, saw the shape of them coming together, her cheek pressed into his chest. It should be him. With her. Giving comfort.

"Katherine, sweetheart..." he emphasised each word at a time, " I do not...know...this guy. Sincerely. Jimmy has flipped. He was always gonna flip – I told you that when you were persuading me to take him on. The guy is unstable and unreliable. Look: someone somewhere has their story muddled up. I mean, I got a glimpse of this Hereward guy in London, but he did not strike me as a dude who's playing with a full deck, right?"

Kat let out a small gasp. "You know what? I really don't care about any of this, or any of these people. All I care about is getting my little boy back."

"I know, I know, kid. So now you've seen a picture of the guy who's got him, right? Which means a) Alfie is okay and b) we're one step near to finding him. Look: if it helps, I'll go in there right now and answer any question your Bridger guy wants to ask. If there's anything – anything at all - I can say which might help, I'll say it. Okay, baby?"

There was the sound of shoes scuffing against concrete as Lefevre approached the entrance again, the automatic door sliding open. "Wait for me in the car? It won't take long."

Kat sounded tired. "Being stationary is not great for me at the moment. Think I might wander for a while. Stay busy..."

"Sure. But don't go near the front of the building," said Lefevre. "There are a load of reporters out there. Don't let yourself be recognised." He gestured beyond the car park. "If you need to go get into a wide open space, the park's in that direction. Keep your sunnies and your headscarf on at all times. You should be good.

"Sure," she said. There was a slight pause "Call me when you're done?"

Jimmy pictured his wife walking away.

Stepping out, he watched her move towards the open space of the town parks. He thought of those times when he had admired that confident stride down some red carpet or towards the platform in an awards ceremony. Powerful. Female Now, from behind, her frame was hunched, her elbows jutting out as she hugged herself. He should have been there for her.

He turned his mind towards Lefevre. Casting a determined eye towards the smoked glass of the building, he reached again for his cigarettes. When that man made his exit, Jimmy Dunbar would be waiting for him.

Fifteen.

Jimmy didn't have long to wait. Within fifteen minutes, Lefevre was in plain sight through the glass walls of the building. Jimmy knew that he'd been seen – indeed, he had intended it to be so. Lefevre hesitated before emerging once more.

"James…" He touched the knot of his tie. "So I told Bridger all I know. I took him through what happened in London." He searched Jimmy's face. "God, I feel for you guys, I so do. I've said this to Katherine, but I'll say it to you too: if there's anything I can do, anything at all…" His mouth constricted into a grim line of sympathy.

Jimmy took Lefevre in. The Italian suit. The razor cut. He felt appalled by the assiduous detail that this man had afforded himself during these harrowing times.

He took a step closer. "So, come on. Donnae leave it there. What did yous tell him?"

The crease at the bridge of Lefevre's nose furrowing. "Tell who?"

"Marge Bloody Simpson…who d'you think I mean? Don't piss me aboot. Bridger. What did yous tell Bridger?"

Lefevre unbuttoned his jacket.. "Like I said: questions about Southbank. What happened, what was said… general stuff…"

Some way off in the car park, the siren of a police vehicle pierced the air.

Jimmy folded his arms, his head to one side. He planted his feet wider apart. "Must try harder, Lefevre."

Lefevre swallowed and narrowed his eyes. "Okay… well… they want to know more about the guy who caused trouble at the signing – the one that they think took Alfie." His gaze dropped to Jimmy's lips as he caught the scent of bourbon. He nodded.

Jimmy stepped closer. "Interesting - that it's taken this much for you to remember the wee lad's name."

Lefevre smiled. "Look – I can't pretend to imagine what this is like for you guys. I have no kids. But don't you think it might be more productive to focus on getting the kid back?" He patted Jimmy's shoulder. "Hey. We'll keep talking. But if it's good with you, James, I'd better be getting off…"

He made to walk past, towards the car park. Jimmy grasped the breast of Lefevre's jacket. Lefevre looked down at the mottled fingers. "James. Sincerely, this is not a good idea. If this is about you being pissed, because I dropped you from my books…"

Jimmy Dunbar's voice was a low growl. He bared his teeth. "You think that matters remotely at this point in time? I want some fucking answers."

Lefevre's tried to grasp Jimmy wrist, but Jimmy's hands were already tugging his lapels. The Canadian looked above the door of the station where the CCTV camera suspended high above them.

"Answers," Jimmy repeated. "You were there in the bookstore wi' that fucking rocket; the police have now told you that the same guy has been seen with Alfie. What I need tae know about is before all o'that. And that's what the copper wanted tae know too, hey? The time before. The time Hereward saw you in a café with that prick."

Lefevre was measuring Jimmy. He still held Jimmy's wrist, but the grip had weakened. His voice was higher than normal. "There will come a time, James – if that time hasn't come already – when you make decisions about who is on your team and who isn't. You need to make informed decisions. The guy you're talking about – his name was Hereward? This is a guy who's had a series of strokes and barely remembers his own name, yeah? Jeez. I'll tell you exactly what I told Inspector Bridger. Before Southbank? That guy? " He shook his head. "Never seen him in my entire life. "

Jimmy was still for a moment. Before he knew it, in a sudden movement, he was pinning the other man against the wall, his forearm across Lefevre's neck, his nostrils flaring, his large teeth bared beneath his beard.

"You're a bloody liar." His fingers crawled over Lefevre's cheek. Lefevre raised himself onto the balls of his feet, his back tight against the tall glass panels of the building. "Understand this, Lefevre: that lanky streak of shit has my boy. Christ only knows what he is planning tae do with him, or what he's already done." He shook him again. "Southbank, Wednesday - I know what I saw. Outside, in the lobby, when he was stirring up shit. I saw you slip something intae his pocket? What was it, huh?"

Despite his vulnerability, Lefevre forced out a scornful laugh. "Isn't it obvious? I bunged him a couple of twenty pound notes to make him disappear. Nothing more, nothing less. We didn't need an idiot like that spoiling the party." There was a rasping catch at the front of Lefevre's throat, as Jimmy's fist pressed into his Adam's apple. "You need to drop this tough-guy crap, James. It's not helping you, it's not helping Katherine and it's certainly not helping your boy…"

Like a rat terrier, Jimmy shook the other man with controlled violence, hissing through clenched teeth. "I don't wannae hear my son's names on your lips again, d'ya hear?" he pressed his face into the other man's. "You're a bloody liar. You're lying about this, like you're lying about Kat…"

"Katherine?"

"You and her, you bastard. I know you're fucking her. You've always had a thing for her. And now – the perfect time to reel her in - when her son's gone missing and she needs someone..."

Even though in a compromising situation, Lefevre had the capacity to disarm. His breathing had quickened, but his smile was cold. "You're the husband, James."

Jimmy's held his fist to Lefevre's face, the knuckles digging into the cheekbones. He drew his fist back and spoke between gritted teeth. "Give me a fucking excuse."

Lefevre looked to one side, and Jimmy became aware of other people moving behind him.

There were three of them: Bridger, and two constables, each stood either side. "I appreciate your timing, gentlemen," said Lefevre.

Jimmy released Lefevre and swung round on the DSI. "What did this bastard tell yous?"

"As I said inside the station, sir: we will inform you straight away if there are any further developments. Mr. Lefevre here has been helping us with our enquiries and there are no new significant developments." His expression was grim, his feet planted apart. The uniforms either side looked alert, hands poised on radios.

Bridger moved between Jimmy and Lefevre. "Look: I don't know what's going on here, Mr. Dunbar, but an arrest for a public order offence is the last thing you or Ms. Kennedy need right now. The next twenty-four hours are crucial in cases of these kinds." He looked to Lefevre. "Did you wish to make an official complaint, sir?"

Lefevre's face exuded magnanimity.   "It was nothing." He moved his fingers around his own neck.

Jimmy jabbed a furious index finger towards Lefevre and tried to push past Bridger. "Nothing significant my arse! I want to know what connection this bastard has with the disappearance of my son." One of the constables took his upper arm. "Will you let go of me..."

Lefevre stepped back. He brushed the shoulders of his suit and fastened his jacket buttons. "These guys are going through soul-destroying times. Unimaginable." He took his car keys and phone from his trouser pocket, and made to walk away. But he paused. Moving close to Jimmy, he placed his lips beside his ear while the constable still had hold of him. "One thing to clarify though, James. The thing about fucking your wife? I never lied to you because you never actually asked me."

***

Later that evening, Katherine Kennedy sat on the edge of a kings-sized bed in a thick, white bathrobe, her knees pressed together. To her side, she saw herself in the mirror of her dressing table. Tracing the dark rings under her eyes with her fingers, she pulled her fingertips down over her cheeks, following the lines that joined the side of her nose to her mouth. She flashed a smile, as was her habit when checking her reflection, but it was the fleeting ghost of an emotion she'd abandoned over the last few days.

Behind the door to the en-suite, the shower stopped. The door opened. Lefevre was combing back his hair, a large bath towel wrapped about his waist. A purpling swelling curved in a semi-circle around his left eye. He placed his comb on the dresser, and prodded the tender wound with the tips of his long fingers.

"He's lucky you didn't press charges," Kat said.

Lefevre walked over to a low chest of drawers. "And that would have helped how?" He opened one of the drawers, and took out his wristwatch. "They took him in and cautioned him."

She fell silent for a moment, then said:, "Bridger called again."

Lefevre turned his head. "Oh? Anything new?"

"The man who was seen with Alfie. They have his name."

Lefevre pulled his watch onto his wrist, and fiddled with the catch. "Yeah? Who is he?"

"Apparently, he's already known to the police. His name is Butcher. Luke Butcher."

He didn't look up. "That's great news, huh? I'm telling you: it won't take long for the cops to close in him." He moved over to the bedside cabinet, and opened the top drawer. Turning round, he looked again at Kat. "You seen my phone, kid?"

Kat gestured towards her side. "It's here. It rang while you were in the shower." She paused. " I thought I should take it. In case it was connected to Alfie in any way."

Lefevre took a step towards her, hand held out.

Her eyes were on him still. "Your phone: why d'you lock it?"

He laughed. "I'm in PR, honey. It's about the people I know. There's all sorts of crap in there I don't want the world to see. " His gestured again for the phone.

She looked down towards her feet in thought before passing the phone back. "The thing Jimmy said about you and me sleeping together? Why didn't you tell him the truth outright – that we're not? Why didn't you deny it?"

He shrugged. "It was the way it came out I guess. If James took it the wrong way, that's not my problem. Now, can I have my phone?"

She nodded towards his bruising. "Evidently, it was your problem in the end." She handed the phone back over.

"Hmm." Lefevre looked down at his phone, his thumb moving over the screen before he realising that she was still watching

THE GOOD MORNING GIRL

him. He held it out on the flat of his hand. "You want it back? I can unlock it. If you want me to."

Kat frowned. "Why would I want you to do that?"

Lefevre looked confused for a moment then smiled. He turned and walked towards the dressing room but stopped in the doorway. "Generally, Katherine, it pays to have some faith in human nature."

Sixteen– the morning of Wednesday 7th December

Simon looked down upon the body of Oleg Kowalski. With abject care and concern, he took in the inert old man. The little wizened face was turned away, those watery languid eyes fixed to a point beyond their present plane. Simon there was no other way but to come right out with it. "I understand they spoke to you about the test results. Is that what this is about?" At first, there was no response. "Mr. Kowalski?"

The old man blinked as if coming out of a dream. **Something here,** "Not at all. I am old, and my days are numbered. For some time, it has become clear that my fate can be read on your faces." He sighed. "Instead, I have been pondering practical questions regarding the young woman who came to visit me." He was piecing the events together in his mind, counting them off on his fingers. "After her visit, she disappears. Not long after this, the child – her half-brother – is taken. These events are connected only by the father that they both share – the poet." His old eyes narrowed. "If there was the slightest possibility that she was involved in the child's abduction, why would she pass on a book of her father's poetry that contains his telephone number scribbled on the inside cover?"

Simon pulled a face. "I don't know, Mr. K. Are you sure that these are the kind of things you need to be worrying about?"

Oleg Kowalski afforded himself a rare laugh. It was, he knew, the sound of dried peas being poured along a tin tray. "Young man, all my life, I have tried to convince myself that I adhere to the key principles of the great world faiths. Nevertheless, the irony remains that I have spent little time considering matters of religion. But you get to that stage in life when such thoughts become inevitable." He smiled. "Lately, I have entertained the possibility of there being a presence, benign or otherwise, looking down on us mortals. He – or she – places a game of chess with challenges and opportunities, placing the pieces at unexpected points along our journeys." He halted, trying to find the words. His lips were dry. "For example: the young woman, Hope Kelly. Could there have been a reason why our paths crossed as they did on that fateful evening aboard the train? She almost asked me as much as much herself." He looked at Simon now, his face a picture of concentration - bright, moist eyes moving from side to side. "A lonely train carriage in which a remarkable young woman talked about the kindness of strangers. Talked, despite all the hard knocks in life that she was dealt. You know, I remember almost every word she spoke that evening. Every one has resonated. She has opened my eyes, this remarkable young lady.

He tried to get more comfortable as he pointed towards the window. "Not far from this hospital, there was a terrible hospital. It sat on a hill overlooking a motorway. An old woman sat at a window staring at the threads of headlamps that headed towards the city. She had occupied that chair for over thirty years, and not once was its upholstery cleaned. This hospital – it was not a good place. The staff were lazy and unkind – some cruel, even- and in the Autumn of 1985, the City Council finally decided to move the remaining patients elsewhere and close the institution down.

"One of the final patients to be moved was the lady of whom I speak. She was a fragile creature, who had, many years since, lost her mind and her memory to the traumas of losing a child. She had no friends or family to visit her, save her husband. For many years, he had visited with the regularity of clockwork - three times a week, month in, month out. Gently, he had persisted with quiet questions about the dirty bedsheets, the cold food, the scarcity of the staff, but no-one there heard or cared. During his visits, his wife neither looked at him or spoke to him as if he had long gone from her mind. Nevertheless, he continued to visit, haunted perhaps by the selfish actions that he suspected may have driven her to those dark places in the first place.

"The husband was much happier with conditions In the new care home: friendlier staff, freshly-laundered beds, soft cushions. But, sadly, these had little effect on his wife's condition. She continued to look past him to the grounds that stretched beyond the tall windows of the rest room. With patience, he would talk to her about the life they had together before the bad times. He found it easiest to dwell on details: objects they collected for their little basement flat in Bristol, wild flowers they found on their long walks across the Bedminster Downs.

"Sometimes, he faltered, running out of things to say when he sat with her, making excuses to find the nurses and speak with them about domestic arrangements. After a time, knowing himself to be unnecessary, he found reasons to curtail his visits: they became weekly, and after a time he curtailed his visits to once a fortnight. When, one cold Winter, he was hospitalised with a bout of pneumonia for a three weeks, he went a whole month away from her. He was surprised by the sense of relief as well as release that came with the break. From that time, it became more difficult to return – or, rather, easier not to. He would send letters instead – trivial words that the carers would read to her emotionless face. The letters became cards – one at Christmas and Easter, another on her birthday, flowers and a note on their anniversary. They were gestures that filled the long gaps between his infrequent visits until there must have come a time when he told himself that the woman he had loved had long since gone."

Simon remained silent. The corner of the old man's eye twitched, and a small ball of saliva gathered in the corner of his lips. "Nancy," he whispered. Simon wondered how many years it had been since he gave voice to her name. The old man's face was sad. "I had only her shell. When I realised this, I am ashamed to say that I never visited that care home again again."

Simon looked down to where Oleg Kowalski's useless legs lay still and straight beneath the sheets. Her voice softened. "If you wanted to go, it's not too late, you know. We could sort out a wheelchair. One of the off-duty drivers could get an ambulance out there."

The elderly patient shook his head. "Someone once told me that old age is the woodcutter stood before a mighty oak," he said. "The trunk is your core; the boughs family and friends; each leaf, a memory. This woodcutter watches you grow, safe in the knowledge that his time will come. He watches you reach your heights, and, after, he begins. This woodcutter, he chops segments of your life away: your work, your faculties; he hacks away some more – old friends tumbling to the earth to rot into the ground, until a single splinter, the size of a toothpick, remains." He paused. "Here I am. With the very last splinter. It is too late to return," he said. "She would never recognise me. Nancy and I have looked upon each other's faces for the last time." The corners of his mouth twitched into a sad smile. " Even if, after all this time, something of my wife of old should be there, hiding in the shadows…" In an absent manner, his fingers traced the outlines of the scar on his other hand and shook his head again. "No, my young friend. Her disappointment in me is far too painful to conceive."

Oleg Kowalski pulled himself to, and took hold of the younger man's wrist. His languid, soulful eyes found Simon's. "Last night, when the ward had fallen quiet, I found myself looking down upon my own body. It seemed part dream, but also very real. How old and consumed I looked down there. I felt myself rising higher and higher, and it would have been easy to concede to the sense of pure serenity that I was experiencing. But there was an invisible chord between us, as if the sleeping old man beneath me was pulling back. And I saw his eyes open. After this, I was back again, lying in this hospital bed." He sighed. "I am near the end, but there is unfinished business. My one regret, I now understand, is that I never said sorry to her. To my Nancy. On the train, before the accident, this young woman, prepared to treat me as her confidante when we had only recently met. It has been a sore reminder of my failing the one person I had solemnly promised, before God, to stay beside in sickness and in health." He fell silent for a few second, taking Simon in. "Young man? Will you go to Nancy for me? Will you tell her that I am sorry for not trying harder to understand? He pointed to his bedside. My diary is there in the bedside cabinet. I have the address of the care home written down."

Simon looked down it the cold purple fingers that clutched his wrist. He felt a faint moment of panic. "I do think it's better coming from you. When you've recovered a little perhaps?"

"Please," said the old man, in a whisper. "Miss Hope Kelly was an angel sent to remind me of my duties before I reached my deathbed. My wife may never hear, but the words I want to be said before her will have been spoken. After this, I can have some peace."

Simon watched the old man. It was not the first occasion upon which he had seen old men look into the shallow pool of their end time. He also knew their stubbornness and tenacity. Talking Oleg Kowalski out of his wishes would be futile. "I'll go. If that's what you want."

"It is what I want," said Oleg Kowalski. "I will ask no more of you."

Seventeen –the morning of Thursday 8th December 2016

"Jimmy. We need to talk."

Back at The Old Schoolhouse, Jimmy stubbed his cigarette out against the wall next to the back door of the Old School House, and flicked the stub into a dark corner. He checked the time – 5 A.M. To the West, the sky was bible black. He hadn't slept since the previous night. Now Kat was on the phone. He asked her, "Have y' heard something?"

"Nothing more since yesterday. Listen." She hesitated. "It's Lefevre. The stuff you were saying about him – it's been playing on my mind. I need to talk it through with you, if only to be able to tell myself that it's complete nonsense."

"Where are you? I'll come to you."

"No. That won't work. Lefevre's got me a hotel room to keep the press at bay, but they already know. There are cars and TV vans parked right the way down the road."

Jimmy stepped away from the building. "So where is he now – Lefevre?"

"Sleeping on the sofa."

Jimmy whispered into the phone. "If there's anything you have on Lefevre, you need to let me know. You cannae protect him if he's keeping anything back."

"For God's sake, Jimmy, give me some credit...." Her voice broke off and there were background noises. "I think he's coming. I have to go. I'll call again..."

Jimmy scanned the dark hills rising and falling before him. "Come to Hereward's place. I'll wait for yous. Meantime, get rid o'any traces of calls or messages between us." His voice tailed off. Silence at the other end of the line. He didn't know how much she'd heard.

Within the hour, a taxi arrived. Beyond, the first rumours of day crept over the lip of the Downs and invisible birds conjured up a harsh, atonal chorus. Kat emerged, and was rummaging through her bag. She cast a quick glance over to Jimmy, then leant back towards the driver's window. The driver lit his carriage as she handed over the fare.

Together, they watched the taxi disappear. Kat turned to Jimmy, unsmiling. "I got here as soon as I could. Then there was the usual round the houses game with the gentlemen of the press. Took a long while, but I think the driver managed to shake them off."

As she spoke, they both watch the taxi's headlights vanish down the narrow lanes. "That driver should be living off the bloody tip for the next year." She wrapped her arms around herself. "It's cold," she said. They both looked past the tall building, and over the downs. Jimmy knew that her mind, like his, would have been trawling that fateful moment when they both realised that Alfie had been taken. The vivid red slit of sunlight threatening the horizon proffered no more hope for either of them.

Kat continued. "There's no time to beat about the bush. There's stuff I need to say. About the past. It's why I had to see you. If we're gonna work together to get Alfie back, I need us to start with a clean slate."

Jimmy took Kat in. She looked immaculate, as always: even in the galling terror of their ordeal, he was always astounded at the way she found time to choose outfits, apply make-up. But now she was removing her sunglasses, as if she needed to reveal her real self to him. The rims of her eyelids were livid and raw, her face more lined than he'd ever seen it. Her voiced was bereft of its usual keen edge. "You're going to hear things you won't like. About Lefevre." She gestured towards the path. "It's easiest for me if we're walking while I do this."

Jimmy stood still for a second as she moved off without looking back. After a short while, he followed.

He watched her pull her headscarf away as she broke into a strong stride. It unravelled from around her neck, and she shook her dark hair back, running her hands through. She put a hairpin in her mouth.

Jimmy caught up with her and walked by her side. Taking out the pin, she glanced down towards his mouth. "Look, Jim: the crap that happened between us before this – we need to put that on hold. Bridger said it back at the police station: we need to work together to get Alfie back." She was looking at his mouth again. "Back then. When we were talking to the police," she continued. "You'd been drinking. I could smell it on you." She dropped her gaze. "And I can now." She finished tying her hair back into a ponytail, and raised her hands in frustration. "All the time when we were together, after Alfie, you stayed sober. You made that vow when I got pregnant, remember? Why, in the name of God, you choose now to fall off the wagon is beyond my understanding." She was staring at him, a quiet anger building. "God, you've bloody let me down, Jimmy."

Jimmy struggled to keep up with her. "You've got this wrong, Kat: there's nothing here I cannae control." A wave of hopelessness engulfed him. "It had a wee slip after you talkin' about divorce and everything…"

She stopped on the path, and she turned on him, a finger held to his face. "There you go again! Don't you dare pin your weakness on me, Jimmy. There has been no 'we' for a long time. But, irrespective of everything anything that happens between you and me, we are still Alfie's parents." She seemed restless, exasperated. "You know, it would have been such a relief knowing that, for once, you could be the one who was carrying us."

Jimmy moved closer. "And I can... I will lass. You will never know how bad I feel about letting that boy outta my sight." He felt a pricking behind his eyes. "It was a mistake. My fault." He reached out but, catching the slight tremor in the thick tips of his fingers, plunged them back into his jacket pockets again. "I'll try tae keep a handle on things. I swear."

She reached into her bag for a tin of lip balm. Running her finger over her lips, she looked out towards the Downs again. Before them, as the light of the morning came up, field and scrubland and bush stretched out in a blurred patchwork of muted blues and greys. In the distance, the slab of sea against the sky had become flat, drab and unforgiving.

"Where in God's name, is he?" she whispered.

Jimmy followed her line of sight. Both of them were an unknown measure of space away from a drop into an unthinkable abyss of bleakness. He thought back to that moment: the stuttering across sketchy dark pathways, shouting his son's name into the great, foggy void.

"I need to keep moving." She wrapped her arms around herself. "Else, I'm in danger of freezing to death."

As they walked, he was aware that they weren't touching. In those early days, they'd get a bus somewhere and walk for miles and miles along coastal paths, woodland, following streams and rivers and drovers' roads, all walking boots and plastic-coated maps; arms folded across each other's backs, grasping fingertips or elbow touching elbow –no space between. It had been a long time since they had walked those paths together.

"Lefevre," he said. "You told me yous wanted tae to talk about him, remember?"

Kat was sure to keep half a step ahead of him. "Maybe it was nothing."

He struggled to keep up with her long, loping strides. "I'm guessing you wouldnae come out all this way otherwise?"

"Okay," she said. "You know that I've known him for a long while– before we got together - before I got him to represent you?"

Jimmy hesitated. "Aye. I remember you once told me the two of yous had something going on before I was around." His body froze. "So it's true? You're back wi' him?""

She stopped to and turned back to face him. "For once in your life, listen carefully to what I'm saying. I'm trying to tell you all of this to clear our heads of all the crap in the past? So that we can focus on getting Alfie back? What I can do without, is your poetic histrionics right now."

Jimmy ran his fingers through his hair and stared at her. "Ok. Fine. Tell me about Lefevre. No dramatic reactions, I swear tae God."

She turned and walking away, her pace more brisk than ever. They reached a bridle gate, and Jimmy moved ahead, fumbling with the catch. Leaning across, Kat pulled it to. She talked more to herself than to him. "If there's a small chance it'll take my mind off the hell we're in…" She took a breath. "The Summer of 2010 – the one when I was over in the States filming a pilot show for three weeks with Dalton. Lefevre flew over in the second week to give some direction with interviews and promo shoots. That time before – before me and you, I mean – the relationship had burned out quickly - at least as far as I was concerned. I'd found him to be very intense and had broken it off, feeding him some line about not wanting to mix business with pleasure. Sure, he was very upset, but he wasn't prepared to lose his most lucrative client. So things settled back to normal. Then, years later, Florida happened. It was 2010. We got involved with some creatives, and there was too much money being thrown around – our American backers were very eager to please. Things got a bit crazy: parties, champagne, coke -you know the kind of thing. "

"Cocaine?" said Jimmy. "I know Lefevre's partial, but you've never told me it was your bag."

"It's not. At least, it wasn't until then. I found myself going along with it. I haven't done it since. Part of it was the buzz of being out there: I'd been used to being in the limelight over here for a few years, but it was cranked up to this whole new level when we went Stateside. Lefevre was very attentive. He watched over me, pulled strings, made sure every deal, every decision worked in my favour."

"And you ended up sleeping with him again?"

"I'm not proud of it, Jimmy. Just as I never saw myself as the type to do a line, I also never imagined I'd have an affair once I was married – least of all with Lefevre after the last time. But everything seemed different out there – as was as if anything could happen. Anyhow, like last time, he was coming on strong. Before I knew it, he was already asking me if I'd ever thought of leaving you. Alarm bells. I backed off. Made excuses."

"You told him it was over?"

A long sigh drew from her body. "I should have been more direct. But you know how it is. There was a lot riding on Florida. It had to be done carefully."

"That'll be a no, then."

She chose to ignored him. "Once we'd got back to the UK, there was this assumption that the relationship would move on, that I would start to make plans to leave you. I'd never given any indication of that, but Lefevre talked everything through like it was a fait accomplis." Her pace slowed. She turned to face him. "OK: I should have ended it there. But I didn't know how to tell him. And I felt I couldn't risk it. I – we – had so much riding on his backing; I was worried that ending it might result in my career going down the pan and, worse still, him telling you."

Jimmy stepped past her, and looked out over the waking Downs. He kicked at the root of a shrub with the toe of his boot. "How much longer did it last?"

"A month. No more than six weeks. There never seemed to be a good time to tell him. But I did in the end. And then he threw a curve ball. He told me that he'd fallen in love with me."

Jimmy stopped in his tracks. "In love? Lefevre? Christ, Kat..."

Kat sighed. "I know, I know. My reaction, too. Yep, he could be very attentive and considerate, but I always thought him too narcissistic to love anyone more than himself."

Jimmy shook his head. "Shit. Lefevre. Of all people."

She threw him a withering look. "Well, evidently, I've never been the best at picking men," she said. She turned and they carried on walking. "To say he was upset is an understatement. Believe me, you do not want to see Lefevre cry. He begged me to give it a go, but I held fast. He went silent for two weeks – I thought he was plotting. When he came back, realigned and eager to continue the relationship on purely professional terms, the relief was immense. With hindsight, I suspect he'd realised how off-putting I found his intensity – that a calm Lefevre was more likely to win over my affections than a grovelling one. So the relationship turned professional once again. After all, you and I both needed Lefevre. We still do."

Jimmy grunted. "You speak for yourself, love. He's given me the bum's rush. From now on, I am no longer represented by Fox-Lefevre PR."

"Yeah - he told me," said Kat.

They approached another gate. "Jimmy leaned against one of the posts. "Lefevre. So why tell us now? He looked her in the eye. "Are you still shagging that bastard?"

She climbed up the first rung of a battered crossbar, facing away from him. For a time, she sat on the top bar, legs dangling over. Then she slipped over to the other side and turned on him, her finger pointing out over the Downs. "You think that even for one tiny moment, I would even entertain the thought of having sex with someone while Alfie is still out there? The fact remains, Jimmy, that Lefevre has become someone who I have been able to rely on. While you were scurrying around trying to chase your sordid past, he was sorting out chartered flights to help me clear up after you. He tied up loose ends, booked hire cars. Got me here. Here to find…" she gestured all round her, "…this!" She placed her hands on her hips. "The press is all over his office and his home, so he's sharing the hotel suite that he booked for me. And I have no shame in telling you that some nights I've needed to be held. To be frank, Jimmy, it makes staring into the mouth of Hell more bearable if you're being comforted by a man who isn't pissing every precious minute up against a wall."

"Okay! Fine, fine…I get that. " Jimmy reached inside his jacket pocket and extracted his fag packet. He grabbed a couple between his thick, mottled fingers, and shoved them between his lips, lighting them one at a time. He took the first cigarette out, took a long, low drag from the second before passing it across the gate.

Kat pursed her lips and pushed out a long, slow breath, watching the glowing tip for a while. She pinched it from his fingers. "It's been over five years," she said.

"Since you had a fag or fucked Lefevre?" he asked. She quickened with anger made to answer but, upon catching his sardonic smile, she softened. He had always made her laugh.

Jimmy lifted his chin upwards and blew a long, straight plume towards the sky. He thought back to that moment outside the houseboat before going in, where he watched Hope doing the very same. He realised now that this had been the very first moment of his life when he had truly recognised himself within the actions of another person. He sighed. A young woman. A boy. Drowning somewhere in a dark and dangerous sea.

Kat took a drag, then slipped her phone from her bag, glancing at it before pulling the latch and stepping back through "We need to head back - the signal out here is crap. What if someone's trying to get hold of us?" She drew from the cigarette again, before throwing it upon the ground.

"Hang on," said Jimmy, "You haven't actually told me yet? Lefevre. The things I'd said were playing on your mind, remember? What else is there?"

She looked towards the horizon. "It seems stupid now, out here."

"Try me," said Jimmy. "If it's about Alfie, anything could help."

"Firstly, it was the thing you said about him being linked to man in the CCTV image. I confronted him about it. He totally denied it, of course, and he denied it again at the police station when Bridger spoke to him. Said the one and only time he'd seen this man was at your thing at Southbank. And this friend of yours who had seen him..." She gestured back towards the hostel.

"Hereward?"

She nodded. "Him. Lefevre played on the fact that he'd had a couple of strokes and his mind was all over the place. Bridger was satisfied that he'd made some mistake and that Lefevre had no connection. No evidence. No motive. Lefevre even played that to his advantage. It turns out that one of his production companies was looking for someone who could act as executive advisor for a BBC police drama."

Jimmy grunted. "Lefevre always says that anyone can be bought for the right price. You must know he's a slippery shite. You must have doubts to be telling me this?"

Kat carried on walking, her head down.   "Like all PR gurus, Lefevre tells lies for a living. When you're closer to him, beyond a working relationship, you become much more aware of that – even paranoid about it – more so still when you're vulnerable. So, when he got back from the police station, after the fight with you, I had it out with him. I asked him why he locked his phone; why he was dashing out late at night with no word of where he was headed? I pushed, and, for the first time I can remember, he got a bit shitty with me. He said that he was stepping up where my husband was failing…" She pulled a face "– which wasn't too wide of the mark."

"Thanks very much."

"The point is, he was rattled. And that wasn't normal. And also, if it turns out that Lefevre isn't straight and the past comes out… well, I wanted it out there without risking everything by sharing it with the police. Maybe you can do some poking around. Go back to your mate. In the meantime, it's best I stick close to him."

Jimmy the stub of his cigarette to the ground and stamped on it. "Either that or I pin the little shit against a wall again and force it out of him."

"Jimmy. Your life is a series of inelegant scrapes. You did nothing to help us get our son back by thumping Lefevre yesterday. In fact, you were bloody lucky that he didn't take it any further." She took another long drag of her cigarette, before taking a long hard look at the tip. "Leave Lefevre to me." She stopped as the tall gables of the Old Schoolhouse rose before them. "Anyhow. Quickly - tell me about this girl."

"Girl?"

She rolled her eyes. "Oh, come one! The girl, the girl. Your bloody daughter, Jimmy."

"Maybe we can save that for another time. Not now, lass."

Her voice rose. "Oh come on! It's hardly irrelevant. There's a link between her and the man who's been seen with Alfie."

"There's no' much to tell. The book launch was the first time I'd set eyes on her."

"Then how d'you know she wasn't a fake? Some crack-head trying to extort a quick buck out of you - or even me? She could have been anyone."

He raised his head. "I saw myself in her. Small, physical things at first, then deeper stuff. It's hard to put intae words. Hereward helped us tae trace her to some shitty houseboat in Shoreham. She's cooped up there with her mother – Jasmine, my ex. I found them there on the Friday – this was two days before Alfie went missing. I tried tae talk but... well... I guess too much water had passed under the bridge. She didnae wannae know. Said I'd made a mistake by turning up. Then she took off. Next I heard of her was that call in the police station. The old guy who said he'd been on the train wi' her when it derailed. Then she did another runner from the hospital. I've no' heard anything since."

"And the man with Alfie on the CCTV image?"

"They call him Spider. He's Jasmine's fella – fine piece o' work. He was there with Hope at Southbank. I'm guessing he must've clocked Alfie then and there, though God knows what he's got in his head."

Kat covered her nose and mouth and closed her eyes. As with him, the horror came in waves.

Jimmy felt unable to comfort her. "Dunnae think the worst, lass," he said. "Look – if he's after anything, it'll be money. He knows you've got money. Everyone does. And he'll know that harming a wee hair on that boy's head will end any chance of success."

She pulled her hand away, tears in her eyes. "But if that's all he wants, why hasn't he contacted us? It's been almost three days, for Christ's sake! Who kind of person could take a boy away from his mother for that long? What else might they be capable of?" She pulled away and her eyes brimming with anger and frustration. "I don't know how much longer I can go on without knowing where he is and what's happening to him."

She turned and looked out again towards the Downs and laughed through her tears. "It's so fucking beautiful out here. It's like, when you're here, there is nowhere else." She was quiet for a moment. Her fingers moved over her lips. "D'you know what I keep thinking? How can the world carry on? Putting the bins out, school runs, the sun moving across the sky. There should be... some massive pause button that you can press when things like this happen. So everyone can look for him." She spoke through gritted teeth.. "Everything I do – put make-up on, eat, sleep, breathe, even being here talking to you – *everything* makes me feel guilty, like I should spend the time doing something to get him back..."

Jimmy moved nearer. He felt the damp warmth of her breathing as the ache in the pit of his gut rose like a swelling tide through his ribs. It took everything he had to hold back from being tipped over the edge. He wanted to hold her. "I feel that too," he said. "All the time."

She remained rigid and still. A tear held at the corner of her eye, but she brushed it aside. "We need to keep our shit together," she said. "We're all he's got." She sniffed, took a deep breath. "I really don't know about Lefevre," she said. "I may be very wrong. Perhaps coming out here was more about being closer to you; because it might make me feel like being closer to Alfie."

She looked at him for a moment, and Jimmy felt that she might be trying to find Alfie in him. Her eyes fell. "Come on," she said. "We need to get back to where there's a signal."

Approaching the path to the side of the Schoolhouse, they followed the iron railings when both of their phones came into range of signal, and burst into life.

Jimmy reached into the pocket of his duffle coat and got there first. "Shit. Five missed calls from Bridger. And a message."

Kat, staring at her own mobile, was opening the very same message. "Jimmy," she breathed. "There's another CCTV picture. Bridger's sent it through."

"I've got it."

There was stillness as they both took the new picture in. It was much clearer than the first and had been captured from above.

Once more, in some nondescript street in the corner of an anonymous town, the very same gangling, unkempt man loomed over a small boy – their Alfie. The man had his arm around the boy's back, grasping the scruff of his green hoodie.

But there was someone else there as well. Jimmy's heart leapt into his throat.

The third figure was female and had cropped hair; she was bent over the boy, and her tattooed shoulder was exposed as a baggy top slipped away from her arm. The arm itself was held in a sling, and she held it tight against herself. She appeared to be talking to Alfie, or perhaps giving him something – her head cast a shadow over the rest of her body.

Jimmy held his breath, terrified in anticipation of the inevitable questions to come.

Kat's face was intense and alert. "Well?"

Jimmy gawped at the image. "Aye," he said, after a while. "That's her. That's my daughter."

Eighteen

Later that day, many miles away, a low December sun threw long shadows across the grounds of the care home. They crept over the lawns, across heavy slate paving stones of terraces and through the tall French windows to herald the chill of a late afternoon.

Within, the rooms were lined with a heavy cream wallpaper that bore a large crimson and green floral motif. Standing lamps cast meagre light across bookshelves laden with unread volumes never; and between each set, nondescript pastoral prints harked back to another era.

The room's occupants were scant in number: hollow shells of people, dozing with their chins on their chests, or playing threadbare memories over and over and over before staring eyes

One of the tall-backed chairs was angle to give its incumbent a view of the world beyond. As the sun began to disappear behind the far boundaries the lawn, it cast a strange halo of light around this one sedentary patient. From the doorway, her still, small head of tight cotton-white curls was discernible, rising inches above the rest of the chair, her thin fingers motionless on the arm rest. Moving nearer, the thinnest of arms became visible, clad in a thin olive green cardigan that had been new on that morning. A tartan skirt ended below knees which were pressed together, the legs, stick-thin and starved of light, in flesh coloured stockings, capped with claret carpet slippers.

A voice carried through the drawing room. "Nancy? You have a visitor." The care worker appeared at the doorway with Simon – the nurse from Oleg Kowalski's ward - following close behind. She made no attempt to lower her voice as she turned to speak to him. "I wouldn't expect to get much out of her, if anything at all."

Simon looked to the back of the chair and removed his scarf. "It's alright," he said to her. "I don't know her. I'm here to deliver a message from her husband."

The care-worker paused. "Her husband? I never knew she had a husband. There have been no visits. Not in my time here, anyway…"

"He's in hospital – I'm a nurse on his ward. Spine injury – he was in that train accident that made the news the other week. He was left him paralysed from the waist down. It's left him feeling… well… as if he should be tying up a few loose ends." He gestured towards the patient. "This is why I'm here – he's got a message to pass on."

The woman pulled a face. "Oh. I see." She gestured towards the chair. "It's afternoon tea soon. Can I get you a brew while you're here?"

"That'd be nice." Simon gestured towards the woman staring out of the window. "I'd best go and see her."

He walked around to the sofa that faced into the room, one that lay adjacent to the high-backed chair occupied by the old woman, and looked into her face for the first time.

Although petite, her posture was good: she held her back straight against the back of the chair, her thin neck stretched and holding a small, neat head high. Where her teeth had gone over time, her bone had atrophied, her bite collapsed. Yet, from her cheekbones upwards, her skin was translucent and almost flawless for a woman of her age.

Simon walked towards the sofa and perched on the edge of the cushion. The old lady showed no awareness of him. He cleared his throat. "Mrs. Kowalski? I have a message for you. From your husband, Oleg?"

Still nothing. He took in her frail fingers, the skin stretched like parchment over her swollen pink knuckles; those fragile wrists. Someone had done her nails, each one garish and different: stars and stripes, spots, glitter – someone else's indulgence, he thought, and most inappropriate.

Her index finger twitched a little, and Simon looked to her face again, but it remained unchanged. He tried to stay chatty. "He's very poorly in hospital, Mrs. Kowalski. He's sorry that he hasn't been here to see you, but he wanted me to pass on a message." He hesitated and twisted the scarf in his hands. "He wanted to say sorry. For everything." Despite all his training and experience, he didn't know what to expect in terms of reaction. Only the persistent twitching of the finger on the arm of the sofa. He added, with care, "Actually, I think he probably wanted to say goodbye."

Outside, there was a split in the dark, low skies, and a sliver of late sunlight broke through. It caught her cheekbones, the tip of her ears. Something had touched her. Her top lip twitched with movement, slipping over her collapsed lower palette, and tiny strange guttural noises rolled and gargled at the back of her throat.

He wondered if she was trying to speak. Now, all of her fingers were moving, crawling like a stunned spider across the arm of the sofa. Simon had caught it in his peripheral vision and he realised, with faint horror, that it was trying to find his own. He kept his own hand still, waiting for hers.

The surface of her palm was a thin, cold, pallid flesh upon his own.

He watched her face. Nothing had moved, save the queer glint of her eye, and the tiniest inflections of her throat as she gave sound to her thoughts in a faint, gargled whisper.

The word was unmistakable. "Oleg."

"Yes." said Simon. He tried to smile. "I have come with a message from your husband, Oleg!"

She turned her head, the movement so slight it could barely be discerned.

Simon leaned forwards. He had, for a time, worked in a geriatric ward. It was a rare thing, but he had seen it happen before: the temporary lifting of the mist was like lifting the years of dust and grime from the rich colour of a neglected painting. But time was always the victor.

He looked into her eyes until it dawned on him: for her, he was no longer the messenger. He had become Oleg Kowalski.

Nineteen – Friday 9th December 2016

Another twenty four hours had passed and the new image appeared to move them no nearer to finding Alfie.

An uneasy impasse hung between father and the mother: Jimmy found himself unwilling to be drawn on Hope's involvement. He could not square that apparent truth of the image with the impression that had been conceived by their brief time together. For her part, Kat continued to press him on his daughter's connections. What had she said? Had her actions given anything away? Where had she been heading on the train?

Returning to one of the interview rooms at the police headquarters, Bridger was keen to impress that the net was closing in in Alfie's abductors. His use of the plural had not gone unnoticed by Jimmy. In addition, the investigation had gleaned more information about Spider: "I think we can be comforted by the fact that we're not talking about some master criminal here." He'd pulled some printouts from a document wallet and painted a quick sketch of Luke Butcher's criminal profile: a series of low level misdemeanours, beginning with his expulsion, aged thirteen, from secondary school for peddling cannabis. There followed, said Bridger, the usual offences: theft, GBH, dealing, possession. He'd spent some time inside, a lot of time on probation – mainly for supplying. There was little to suggest that interested in Alfie was motivated by anything more sinister than bribery or blackmail.

"I think we can expect a demand for money soon," said Bridger. He turned to Kat. "With respect, madam, it's the one thing you have that someone like him would want."

"But it's as Kat said," said Jimmy. "Would we no' have heard something by now? Like a ransom note?"

Bridger nodded. "I would have thought so, sir. Although, in some cases, if the kidnapper can hold out, parents are likely to become more desperate, and therefore to pay more. It's a strategy not without risk. For a start, it gives us more time to track him down. Butcher's not the sharpest knife in the drawer, which is why we remain optimistic of a quick resolution."

Bridger was keen to shift the focus of the conversation. "Anyway. If I may, I'd like to move on to this." He placed another buff folder on the table, this one newer and thinner than the last. He extracted the newest image and pointed to the female in the picture.

"Hope Jasmine Kelly. DOB: 28th July 1988. Daughter of Jasmine Adela Kelly. Father..." His voice tailed off, and he gestured in Jimmy's direction. "No police record except a caution for possession of cannabis at a music festival in 2008. She dropped out of education at the age of fifteen, registered as full-time carer for her mother; held down a series of small part-time jobs, then enrolled on a series of college courses as an adult whilst moonlighting in local shops and pubs." He focused on Jimmy. "I'm assuming, Mr. Dunbar, that a lot of this information is new to you as well."

Jimmy remained silent. Bridger held out. Jimmy shrugged. "That was a statement. It wasnae a question."

Bridger scratched the inside of his wrist. "Let's go with it as a question, then."

Jimmy leaned forward over the desk. "I didnae know about going tae college. We only spoke once – never got intae that kind o' stuff."

Bridger lifted the top sheet. "Alright. Well, not that it's relevant, but she has degree in Creative Writing. Currently applying for Post Graduate research."

Jimmy scratched his beard. "Wow. Never knew."

Bridger let the top sheet drop again. "Mr. Dunbar. I need to ask this question again: can you think of any reason at all," his finger tapped out the syllables on top of the printout, "why your daughter, Hope Kelly, might agree to be an accomplice in the abduction of your son?"

Jimmy's mind went blank. He stared ahead.

"Jimmy?" It was Kat's voice.

He looked across to Bridger. "What? No. I can only tell yous what I know. The book signing in London– that was the first time I'd seen her. She was with this Spider or Butcher or whatever he calls himself. Before she spoke tae me, I thought they were a couple, despite the obvious age gap." He squinted. "I do remember her clocking Alfie when she approached me in the queue, but looking back, that's not surprising given, you know, their connection. And the resemblance –" he shrugged, " quite a strong resemblance – between us..." He looked down at the new image again, and moved it closer. "Where did you say this one was taken?"

"I didn't. It's a street in Brighton. About five miles away from where the first image was caught. Uniform have been all over the area, we've done door-to-door questions and the like. This one is a reflection from a shop window." He tapped the top corner, "You can see that the shop sign is backwards – the tech guys managed to enhance it."

Jimmy moved his fingers over the picture. His son. His daughter. What were they saying to one another? Looking more closely, he saw damage in her posture – the slouched stance, the arm held in a sling. "She's had her hair cut," he said. "It's much shorter here. But, yeah, I'm pretty sure that's her." Bridger was happy to let him take his time over it. After a while, JImmy straightened his back and looked up again. "Look: I know how it looks in this picture. The two of them with Alfie. But how can we be sure..?"

Kat couldn't contain her exasperation. "Christ, Jimmy. Look at what's in front of you. She's there with our child. She's knows where he is and who he's with. If she wanted to help, why hasn't she contacted the police? Why hasn't she contacted you? Didn't you tell me you wrote down your number for her?"

Bridger's mouth was set in a grim line. "Your wife is correct, Mr. Dunbar. The first image was captured on Monday afternoon; the second, the day before yesterday. Both were taken after your daughter discharged herself from hospital in the early hours of Sunday morning." He fell silent for a short while, choosing his words with care. "If any tiny part of you is holding back in order to defend that young woman, Mr. Dunbar, I'd urge you to think again. As it stands, the female in this picture is, at the very least, an accessory to the abduction. If there's anything that you either know or can remember about this woman or man that will help us close in on them sooner, I can only stress how critical it is that you share this with us." He looked across to Kat. "Many cases like this end with the safe return of the abductee. But we know that this this man, whilst low-level, is something of a loose cannon. We need to get to your son before this man becomes more desperate."

***

Later that afternoon, Jimmy was stepping out of an off-licence, shielding his face against a low sun. He set his sights on a newsagent's across the way. Before crossing, he sat himself on a bench awhile, and pulled opened a white plastic carrier bag. Extracting a plastic water bottle, he unscrewed the cap and poured the water onto the path. Inside the bag, he half-filled the bottle with the half-bottle of vodka he'd bought. He raised the plastic bottle to his lips, and drew from it. Drawing his lips over his teeth, he replaced the cap. Getting to his feet, Jimmy stood, swaying on the spot for a moment, before crossing the road in the direction of the newsagents.

The day's papers lined the rack outside the store. Bridger had warned them: the front pages were saturated with the CCTV images of the Hope and Spider with Alfie. Although he'd seen similar online, the impact of hard print was more painful to absorb. The more salacious titles had seized upon the arresting idea of a young blonde outcast as some femme fatale in the guise of angelic drifter. The words leapt out at Jimmy: 'abandoned', 'desperate', 'estranged'. One of the papers had found an incongruous picture of Hope in a graduation pose, smiling with the sun behind her, clutching a scroll with blonde hair spilling from beneath the mortar board and a borrowed gown. "The face of evil." With growing horror, Jimmy realised that, before any real harm may even have come to Alfie, his daughter was already being cast as the next Myra Hindley to Spider's Brady, their unspeakable, and as yet uncommitted crimes scribbled over their faces.

Jimmy picked two of the papers from the rack. Much like his own, Spider's star, that had occupied column inches twenty-four hours earlier, was already on the wane. With the obvious exception of Alfie, there were two key players in the sordid events that were unfolding: despairing celebrity mother, all dark glasses and muted shawls, flanked by policeman as she fled towards an escape vehicle; and the new lead – the troubled and vengeful step-daughter who had been seen, within the last twenty-four hours, man-handling the young, defenceless abductee. Disparate pieces of a puzzle, thrown together with little or no logic.

Jimmy was exhausted. He went to close the last paper he'd skimmed through, when the sight of his own name caught his eye. They'd printed one of his recent poems – verse taken from the very same volume that Hope had taken the week before. His heart jumped in his chest, but any hubris was soon displaced by guilt. With grim fascination, he read on. The Arts Editor – who Jimmy admired and knew, had, with a grim brutality, dissected the poem, stanza by stanza, line by line. By the article's closure, Jimmy Dunbar was exposed as a trite, hypocritical narcissus living off 'unoriginal, sentimental doggerel'.

Jimmy's heart sank. The capacity of a human being to kick the crap out of his fellow man whilst he was down beggared belief. He ambled through the narrow doorway of the shop, slid a few coins across the surface of the counter, and, without knowing why he wanted to keep it, dropped the paper into his plastic bag. The newsagent scooped up the coinage and dropped it into his till with an invasive clatter.

Outside, the sun had disappeared from the sky. Since the days of the snowfall, a milder front had crossed over from the channel. The streets were dank and grey now, a uniform drizzle rendering the world a limp, lifeless place of rounded-shouldered strangers with faces contorted against the rain and the perpetual smell of damp. Everything he touched was coated with that thin layer of slime that fouls every surface in dreary weather. Feeling the weight of the plastic bottle in his bag bumping against the side of his knee, Jimmy looked ahead for a place in which he could drink, unseen and uninterrupted.

When he reached the park, there were two benches ahead: one with a teenage couple wrapped up in their private universe; the second occupied by an older lady petting a Scottish terrier on her lap. Jimmy chose the latter, but sat at the opposite end of the bench.

His voice was gruff. "Afternoon," he nodded. She smiled without making eye contact, and put her dog on the ground.

He'd left enough room to his right to place the carrier bag in a way that its contents could not be seen. He took the newspaper and opened it to his poem, resting it on his lap and flattening the page down. The weight of the liquid within the plastic bottle satisfied him, as he rested it on the paper and began unscrewing the plastic lid.

"I'm so sorry."

He was startled by her voice. Looking up, he saw that the old lady had turned towards him. She nodded towards his newspaper. "You're that Katherine Kennedy's husband, aren't you? The one with the missing boy."

Jimmy's fingers drew back from the plastic cap. "Aye."

She looked down at the carrier bag and, at that moment, he knew that she knew what he was up to. This lady had a careworn face, with little wisps of peppered hair that poked out from under a bottle-green bobble hat. The dog wore a matching knitted coat. She looked tired. A long, tired, life; a demanding family; troubles of her own. Where in her life, Jimmy wondered, had there been some sad fuck-up like him – some father, brother, husband who let her down time and time again.

Nevertheless, she smiled reassuringly. "I'm sure they'll find him," she said. "They're pretty clever these days, you know. There's the Tinternet." Jimmy made an attempt to smile back. "It'll be alright," she said. She rose to her feet with a slight groan, and tugged at the lead. "Come on, Toffee." The dog resisted. With an obstinate strain on its lead, it moved towards Jimmy's boot, sniffing the heel. *Go ahead: piss on it you little bastard,* thought Jimmy.

When she'd gone, he stretched his legs out in front of himself, the joints in his knees clicking. Unscrewing the cap again, he held the bottle aloft, watching the clouds move through it. He placed his index finger into his mouth and bit down hard on it until it hurt. He thought of Kat, of her sadness, and her words in the station:

God, you've bloody let me down, Jimmy...

Fighting the urge to weep, he tipped the bottle until the contents poured in a clear, twisting ribbon upon the dark path at his feet. The tiny streams followed the gradient of the hill. He watched until the trickle ceased, and then he rose and dropped the empty plastic bottle into a nearby bin, followed by the plastic bag and the newspaper.

He tipped his head up to the sky and stood there for a while. "Holy Christ," he mummbled, the tears rolling down his cheeks, into his beard.

Walking back along the park path, the ringtone of his phone sounded once more. It was Kat.

"Get here now," she said. "I'm in Lefevre's hotel room. I've sent you the location." Jimmy's grip on his phone tightened. "It's happened."

Jimmy blinked. "What? What's happened?" But she had already hung up.

Twenty: the evening of Friday 9th December 2016

At the entrance to the hotel, an unsmiling concierge guarded the glass doors.

Behind Jimmy, a scrum of reporters and photographers grappled beyond an outer gate, their voices playground taunts: *Jimmy – any developments? How's Katherine taking things at the moment? Is there any truth to the rumour that your daughter is connected with Alfie's disappearance? Jimmy? Mr. Dunbar?*

Jimmy pushed against the glass door. For so long, he'd craved and fed on their attention. Now they owned his arse. He felt tired.

The concierge raised a sardonic eyebrow. "Can I help you, sir?" he inquired, with a distinct lack of awe.

"I'm here tae see Ms. Kennedy," shouted Jimmy, looking up from the marbled entrance step. He presumed that this man could see the crowd baying for blood behind.

Again, the full body scan over the black duffle coat, the scuffed boots with toes curled up at the ends. Jimmy bridled, and cast a brief backwards glance at the scuffle to his rear. He moved forwards with a slight hint of malice and affected his strongest Glaswegian growl. "I'm sure you can appreciate, matey, that it's a matter of some urgency. There isnae time to fuck aboot."

The concierge took one neat step backwards, and made a slight deferential bow. Jimmy presumed that this was the invitation to enter, and moved through into the lobby area of the building. "Please take a seat. I'll call Mr. Lefevre. Would you like something brought to you while you wait? Tea? Coffee?" There was the slightest twitch of his cheek muscle, as he added, "Something from the bar, perhaps?"

"Nay, yer alright." Jimmy mumbled. He moved over to where two leather chesterfields faced each other, a low scattered with a contrived selection of design magazines placed between. The concierge had not stopped watching, but held a phone to his ear, mute and awaiting instruction. Jimmy picked up a magazine and flicked through it, before tossing it back down on the table again.

Beyond the hotel, the light was dying and, in the adjacent buildings, lights flickered on in the adjacent buildings. It was difficult to shut out thoughts of all maleficent forces lurking in the shadows; the corrupt and twisted self-servicing creatures who would give no thought to do a thousand terrible things to a terrified child. The tall buildings, the low, driverless cars gliding by with their dim interiors, tyres hissing against the wet tarmac of the roads. He wondered what was it that Kat had to tell him? *It's happened.* Where was he? Who had him? He tapped his jacket pockets until he found his cigarette packet, extracted one, and put it between his lips, before remembering where he was.

The concierge replaced the receiver and walked towards him. His eye trailed down to the cigarette, but his manner had softened. "The top floor, penthouse suite, sir. The lift is in the far corner – I'll buzz you in when you get there. And, erm," he inserted a diplomatic pause, "I'm afraid that the whole building has a strict 'No Smoking' policy, sir. Unless..." His eyes flitted over to the designated smoking area – a point at the precise centre of where the throng of reporters occupied the front of the building.

"Yer alright," said Jimmy.

A minute later, Kat met him at the door to the suite. She pulled him through the door, and shut it behind both of them. Jimmy glanced around. "Where's Lefevre?" he asked.

"Never mind Lefevre," she said. "Read this."

She pushed a crumpled sheet into his hand – an unfolded page that had been torn from a notebook. Jimmy squinted at the writing. There were two hands. The first was unmistakable – Alfie's name in huge, crude letters with the awkward loop of the 'f' curled with the ostentatious fashion they had insisted upon at his French elementary school. Beneath, the untidy and semi-literate print of an adult hand, spelling out an address. He read it aloud: "Flat 18, Nelson Place. No pigs." He glanced up from the note. "When did yous get this?"

Kat gestured towards the foot of the door. Her breathing was shallow, her eyes wide with excitement. "I found it seconds before I called you." She pointed to the floor. "It was down there. Someone must had slipped it under the door."

"How long has it been there?"

She shrugged. "I guess a while. I went out into the corridor and there was no-one around. The concierge said he saw no-one coming or going either."

"And Lefevre? Where was he?"

"I'm right here, James." Jimmy swung round to where Lefevre filled the doorway to the main living area. Dressed in a long-sleeved t-shirt with a Breton stripe, and dark, slim-fit jeans, he had moved barefoot into the doorway.

Jimmy's hackles rose. Here stood a man who had conducted a series of affairs with his wife; now he stood in the way of them finding their son. "You need to fuck right off, pal, before I do something I might regret."

Lefevre held his head back, and spread his arms in apology. "James – wait. I gave Katherine my word that I'd stay out of it – I'm well aware that I'm an obstruction as far as you're concerned – but I think I can help." He padded towards them, his feet making no sound on the parqueted floor. Jimmy's irritation rose as the subtle scent of Lefevre's parfum filled his nostrils.

Lefevre took a corner of the paper between the tips of his finger and his thumb. "I've looked up zip code. I know where this is." He jingled his keys with his other hand. "I can drive us there in, say, forty minutes?"

Kat looked between the two men, Jimmy being the key point of focus. Her lips were parted and there was no way of knowing what she was thinking. Lefevre fell silent, content to wait for an answer.

Jimmy looked at them both. "Are yous both off yer heads? We shoudnae be wasting time even talkin' about this – why hasn't anyone phoned the bloody police yet?" He went for the mobile in his coat pocket but, in a lightning movement, Lefevre had hold of his wrist before he could get there.

"What the…" Jimmy looked down at Lefevre's soft, well-manicured nails, the smooth, fawn-brown flesh juxtaposed against the mottled pink of his own. He spoke through gritted teeth. "If you want tae live the rest of your excuse for a life with both o' those girlie hands, pal, you'll take them the fuck off me right now."

Kat tried to move between them. "Listen to him, Jim. I think he can help us."

Jimmy never stopped watching the other man. "If you have something to say, Kat, say it now. If this here piece o' paper is telling us where Alfie is, I for one dunnae wanna waste any more time."

Kat took the note. "The guy who has Alfie knows I'm here – he must have followed me to the hotel. Now he wants me at this address. I'm presuming that a demand for money will follow.

Either that or it's some kind of tip-off."

"What we do then," said Jimmy, "is call the police. We phone Bridger."

Lefevre cut in. "James: think. I know where this place is. If you call Bridger, and he sends his cops crashing in, whoever is here at this address will see them coming from a mile off. You're up against a local: someone who knows the area and his way around the law. You have zippo chance of seeing your son if you play this wrong. I say we get to this place and we find out what this person wants. We deal with them on our terms."

Jimmy glared at Lefevre. "We? There is no 'we', Lefevre. What the hell has the disappearance of mine and Kat's son got to do with yous?"

Lefevre raised his hands again, shaking his head. His speech careful and deliberate. "You're right of course, James. It has nothing to do with me, James. And I totally get that calling the police seems the right thing to do. But I've been a colleague – and I'd like to say a friend - to you guys for some time." He shrugged. "All the shit that's happened between us over the last few days? We put it behind us, right? Forget about it – at least for the time being. You know that this is way more important. I'm here. I have a car." He paused and studied Jimmy for a moment. "And I have something else." There was a dramatic pause while he weighed the other man up. "Wait here."

Trotting back down the corridor, Lefevre ducked into one of smaller rooms. Jimmy and Kat watched after him, neither knowing what to expect.

Lefevre was quick to return, and he did so bearing an object wrapped in a light blue cloth. He held it before them on one splayed hand. "Pull the cloth away," he told Jimmy.

Kat gasped as the black steel of a handgun glinted with malevolence in the low light of the hotel suite. "My God, Lefevre! Where did you get that?"

Jimmy looked down on the object. The sight of this sleek, well-groomed man brandishing such a lurid object was incongruous to say the least.

Lefevre pulled it out of its shoulder holster. "It's a Beretta 92 semi-automatic. When I worked for Jabba Dre – you know, the American rapper guy? – a couple of years ago; he gave me it as a gift when he was touring the UK. This was before he got killed, obviously. I didn't know what the hell to do with it - but Dre wasn't the kind of guy you'd want to piss off by offending his generosity. He told me at that time that it was loaded, but I never checked. And besides, I was representing him – I wasn't going to turn in one of my clients for possession of a weapon. So I figured I could hide it away somewhere for a rainy day." He looked Jimmy in the eye. "This is the rainy day, James. And here's the gun. Take it."

Jimmy stared down at the weapon. Kat looked on in in horrified silence. "This is starting to get bloody surreal," said Jimmy. "I mean... a gun? I wouldnae know how to use the fucking thing..."

Lefevre now held it in his hand, his finger sliding against the trigger. The fingers of his other hand curled around the barrel. "Yeah, well I do. I'm Canadian, remember? My old man used to take me into the forest with a rifle when I was a kid. It's in the blood."

Kat broke her silence. "Look: the sight of that thing scares the shit out of me. I don't want any guns near my boy." She turned to Jimmy. "We can't waste any more time. I say we get Lefevre to at least drive us to this place so that we can at least check it out from a distance? Then if we feel we need to, we call the police at that point?" She held the piece of paper close to Jimmy's face. Her voice was cracked, her expression desperate. "Jim, come on. This is our boy's handwriting. He needs us."

Ten minutes later, the barriers of the car park beneath the hotel lifted for Lefevre's car to pass through the exit and into the twilight. In the front passenger seat, the streetlamps caught the angles of Kat's anxiety. Behind her, Jimmy occupied the middle of the rear passenger seats, crouched forwards, his long arms spread across the backs of the seats.

A car that had hugged the pavement ahead of them now switched its headlights on and pulled out as they passed, now tucking in behind them. Lefevre checked the rear-view mirror. Indicating right, he turned off down a side street and the other car followed. Kat wrapped a scarf around her head, and slipped her sunglasses on. The headlamps of the car swept across deserted rear entrances and alleyways.

They cut through the streets and then the suburbs in silence, the night falling around them. Leaving the city behind, they headed southwards along a dark dual carriageway. Jimmy turned and looked out of the rear window; the other vehicle had dropped away. Kat remained entombed in silence, moving to pull the scarf from back around her neck, before slipping the sunglasses back into her clutch bag.

Jimmy watched the back of Lefevre's neat head for a while. None of them had spoken of the gun since their time in the hotel. He felt the edge of his phone in his pocket. With a surreptitious movement, reached for it, pulling it onto his lap. Pressing the home bottom, he covered the screen in alarm as a faint green light troubled the car's dark cabin. The sleek head in front of him was held still. With one eye on Lefevre, Jimmy scrolled through his contacts until he found Bridger's direct number. He sent a text: 'F O L L O W'.

Minutes passed. As the car pushed forwards through the night, Jimmy felt every gear change, every bump in the road. His jaw ached as he ground his teeth, a tight ball of twisting nausea rising through his stomach towards his throat. He needed distraction. Leaning forward, he asked, "So where we headed tae, exactly?"

Lefevre turned his head towards Jimmy. "It's a Brighton address in the Whitehawk district. A place called Curtis Rise." He enunciated the words with care. "Three tower blocks – not the most salubrious of locations, to warn you."

"Warn me? You already know who we're dealing with," said Jimmy. "Your pal in the bookstore, remember? That's the guy who's taken our son."

Kat turned away from them and looked out of the passenger window.

Lefevre remained focused on the road. "How many times, James? I already told you: I was the guy who paid him to disappear."

Jimmy made a scornful noise. "And a bloody good job you did o' that." He looked out into the darkness. "I grew up in a high rise in Glasgae: any eejit who's messed with my son has me tae deal with."

Kat's voice was low and weary. "For God's sake, Jimmy..." It was the first time she had spoken since Lefevre had produced the gun. "We need to drop this. We need to focus on what's ahead. And another thing..." She turned back towards Lefevre. "The gun. I don't want it anywhere near Alfie. I want him back. Unharmed."

"The gun's in the trunk," said Lefevre. "That's where it'll stay, if that's how you want it. I promise."

Jimmy stared at Kat's back as they drove on. The first thing he had noticed about her, his first reason for loving her was her surety of purpose. Every decision she made was built on a solid foundation of reason, and a confidence in herself and the people she chose to surround herself with. Katherine Kennedy was a woman who believed in herself and her own talents; she had believed in their family unit; and, until the last year or so, she had believed in her husband too.

"I wish I could be the person you want me to be," he had once said to her.

She had held his face between her long, delicate fingers. "You're doing fine, Jim," she had said. "Carry on being the best version of you."

But Jimmy knew that he had fallen well short, even in those early years of their relationship. Something – boredom, lethargy, jealousy - had led him to settle for less.

The dark shadow of Lefevre loomed in front of him, propelling the car into the night. They travelled on in silence, time becoming something that stretched and recoiled with each spasm of fear of an unknown sequence of events that lay before them. Outside, the darkening landscape became an indeterminate blur, an obfuscation of high roadside banks with loud advertising hoardings, low fences, and flat, featureless fields that span backwards into the darkness. They hurtled on in silence: roundabouts, dark wayside burger vans, empty laybys. In silence, Lefevre tapped the satnav with his gloved finger, and it shed an eerie light over the cabin.

In time, the roadsides became more crowded, haunted with dark, shivering terraces and boarded up shopfronts that sat some fifty yards back from the carriageway. Many windows were dark, but some were bothered by the occasional signs of life.

Another ten minutes passed and Lefevre indicated left without speaking. He pulled into a layby and switched off the satnav.

Ahead of them, lit by a series of crooked streetlamps, lay a wide semicircle of patchy grass. It was bordered by concrete, and preceded a tall wire fence riddled with litter and holes. A skinny lurcher, collarless and with no apparent owner, ventured before the headlights and took a quick piss against the twisted carcass of a shopping trolley. Beyond, a bleak distance of parkland stretched towards a playpark.

Some distance ahead, the three brooding tower blocks stood appeared to Jimmy as grim sentinels to a modern-day Hades. Kat cast a sidelong look at Lefevre. "Are we there?" she asked in a small voice.

Lefevre nodded. Turning his whole body round, he faced Jimmy. "So how d'you wanna play this?"

Jimmy looked at the dark shadows over the other man's face. The Canadian's eyes were taking in a car that had pulled up some forty yards behind. It killed its lights, and Lefevre's face fell into darkness once more; save the smallest glint in the whites of his eyes.

"Turn the car light on," said Jimmy. Lefevre complied, and Jimmy fished the notepaper from his pocket again.

Lefevre wound the driver's window down by three inches. The night filled their space, an invasion of sirens, speakers, distant traffic. He pointed towards the three towers. "One of those. No idea which. Take your pick."

Jimmy heard Lefevre unfasten his seatbelt. He scrambled from his seat and got out of the car. He could smell rain in the air. Turning towards the lowering driver's window, he addressed Lefevre. "Me and Kat'll go. You stay here."

Lefevre looked back to where Jimmy's big face hung by the window. "Sure," he said. "You got my cell phone number. You sure you don't want me to hang a few yards back –in case you need an extra body?"

"I'm completely sure," said Jimmy.

Kat and Jimmy turned to look ahead towards the three high-rise blocks. Their silhouettes were stark against a starless, purple-grey sky and, at their feet, a garland of scattered lights marked a smattering of dwellings. Each knew the other to be thinking of one person: Alfie. Their boy. He was out there. Somewhere.

Jimmy spoke in a low voicer. "Put your phone on silent," he said. Like a kid terrified of losing his first concert ticket, his fist curled around the notepaper bearing the address.

Taking a tentative steps forward, the presence of the place became palpable. In Jimmy's hometown, every backstreet and outbuilding had been familiar: the safehouses, the alleyways, the broken lift shafts; places to find sanctuary, places to steer clear of – he'd known every inch like the back of his hand. This place, though, was something different: stark, bleak, bleeding like a wound. Every square foot stank of disappointment, neglect and despair. Buried into the fabric of that place were the crackheads, the abusers, the abused and the shat upon. And somewhere, mixed up in the middle of it all, was their five year-old son.

Kat stalled. She was a few yards behind him, staring ahead as he had been. "Hey, Jimmy." He looked back to her. "Don't read anything into this," she said. "But will you hold my hand?"

His face softened. "Aye, lass." The stubby tips of his fingers touched hers, and hers shrank away at the suddenness of his response. "Sorry," he mumbled. With some relief, he felt her slim, cold fingers return to wrap around his own.

She asked him: "D'you think he's out here, somewhere?"

"Aye. We need to believe that."

She said: "In both pictures, he was wearing the same clothes. Did you notice?"

"Aye, I did."

She shivered in the cold evening. "Did he have his coat with him? When he went?"

Jimmy shook his head. "A couple o' days ago, I got his gear together in one place back at the hostel. I'm sorry to say he didnae take his coat."

At some distance behind them, Lefevre watched their silhouettes being consumed by the semicircle of worn parkland, as they passed through the tall gates interspersed between the wire fence. The figures grew smaller as they slid past the tiny playground, now dwarfed by the three tower blocks. He stepped from his car, and tapped his breast pocket , feeling the steel weight within pull the fabric of his jacket tight against his shoulders. He clicked the key fob and slid the gun from within his jacket pocket, to rest it on the roof of the car.

Twenty-One

Eighty miles away, in the small district hospital, two figures whispered at the far end of a ward. Both cast the occasional glance towards the furthest bed, where the old man, Oleg Kowalski, lay.

"I feel bad about getting you out on your week off, love," said the first. "It's just that – these last couple of days - what with the confirmation of permanent paralysis - he's given up the ghost. It's like he's not with us anymore."

The second person hung his coat on a peg near the door. "Can't say I'm that surprised. He wanted me to do him a favour - say goodbye to his wife for him. She's in a nursing home about twenty miles away."

"And?"

He nodded. "Yeah. I did it. There's not much to tell, so I thought it could wait until I came back from leave. That said, if anyone hears it first, I suppose it should be him."

He made his way towards the bed. He took a chair – and rested in the same area that had been occupied by Hope Kelly some five days earlier. Sitting down, he took in the frail, inert figure before him, wondering what could be said to make him feel any better about living or dying.

Twenty-Two – the evening of Friday 9th December 2018

"There's something about abandoned kid's playgrounds that gives me the willies." Kat shivered as they walked adjacent to the iron railings.

"You and ninety-five per cent of the population," said Jimmy. "Anyways, this one isnae abandoned." He nodded to where three young men moved out of the shadows. Two, who had been draped over a decrepit climbing frame wore hoodies and were sharing a spliff; the third stood on the ground and wore a red Santa hat.

All three were thin, wiry and watchful. As Jimmy and Kat passed by, two dropped down from the frame to half-face them The third remained still on the ground.

Jimmy put a light pressure on Kat's arm beneath his own, indicating for her to stop. He turned to face the nearest man. "Excuse me, pal," he said. He gestured towards the three tower blocks. "Which one of those wee beauties over there is Nelson Place?"

Santa stepped forward, and inclined his head towards them, his face hidden. Kat touched the arm of her sunglasses. Santa spat onto the ground, grinning. "Middle one, mate," he said.

"Cheers," said Jimmy. "And a Merry Christmas to yous too."

They walked on. "Dunnae look back," said Jimmy.

"I believe that the charming young man with the hat may have recognised me." Kat said. "This place is bloody terrifying."

"I'm no' sure having grown up somewhere like this helps as much as it should," said Jimmy. "The only difference is that you know more about what's out there…"

"Are they following us?"

He cast an quick look behind. " I dunnae think so."

They found a walkway that led them beneath the bridge of a car park that preceded the towers. Beyond, a young girl, no older than fourteen or fifteen, was sat on a blanket that covered the pavement, her legs pulled up under her chin. She drew from a cigarette. Alongside, there was a frayed backpack, a can of cider – she appeared oblivious. Jimmy thought of Hope and her destitute existence.

The sound of a distant siren brought him to his senses. "Something I should say. In the car, before we got out: I sent a message to Bridger. I thought he should know where we are."

Kat withdrew her arm. "What?"

"I was thinking of the lad."

She took off her sunglasses and fell quiet for a moment, looking over at the towers. "Well, if you must know, you weren't the only one," she said after a while. "When I went to the loo, before we came out? I text him as well. Seeing that bloody gun was the final straw. Enough." She looked around them. "You think they're on their way?"

"Dunno. I keep hearing bloody sirens. But that's the way in any city, every night in a place like this. Let's keep moving." They carried on walking. "Any more thoughts about Lefevre?"

"I had no idea that he had a gun" said Kat. "But I'm thinking I was wrong to doubt him. He brought us here. I think he wants to help – even if it's about pleasing me."

They were now walking along a narrow, litter-strewn path that circumvented the first of the towers. It loomed over them as a maleficent giant, dark and foreboding: the thin, narrow recesses on each storey harbouring low, dark windows as eyes that watched them pass. From high above came eerie, sub-human noises: snatches of low conversation; explosive hyena cackles; a perpetual, hacking cough; children screaming. Somewhere near the summit, a young couple tore each other apart with undignified abandon, their curses shattering like glass on the concrete ground below.

The second block, theirs, stood some fifty yards beyond the first. The entrance to Nelson Place was propped open by a concrete breeze block, the top half of the door boarded over where the glass had been broken and never repaired. A forlorn and outdated poster about a community group meeting hung by a single drawing pin.

"Abandon hope all ye who enter here," murmured Jimmy. He pushed at the sprung door and, in silence, they passed through. The corridor before them reeked of cat-piss and damp; it disappeared into the gloom, with an uninviting flight of stairs climbing into the shadows to the right.

Kat gestured towards another door. She held a tissue over her nose: the acidic stench was all-consuming. "The lift's out of order ," she said.

A strange cacophony of descending footsteps filtered back down. Jimmy and Kat stood still at the foot of the stairwell for a time. Jimmy fumbled for the torn piece of paper in his pocket. He'd remembered the number, but needed to look at it again to reassure himself. "Flat 18," he read.

Kat took the tissue from her face and steeled herself. "Let's get on with it," she said.

Within minutes, they had arrived at the sixth floor. The sign for

Flats 15-18 indicated a corridor to their right. Still, there was no sign of the police throughout the park below.

Half way down the passage, two huddled figures spoke in low voices. The long balcony that stretched across the doorways and windows was exposed to the night; and the darkness of the park and the distant lights of the city spread out like a filthy eiderdown.

They had no choice but to pass by. The first of the characters had the deportment of an older man, but his attire and complexion suggested otherwise. A thin, hunched frame was lost within a faded black t-shirt; a pale, untrusting face squinting and wizened beneath the bent peak of a baseball cap. The other, facing away from them, was younger. He wore a black tracksuit, and his head was shorn and inclined towards the other man.

They became alert as Jimmy and Kat approached. The younger man had large, arching eyebrows, heavy-lids, a tight gash of a mouth. He stared at them with a blank expression, as they came near.

Jimmy nodded and took a quick sidelong look at the nearest door. "We're looking for number 18," he said.

The older man gestured with his cigarette towards a door further down. His face was cold and untrusting. "Empty. They served an order on it coupla weeks ago."

"Right," said Jimmy. He looked back at Kat. Her eyes were aflame with intensity, but she remained silent. Jimmy stepped forwards. "We'll go and check it out. This way, right?"

The gaunt-faced man looked to the other. "They don't believe us."

The younger man's mouth curled into a cruel smile. "They never do."

Positioning his body between the men and Kat, Jimmy gestured to her to pass through. Keeping her head down, she walked forwards. Moving to follow, Jimmy felt for a moment that two people in their path might step ahead of him to block his path, but they stood back against the edge of the balcony and continued to watch.

"You won't find anyone in there, mate," one of them said.

Kat got to the door of the flat ahead of Jimmy. The glass above the door was dark, and she traced the words of the closure notice with her finger. Her fingers splayed to rest on the door's main panel, and she leaned in and listened. Silence.

Jimmy peered at the notice over her shoulder. "This looks like the right flat. Maybe it's some kind of hoax?"

Kat was irritated. "No," she said. "I have no doubt that that was Alfie's handwriting. We haven't come all this way to turn around and leave."

There was no handle. She placed her other hand on the door and rested her weight against it. There was a click, and it gave way. Catching her breath, she stepped back and looked to Jimmy for instruction.

"I guess we ought tae go in," he said. They moved forwards into the darkness, staying close to the inner wall to their right. Kat felt the peeling wallpaper, and groped for a light switch. Finding it with her fingers, she clicked it on. The flat remained consumed by darkness.

Jimmy swallowed. "Why don't you go back outside and call Bridger again? I'll take a wee swatch in here?"

"No way," she said. "If there's any chance that Alfie's here , I'm coming too."

Jimmy inched his way forwards. "Hello?" His voice sounded unsteady and strained to his own ears. They appeared to be in a narrow hall, ahead of a sitting room.

Kat followed. "Alfie?" Nothing came back. She turned back to Jimmy. "We should check the rooms. Use the torch on your phone." She motioned ahead of them. "You go in front; I'll check the rooms to the side."

Jimmy moved forwards while fumbling for his mobile in his pocket. There was a dull thud. "Shit!"

Kat called from another room. "What? What is it?"

Jimmy clutched the lower half of his leg and hobbled sideways. A web of cracks crawled over the screen of his phone. It emitted a meagre light. He gritted his teeth and called back to her. "Nothin'. Cracked my shin on a fucking table. And broken my bloody phone."

No sooner had he finished speaking, than something sprang to life before him. It was a cheap mobile phone on the surface of the table. The screen lit up and it buzzed itself, inch by inch, across the wooden surface. Jimmy leant forward, his heavy features lit by the eerie green glow of the screen. *Incoming call. No caller ID.*

There was more light behind him now, as Kat ran back into the living area, her phone held aloft as a torch. "That wasn't your phone?" she asked.

Jimmy said nothing, but looked from the phone to her, then back to the phone once more. Now that there was more light, they could see that, bar the coffee table and the phone, the flat was sparse, as if someone had recently moved out.

The phone continued to ring. Kat was clutching something she'd found in the other room. She held it up to Jimmy. "Look," she said, holding her phone against it. It was a Cbeebies magazine and a dirty blanket. "Smell it Jimmy..."

Jimmy held the blanket to his mouth and nose. He breathed in. "Alfie!"

Kat made a sudden grab for the phone. She spoke through a gasp. "Hello?" She waited. "Who is this?"

The caller spoke with a whisper, but failed to conceal a broad estuary accent. "Kaffrin Kennedy?"

"Have you got my son? Have you got Alfie?" Clutching the phone until her knuckles went white, a quick succession of shallow breaths wracked her frame until she could contain herself no longer. She spat out the words. "Where's my son, you bastard?"

Jimmy stepped towards her. He touched wrist.

She took a deep breath, swallowed, and managing to regain some control. "Where are you? What do you want ?"

There was no immediate answer on the line – only the low whistle of a thin wind across an exposed space. The caller was out in the open somewhere. A voice came back at last. "Soon as I tell you - you leave your phones on the table next to the one you're speaking into. Someone'll come in and clear 'em out when you leave. I can see where you are and what you're doin'. If I get one sniff of uniform, you don't see your kid. No fuckin' around."

Kat placed her hand over her chest. "Alfie's with you?"

Jimmy drew his head in, close to Kat's. They both listened. The scuffling of feet, the low voice of an instruction, then the breathing of a child. "Mummy?" The voice was anxious, tearful. It was Alfie's.

Kat gasped. "Alfie?" Then, she shouted: "Alfie!"

The man's voice cut in again. "You'll find us on The Whitehawk," he said. "Remember what I said about your phones. And no coppers."

Kat shouted into the phone: "Hello? Hello?"

Jimmy took hold of her wrist. "What did he say?"

Desperate, Kat shouted back into the phone, "I don't know where that is! Where is that?" She paused for a second, then looked to Jimmy again. "Hello? Hello? Shit! He's hung up!"

"Where are they?"

She let her arm fall. "He said, 'The Whitehawk.' "

"But this *is* Whitehawk! It's the name of the bloody district." He felt desperate. "Christ! Alfie could be anywhere..."

Kat stared at her phone. "He said *The* Whitehawk..."

Jimmy shrugged. "Maybe it's a pub or something..."

She shook her head. "No - they were outside." Her fingers scrolled over the phoned, then she stopped, and looked up, holding an image up for Jimmy to see. "There's a chalk carving on the hills overlooking the estate...'The White Hawk'." She threw the phone down, beside Jimmy's on the table. "For Christ's sake, come on!" she cried.

Kat was fitter than Jimmy; she got back to the staircase in no time, her heels echoing back down the cold passage.

"Hold on, lass!" Jimmy shouted, "Don't get intae anything wi'out me..."

Wheezing, Jimmy managed to catch her as they reached the stairwell. They clattered down successive flights in silence, minds projecting forwards to the dark, looming hills behind the estate where their son's life was held by the whim of a stranger.

At the foot of the final flight, a figure was waiting. He had his back to them, but his head and shoulders were discernible in the half-light. As Kat and Jimmy approached him, they hesitated, and the man turned.

His face was obscured by shadows, and now, his hand grasped the bannister. He spoke. "What's going on?"

"Lefevre?" said Jimmy. "Yous were supposed to stay put in the car?"

Kat pointed in a vague direction beyond the estate. "He's got Alfie out there on the hills somewhere. We have to find them."

Lefevre wore a light raincoat and was catching his breath. "The cops are nearby," he said. "I saw a couple of unmarked cars near mine; there's been a helicopter overhead too." They all listened. A faint ripping of blades could be heard somewhere above.

Kat's eyes widened in alarm. "He's threatened to hurt Alfie if the police show – don't let them near us!"

Lefevre looked back over his shoulder. "You both go. If they're near, I'll stall them until you need them there."

Jimmy stepped past him, and pushed at the exit door. "Come on for Christ's sake!" he shouted.

In seconds, they were out in the open air. Both of them looked beyond the tower blocks to the periphery of the estate, where, somewhere in the darkness, the edges of the valley climbed into a darkness that held their son's future on a knife's edge.

Twenty-Three

At the outskirts of the estate, Jimmy was forced to rest. Before now, adrenalin and the compulsion to find Alfie had kept him moving. Now, though the physical strain was overwhelming. His chest was tight and a rasping wheeze drew into his throat.

On the road ahead of him, Kat urged him on with a series of frantic gestures. The occasional car hurtled between them, oblivious of their ordeal; above them, a dark sky fringed with cobwebs of cloud hung like a pall.

By day, dogwalkers and ramblers could flee the chaos and claustrophobia of the estate to climb beyond the valley. If the light was good, it was possible to look past the sprawling estate, to where the Seven Sisters guarded the South Coast. On a good day, it was said that the Isle of Wight was visible. By night, though, the Neolithic hills and causeway became consumed with something more timeless and sinister. Secrets and dark legends ran amok over the dense shrublands, forging echoes of more distant times, when settlers carved causeways and made sacrifices to their selfish gods.

When Jimmy reached her, Kat pointed out towards the hills. "Look," she said. He followed her line of sight to where, on the hill, two spots of light hovered like firefly ghosts. One was less defined and flickering; the other, a pinprick that bobbed about, sometimes to vanish altogether. "Could that be them?"

Jimmy was out of breath, his hand held across his chest. "Let's get up there and see."

As they traversed the edges of the Downs, the first flat drops of rain fell onto their heads and shoulders. Following the days of snow, the subsequent thaw meant that the ground was soft underfoot. Kat and Jimmy took on the hills in silence. As the more experienced walker, Kat was quick to find a crude path that led them around the low thorny shrubs and unseen ruts that threatened to mar their ascent towards the brow of the first hill. Jimmy tried to keep the source of light in view; but his night vision was poor and he was forced to stop at regular intervals, both to catch his breath and to wipe the moisture from the lenses of his glasses. "What if it's all a wind-up?" he shouted towards Kat's disappearing back. But she ignored him, her hopes already too high.

Fifty yards forwards, she had stopped. She was crouched down on the ground, running her fingers across the ground. "This must be the chalk carving," she said. "This is where they should be." She stood up and they looked about them to see simple arcs and lines scored into the earth, forming a shape some fifty feet across. Jimmy could make out the wing, the crude interpretation of head and hooked beak. This was the place: the White Hawk. But where was Alfie?

Kat had turned to face Jimmy now, her finger to her lips. "Listen." To their right, a mere silhouette against the heavy skies, a line of tall bushes and trees crowned the ridge of Red Hill. From behind, the flickering light was stronger now, and the weak beam of a torch sometimes caught the bare branches of trees. They heard the crackling of a fire, the low hum of voices.

Together, they crept beyond the copse. The air became thick with woodsmoke and damp tinder. A battered fire bin crackled and hissed in the rain, spitting orange sparks into the black sky. Behind, stood two figures: man and a boy.

Spider. Alfie.

Spider had Alfie in front of him, his arm curled around his neck, his hand over the boy's mouth.

For a moment, Kat stood very still. Then she crouched down on the ground, tears running down her face. She held her hands in front of her, fingers splayed, willing the boy to run to her. "It's okay, baby," she said. "Mummy and Daddy are here now. Everything's going to be fine." Alfie's terrified eyes glistened in the flickering light of the fire. His body was rigid, occasionally wracked by a violent shiver. He wore a cheap anorak which was far too large for his frame.

Spider called over in the same queer yodelling voice that Jimmy had heard at Southbank: "Shame about the rain, man. Spoilt the family reunion, ain't it? It's normally nice up 'ere, with a little fire on the go," he said. "You can see anyone coming from miles away." He spat into the flames and tugged Alfie's neck.

Kat got to her feet. Jimmy sensed she was all for running towards him, and he had a tight grasp of her arm. "Be careful lass. We don't know what he might do"

Spider grinned and wrenched the boy closer. "That's right. Stay right where you are, unless you want summink unpleasant to happen." His eyes glinted, a queer leer creeping over his long, dysmorphic face.

From the city below, sirens crawled across the streets and parks as the chugging of helicopter blades troubled the far corners of the night's sky. Spider beady eyes scanned the heavens before returning to Kat and Jimmy.

Kat took a deep, gasping breath, wiped the thin streaks of mascara from her cheek with the heel of her hand. She took a deep breath before speaking. "Tell us how much you want."

Spider held his twitching limbs still for a moment, and raised his head up to the night, his exposed teeth glinting. With a sudden movement, he shoved the boy forwards with his knee, arm still muffling his small mouth. Alfie's face came out of shadow, his face pale and dirty. There was a muffled sound as he tried to call out. "I know what you're worth, Kaffrin Kennedy."

"Fucking tell us how much," Jimmy growled.

Spider sniffed. "I reckon six zeros would do it."

The space around them was filled with Jimmy's incredulous laugh. "A million? Your bum's oot the window, man! If you think for a moment..."

"It's yours." Kat's voice cut through her husband's.

Jimmy's mouth hung open. "Are y' mad?"

She ignored him, keeping focus on the man and boy on the other side of the fire. The rain fell harder, and the fire threatened to go out, a low hissing slithering around their them. "How do you suggest we do this?"

They became aware that Spider was looking beyond them, back towards the Swanborough estate below. His sharp, feral senses had caught a movement on the hill. Now, they too became aware of footfall – that of a lone individual - and then the heavy breathing of someone below the chalk carving.

Spider pulled the boy closer. As they all turned, the outline of a man, framed by the lights from the estate below moved to within twenty metres, then ten. The figure flashed a searchlight over them.

There was some panic in Spider's voice. "I said no coppers." He hauled the Alfie backwards. The boy's heels were scraping through the wet earth, his body a dead weight being dragged away from the light of the fire and towards the darkness of the Downs.

"Wait," shouted Jimmy. He shielded his eyes as the figure flashed his torch across their faces. "That's no copper, man..."

The figure stepped forward now, so that his face could be seen.

"Lefevre!" exclaimed Jimmy. "We told you tae stay away and keep the boabies off...."

Lefevre was breathless. He stood some way off and had to catch his breath before speaking. "Exactly what I been doing," he panted. "But the whole place is crawling with cops down there, and your Bridger guy's among them. They caught up with me. I told 'em I'd driven you guys here but that you wouldn't tell me where you were headed. They know about the note and they found your phones in the high rise."

Spider watched Lefevre as he spoke, seemingly unperturbed by the sudden appearance. His grip on the boy still firm, he placed his own torch between his teeth, and reached into his pocket.

Kat gasped as the torchlight glimpsed off edge of a small switchblade. She stepped forward. "For Christ's sake, please don't hurt him – I've told you, you can have whatever you want."

Spider looked from Lefevre to Kat. "Then ask your Yankee boyfriend here to drive you to where you can get the cash. I give you a new location where I know I'm not gonna get followed. 'You hand over the money, get the boy back, and I vanish." The stained groins of his teeth glistened in the half-light. "I got eyes everywhere. One foot out of step, or any word to the pigs..." His other hand crept in front of Alfie's neck, long fingers curling the blade into the boy's smooth flesh.

Jimmy shouted, "Okay! I get it. But where d'yous suggest we get hold o' a million at this time o'night?"

Spider brought some phlegm into his mouth and spat it to one side of the fire. "Shouldn't be a problem for Her Majesty there. She's the famous Kaffrin Kennedy, yeah? A copy of 'er book in every house, blah, blah, blah..."

Lefevre had recovered. He moved around the side of the fire. "There's no way you're getting your hands on Katherine's money, buddy-boy."

"Lefevre!" Jimmy hissed. "Stay the fuck back! What the hell are d'you think you're doing? The guy's got a knife to the boy's throat…"

The Canadian ignored him. A step closer… then another.

Spider scrutinised the man approaching him. Lefevre continued: "A million, huh, buddy? Don't you think that's a little… greedy? Popped your head around the door of an empty candy store, and now you wanna take the whole lot?" He turned his head towards Kat and Jimmy. "This guy here's full of bullshit. Eyes everywhere, my ass." He voice rose to a shout. "Hey, Mr. Smalltown!" He unbuttoned the top two pockets of his raincoat and nodded towards the terrified Alfie. "You really gonna hurt that kid? In front of Mom and Dad? Sincerely?"

Kat looked on, appalled, as his hand fumble inside the raincoat for the inner pocket. "Lefevre, please! I don't want you risking Alfie's life!"

Lefevre held his hand up to her. "Don't worry, Katherine: I know what I'm doing. I've dealt with the losers like this before."

Spider spat into the fire for a third time; his face split into a contemptuous sneer as one who was relishing each moment. Jimmy watched him assiduously: the convulsive twitching and jerking of his limbs while the blade sat snug to the throat of his son. Spider moved his lips close to the boy's ear. "You take care not to move, Squirt. You take care not to shout out. See?" Alfie nodded. Kat held a hand over her mouth, her eyes wide and petrified.

Spider locked eyes with Lefevre once more. "You reckon I'm Mr.

Smalltown, yeah? Two envelopes stuffed with cash, right? One's got fifty grand in it; the other, a cool million." He cocked his head to one side. "Deal or no deal?"

At first Lefevre gave him nothing. The rain had set in now: sheets that fell from a veiled sky to saturate the ground until it could hold no more. It ran down the hill and formed dark pools in ruts and on the lowest ground. A deep growl of thunder seemed to burgeon from every conceivable space around them.

Kat moved nearer to Lefevre until she could touch him. Her fingers crept into the nook of his inner arm. Jimmy could see the angles of her face in the dying flames and torchlight. She was ten years older, every tendon and muscle clenched against the uncertainty of Alfie's fate. From her lips, there came a beseeching tone that Jimmy had never heard before. "I know you're trying to help me," she whispered in Lefevre's ear. Jimmy could see that she was looking to where his hand had slipped inside his rain coat. He remembered – the semi-automatic. She continued. "Please don't do anything that might endanger Alfie. He's already terrified. Let's finish this his way. I can easily live without a million."

As she spoke her last word, the light hacking of helicopter blades began troubling the corners of the skies once more. Spider looked up. "The cops come any nearer, and you know what happens."

"Give the kid up," Lefevre repeated. "Play this the right way before they close in on you."

Spider shook his head. "Nah, you're alright," he said. "Instead, I think it's time Kaffrin Kennedy found out a few home truths about her boyfriend."

Lefevre stiffened. Jimmy saw that the hand that had slipped inside his raincoat was now emerging.

The barrel glistened in the night. The gun. Lefevre lies about its location made its appearance even more palpable. Kat recoiled. Lefevre held it on both hands, index fingers curled around the trigger. "You talk too much, buddy," he said.

Spider ground his teeth, his cheek muscle convulsing. Keeping a tight hold of the boy, he continued to taunt Lefevre. The sight of the semi-automatic didn't seem to put him off. "You told me yerself that you don't know how to use that mutha, remember?"

Jimmy looked between them. "So Hereward had it right all along? Yous twos do know each other?"

Spider sneered. He looked at Jimmy. "Oh yeah, we know each other. I found 'im when I was trying to find you. It's like this: I've never been bothered about who my missus had been shagging before I was on the scene, but when I found a photo of you and her, and realised I was looking at Hope's old man, summink irked. There we was shacked up on a shitty houseboat while some tosser who's shagged and ran, leaving her up the duff, gets getting away with not paying a penny. An' what's more, it turns out that he's now shagging some rich bird off the telly who's worth millions." He tapped the side of his skull with the knife blade. "Well, this does my fucking nut in. But trying to get hold of Jimmy Dunbar ain't easy, not least when you look 'n' sound like me. *Mr. Dunbar doesn't take personal calls... Mr. Dunbar's busy.. Mr. Dunbar's out of the country for the foreseeable future... can I pass on a message?* But they don't bank on old Spider. You see, he's always been the persistent type. A dog wiv a bone. So, after trying a bit more, I get Mr. Lefevre here on the end of the line."

Lefevre cut in. "You gonna believe this guy? A punk who's as high as a kite and talks complete horseshit." He thrust the barrel of the handgun in Spider's direction. "I suggest you let go of the kid and run for the caves where you belong, asshole, before I shut you down for good."

Spider crouched low behind Alfie, the knife dangling in front of the boy's breastbone. He nodded towards the gun. "You ain't got a clue what you're doing with that gun, mate. You pull the trigger, there's as much chance of you hitting the kid as me."

Jimmy glanced at Lefevre. "He isnae gonna pull any trigger. You have my word. Keep talkin'."

Spider measured him up for a moment, then continued. "So I wanna know where we can find Jimmy Dunbar so we can get what we deserve. The bastard hangs up on me twice; then, when I'm thinking I need to go down a different route, he calls me out of the blue." He peered from behind Alfie's shoulder, his head higher than the child's, and smirked. "Remember that conversation..." He affected the accent with a sly grin, *"Buddy-boy...?"*

Lefevre looked straight ahead. "Whatever crap this guy keeps coming out with, ignore him, Katherine. I've crossed paths with liars and psychos in my time; this shit-for-brains is right up there with the worst of them."

Jimmy watched Alfie. He noticed the heavy eyelids, the mouth closing, a slight swaying. "Keep talking," he shouted to Spider. He stepped forwards. "But make it quick, if you wannae take anything away with yous."

Spider gloated. There was a second rumble of thunder, and the air thickened. Thick, straight rods of cold rain continued to smack the earth beneath their feet, pulling a veil between them and the edges of the estate. Spider's beady black eyes moved over the faces of his adversaries. The rain ran off the peak of his cap, and dripped off the end of his snub of nose. "He tells me he wants to talk. Says we both got summink to gain from screwing Jimmy Dunbar over. So we meet up. Jimmy's gonna be in London in November, he says. If I can persuade the daughter to have it out with him there and then; like, make a public scene in front of everyone, then he'd make it worth my while." As the rain trickled down his face, he ran the wrist that clenched the knife across his forehead. He flicked tiny droplets into the fire and it sizzled angrily. "We talk cash. Talking Princess Hope round ain't gonna be easy: she's always been a goody-two-shoes. So I talk him up a bit and, by the end of the conversation, we've come to a bit of an understanding."

Jimmy watched Lefevre's back. The man stood still, concentrated, his arms straight ahead of him, the tip of the semiautomatic trained on the boy and his crouching assailant. He spoke in a low voice. "You got anything to say about this, Lefevre?"

Lefevre was silent for a moment. When he spoke, his voice was low and dismissive. "Sheesh, James. Give me some credit? You think I'd be standing here pointing a gun at this man's head if I was in cahoots with him? You seriously think I'd associate with a moron like this?"

"Southbank," Jimmy said. "I saw you slip this jalkie summat before he left…"

"I already told you: I was paying him to scram, you idiot! To go away and rot in some corner and not shit about with us again. It's the only thing people like him'll listen to…"

But Jimmy was not to be put off. "Then there's Hereward's story. Seeing yous together before…that ties up with what this guy is saying."

Spider was still grinning. He knew that Lefevre was in a corner. Somewhere in the distance, tiny blue lights flickered amongst the huddled buildings of the estate, but he still seemed untroubled by them. *"Get in there with the daughter and stir up some trouble,* he said. Course, she's too soft to go through with it and does a runner before she delivers the demand for cash. So. Plan B."

Jimmy sensed Kat's urge to run to the boy grow with each second that passed. But there was too much risk. He kept hold of her wrist and found that there was no resistance. He wanted her to hear the truth about Lefevre. "And here? Now? How does being in this place fit in?"

Kat moved forwards, so that she could see Lefevre. She searched his face, hers tilted up towards his, blinking away the rain as it fell on her face. Her voice was quiet and more tender now. "Tell me that you're not, in any way, involved in what is happening here. Look me in the eye and deny it; I'll believe you."

Lefevre kept his focus on Spider and Alfie. "This is under control, Katherine. This punk is gonna drop the knife and let the kid go." He jiggled the barrel of the gun. "Come on."

Spider studied Lefevre's face for a moment. His mouth curled into a contemptuous sneer. He jabbed the knife in Lefevre's direction. "It ain't rocket science. How did that note got delivered? Where did he get the gun from?" Again, he imitated Lefevre. *"I'll say I got it from some rapper guy I represented...* Only now it's gone tits up for 'im 'cos I ain't playing by his rules no more."

Kat froze, aghast. "How would he know that?" she asked. "You actually said that about the gun in the hotel room... how would he know about the note and the gun?"

Lefevre wouldn't look at her. He raised the barrel of the gun higher, until it was level with Spider's head.

Kat was desperate. "For God's sake, Lefevre," she pleaded, "Look at my little boy's face! He's going hypothermic. Put an end to this now. Put that bloody thing down. I'll get him his money – I'll do anything he wants as long as I have Alfie."

The boy was shaking more violently now, as the droplets fell down his forehead and over his face. Jimmy watched in horror as his eyes were closing, his teeth clenched and chattering.

Kat's voice was broken with quiet sobs. "I need him to be with me."

Lefevre face was a taut mask. He couldn't look at Kat. His breathing was shallow, his knuckles red raw. He spoke through a clenched jaw, his voice thin and strangled. "You can't see it, can you Katherine? None of this, *none* of it... is about the fucking money." He turned his head, every muscle in his face working with fury. He found Jimmy and there was a rage behind his eyes. "I did all I could to get that fat, lazy bastard out of our lives. He's never deserved you..."

Kat stared at him, disbelieving. She took a step away from him, shaking her head. "Christ," she whispered. "You mean... you'd put... my child through... this?"

Lefevre shook as he spoke, a tremor at the end of the barrel, that sent a shock through his rigid arms and his whole core. He struggled for control. "I needed to do something to get closer to you. To show you what I would do for you. No-one's got hurt." He waved the handgun at Spider. "If this bastard would have played his part, he'd be a hundred miles away with fifty grand in his back pocket, and you'd have Alfie back. But he got greedy."

"So that's it," Jimmy mumbled. "You set yourself up to be the bloody hero. Jesus Christ, Lefevre –how low can a man stumble?" he thrust an accusatory finger towards the Canadian, his head thrust forward, and his voice rose to a shout. "I told you," he thundered. "I told you we couldnae trust this bastard."

Lefevre spat his words into the night air. "You were always punching above your weight with Katherine, James. You and your shitty poetry! You ever think, for a moment, that I wanted to help get that insipid crap published; that I would have gone anywhere near it if it hadn't been about pleasing Katherine? We laughed at that shit you wrote behind your back." The hand holding the gun was thrust in Kat's direction. "You know what she told me that time we went out to the States? That anything she felt for you died years ago. And what, after all, would be mildly diverting about a washed-up, alcoholic mediocrity?"

"You keep talking and I'll punch your face in, Sunshine, gun or no bloody gun," Jimmy growled. He ran his fingers across his beard, wiping the droplets of rain away. Focussing on the boy again, he knew that time was running out: Alfie's legs were buckling beneath him, the grip of his assailant being the one thing that kept him upright.

He had to focus; to reject those primeval, instinctive surges that shunted him between chaotic, self-serving episodes whilst neglecting what mattered. For too long, he had drifted, rudderless, around the centre of a sea, watching everything that mattered drift towards the setting sun.

His boy. His wife. His daughter.

None of this could be about him anymore. Jimmy breathed out. He let his arms fall down by his side, the rain driving hard into his skull. Spider still grinned at the chaos he could raise with glee. "Tell me one thing," Jimmy called over to him. "My daughter - Hope. Tell me she wasnae involved in any of this."

"Why don't you ask her yourself?"

They all looked around. A still, female voice had come from the darkness. Somewhere beyond the fire, behind the tall man and his captive, was a thinly-spread copse stretched against the lighter patches of sky. A shadow stirred therein.

Jimmy's stomach tightened. It was her. Hope.

Shrouded like an old woman in a heavy blanket, she came out of the shadows and edged towards the fire, her face hidden. Jimmy could see that Alfie sensed she was near – he was trying to move closer, only to be reigned back by a vicious tug from Spider's clawed hand. With a vicious energy, Spider turned on the girl. "What you playing at? I told you to stay hidden, you stupid cow."

She had come behind them to position herself beside Alfie. In the light of the fire, Jimmy saw her fingers creep from the shawl to brush the boy's.

Kat spoke to Jimmy in a low voice "That's her, right? The bitch who helped abduct Alfie? Your daughter." She checked Jimmy, to gauge his reaction

Jimmy knew it was her, but found himself unable to say anything that might implicate her. He stepped towards her.

"No closer," hissed Spider, brandishing his knife.

Hope lifted her head now. The heavy throw she had wrapped around herself fell away and, in the light cast by the small fire, Jimmy had glimpses of her ordeal: a purple swelling around her left eye, and a raw wound that across her left cheek. With her closely-cropped head, she was unrecognisable from the startling young woman who had pushed her way into that lecture hall barely one week earlier. But he was her father; he knew her.

His mind played a rapid montage of Hope's movements that he had been aware of: her sudden appearance at Southbank, the confrontation at the houseboat, and her emotional departure. And later, in the police station - the call from the articulate old man with a faint Eastern European accent. *I regret to inform you that your daughter has been involved in a rather serious train accident.* It pained him to imagine what she had been through.

Each of her movements cried discomfort and pain. Her awareness of him contained no less intensity than it had that day at Southbank. Her hand came before her face, and she pressed her finger to her lips, before reaching down to clutch her abdomen. She crouched, her head down for a while, and Jimmy knew that she was suffering physical distress.

For a time no-one spoke. The driving rain continued to slap the earth and the naked boughs of the trees trees against the perpetual symphony of city sirens. It seemed, for a moment, that all were captivated by this strange, resilient woman.

It was Kat who broke the silence. "So how does the girl fit into your plan, Lefevre?"

Lefevre frowned, his arms sill rigid as he held the gun, trembling. "Forget her. She doesn't matter."

"Not to you maybe," muttered Jimmy. "But the lass matters to me."

Hope's eyes shone in the firelight.

Lefevre shrugged with irritation. "So. This lowlife junkie tells me that James Dunbar has a grown-up daughter. And she's living in a fetid houseboat with her junkie of a mother. And that's it - Bingo, as you Brits would say. I have the golden nugget of information that will let the veil fall allow Katherine to see the dirty, selfish piece of crap that she was giving her life to." He bit his lip, and focussed on Spider. "Only this bastard wouldn't play ball."

Jimmy fixed his sights on the tip of Lefevre's semi-automatic. "There's no way to go with this, Lefevre. You're no Reggie Kray, pal. Look around you. How d'yous get out of this a free man? And what d'you take away? You've fucked things up - we all have. Do as Kat says: put the gun down and fuck off. Me and Kat'll pay this guy off and get Alfie back. It can end there."

From the edges of the estate came the sound of baying dogs. Far below, strips of bold flashlight licked concrete and tarmac. Lefevre's voice was strange and broken. "Yeah, sure thing, Dunbar." He avoided looking at Kat. "But what the fuck do I get? I tell you what I don't get: I don't get the one thing I've wanted and waited for, for so long…" His voice cracked. The hand that held the gun shook even more, and he wiped his eye with the back of it. "I have been so…fucking… patient all these years…" He breathed out, long and slow, and drew his lips in. "Enough," he said. "Enough, now. It all ends." He stepped around the fire and approached Spider and the boy, and Hope, the tip of the barrel wavering between them.

Spiders' face changed and Jimmy realised that he was seeing something in Lefevre's expression that he had never gambled on. Spider took an uneasy step backwards, dragging the boy with him. He lowered his body, the boy as a shield before him. "You do anything to me," he said, "And I swear to God, this kid gets it in the neck."

Alfie's body was slack now, his eyes closed. He appeared to be drifting in and out of consciousness.

Kat covered her mouth in horror. She let her arms drop. She was very still for a moment, lost in thought and the agony of decision. Then, she turned and walked up to Jimmy. She faced him full-on, eyes wide and making contact with his. She blinked away tears, almost lost to the rain, and drew the flat of her hand across her mouth.

Jimmy stared at her. "What? What is it?"

"I'm so sorry, Jim," she whispered. "You should never have found out like this. But there's no choice."

Jimmy shook his head, dumfounded. "If you're thinking of giving yourself to him to stop this..?"

"If it were that simple..." She turned and took a few short steps towards the fire. "Lefevre?" Hearing her voice, he inclined his head. "There's something you need to know. About Alfie. Think back. 2010. That trip to Florida – the Dalton contract."

A muscle in Lefevre's cheek twitched. He was silent for a moment. After a while, he asked, "What about it?"

Kat's voice was cold. "Five summers ago, Lefevre. We weren't exactly careful. Alfie is five years of age."

A brief guffaw of disbelief exploded from Lefevre's mouth. "No. You told me it couldn't be the case." He shook his head. "You assured me all the timings were wrong."

She moved nearer to him. She speech was fast, impatient. "I lied, Lefevre. That night back in England when I took you out for supper at Carluccio's – remember? " she said. "I lied about the timings. I lied about the due date. And I lied to Jim too. After that it didn't matter. You'd heard what you wanted to hear."

Lefevre hadn't moved. His face registered nothing.

The heavens opened. The clouds grumbled and the rain came down as though this were the end of times.

Spider's eyes glinted with glee. "Well, well, well..." he muttered. "It's happy bloody families."

Lefevre's expression had hardened, is mouth taught with determination. "She's lying," he said. "She's telling me this to protect her son.."

"*Our* son, Lefevre." She moved closer still. "Think!" she urged in a low voice. "Florida. We were away together. We had sex, Lefevre. A lot of sex. You knew all of this – we talked about it..."

Jimmy stood, his mouth open, unblinking, his life falling apart, piece by piece by piece. He shook his head, his whole body saturated , shivers running through him.

Kat whispered in his ear. "Look at him, Lefevre. Look at his face. See it for yourself. You're pointing the gun at our son, Lefevre – Alfie is yours and mine.

The heavens opened once more.

Jimmy hands swung like pendula as the rain lashed down over him. That it had come to this, extricated from everything that mattered: a neglected son who had never been his; a wife who'd fallen out of love with him love with him; a daughter he had abandoned before she had even come into this godforsaken world. And now, at the point of that hellish journey where all roads crossed, the first blood was about to be shed.

Lefevre. Everything strand of blame seemed to fold back onto this man.

His fingers curled inwards towards his palms, and a rage gathered at the pit of his stomach. He felt the blood come pumping from his chest, thundering in his ears, his brows and cheeks and mouth muscles knit into a tight ball of rage. He assumed the crouch of a fighter. Now he was running; running at the man with the gun. Quick, heavy strides, two three, four, like a bull; on, on towards the back of the man who held a gun to the head of the little boy who he'd assumed was his own for all this time. "Bastard!" he screamed, his rage spilling over the surrounding hills.

Lefevre hadn't seen him coming. He was turning at the point of contact and, as he felt the full impact, his fingers pulled the trigger.

Spider took the impact of the first round to his shoulder. He twisted to his right, dragging the boy away with him, the blade dropping from his grip to the sodden ground. Thumping Lefevre to the ground down, Jimmy saw, through the flames of the fire, the shape of Hope dropping down too. Had a bullet caught her? He buried his face into the back of Lefevre's raincoat, pinning him down with his greater mass and strength.

Jimmy could hear Alfie screaming. He could hear helicopter blades slicing through the sheets of rain, the baying police dogs closing in on them and that queer yodelling voice of Spider's: "Give me the knife, you bitch!"

Without warning, at the flick of a switch they were dazzled with white light – the crude spotlight of a police helicopter that hung, like a gigantic hornet, eighty feet above them. Jimmy and Lefevre wrestled on the ground still, and Lefevre could offer little resistance answer to Jimmy's weight. He kept his body low on top of Lefevre's, but his hands moved to the ground, feeling for the gun. Jimmy's fingers crawled through the sodden tufts of grass until, at last, he found the slippery steel of the barrel. His fingers curled around it, but he felt resistance: Lefevre still had hold of the grip.

Pulling his free arm back, Jimmy tried to punch Lefevre's body, his face. He felt his hold on the handgun weaken, and was able to prise the weapon from him. All he could think to do was toss it into the bushes.

He shifted his weight forward now, so that he was sat on Lefevre's back, underneath the shoulders. He could see over the falling flames of the fire: Spider, clutching his shoulder with one hand, the scruff of the neck of Alfie's jacket in the other. The boy hung like a limp half-filled shopping bag, his head dropped down, knees scuffing the ground and Kat was moving in on them.

"Careful, lass," he yelled. "He still has a knife somewhere..." He had lost sight of Hope.

And then Jimmy realised: she was behind Spider and Alfie. Her movements were agonised but deliberate, the glint of sharpened steel now in her clutches. There was no time to speculate what she might do.

Jimmy saw her arm thrust forward, with a sudden, sharp action. Spider's whole frame convulsed in an instant. His high-pitched scream ripped through the hammering rain. Letting Alfie drop to the ground, Spider's face lifted to the sky, to the full onslaught of the rain; the spotlight freeze-framing his bemusement. For no more than a second, a wide maniacal grin cut his face clean open, and his arms went rigid, before he too fell, face first, to the Earth, the handle of the knife jutting from between his shoulder blades.

Jimmy's head swam. He watched Kat move in on Alfie, crouching over him, folding her body round his as she wept weeping; he saw the two still figures of Spider and Hope. Black and navy uniforms and blue lights closed in. The dogs were nearer still. Beneath him, Lefevre was weakening, his breathing shallow and quick, eyes bulging as Jimmy pinned his shoulders down. With his cheek pressed to the sodden earth, he summoned enough strength to voice his final triumph. As the rain lashed his face, he spat his words through clenched teeth and bubbling saliva: "You lose the boy, Dunbar - like you've lost everything else in your miserable life..."

Jimmy heard the words, dead-eyed. Enough. He shifted his weight from Lefevre's top half. Now he was kneeling over him, his knee pressed into the small of Lefevre's back. He reached forward and grabbed Lefevre's face. He felt the man's tongue and teeth touch the palm of his hand. Now, both of his hands were gripping the sides of Lefevre's skull. He looked down on him with gritted teeth. One fluid motion: jerk and twist. Like a chicken.

Without warning, hands were on him. He his body being hauled off Lefevre's. For a bizarre moment, Jimmy wondered if he was having some kind of out-of-body experience – a dying man being borne to an ulterior plane – but the rough arms around his neck and his waist, the brief glimpse of Lefevre's wrists being cuffed, the driving rain, and the wailing sirens wailing brought him back.

At least two policemen had hold of Jimmy. Another three were on Lefevre, one recovering the semi-automatic from the scene. He heard Bridger's voice. "That one's led us a right merry dance," he said. "Get him down to the van at the bottom. And seal off the road."

Jimmy struggled as his arms were pinned behind his back. "Get off me," he yelled, as Lefevre was dragged down the hillside. "I need to see my daughter."

He heard the police radio was close by: "Victor seven-zero. First suspect apprehended. Air ambulance and two more cars two minutes repeat two minutes away."

"Received Delta Echo. Out." One of the officer's spoke to him. "Okay, sir. We're going to let you go now. Just don't so anything stupid…"

Somewhere beyond the brow of the hill, the dazzling low lights of the air ambulance cut through the rain, the deafening noise of the rotor blades drowning out all.

Beyond the dying fire, lay the still body of Hope Kelly. She was on her side, arm stretched across her stomach, eyes closed.

"Dear God." Jimmy staggered to her. To his side, two paramedics bore a stretcher from the ambulance far down on the road below and were now lifting Alfie onto it. Kat was bent over him, her hands clasped to his cheeks. She kissed the top of his head over and over. "I love you. I love you."

Jimmy crouched down beside Hope Kelly's body. Alongside her still, blood-flecked hand lay the switchblade, its blade doused in blood. Beyond that was the dead body of Luke Kevin Butcher. Her eyelids flickered and a few tiny, intermittent gasps escaped her lips.

The drips from Jimmy's sodden, matted hair fell to her cheek, but there was no response. He found her wrist, lay two fingers across it. Nothing. They moved to her neck. Nothing still. No rise and fall of the chest, no flicker of an eyelid.

Another police officer came beside them both, and looked on. He cleared his throat. "Sir: you need to move to one side…"

Jimmy ignored him. He stared through the rain at the disappearing backs of the paramedics as they bore Alfie down the hillside and through the rain, Kat running alongside. "This girl needs someone's help!" he yelled. Catching his voice, Kat looked back over her shoulder. For a fleeting moment, she stopped in her tracks, and turned to face him. Then she and the others disappeared through the rain.

Jimmy watched his daughter's face, willing her to find life. He scanned her body. Lefevre had fired more than a single round, he was sure. Had a stray bullet found her? Had Spider managed to get her before he fell? There was no obvious entry point, no wound…

The police officer's voice cut through: "Sir: the air ambulance is here. The paramedics will with be with her in seconds. You have to move aside."

Jimmy stared at him. Then he looked down. Her face. His daughter's face. It was bruised and scarred – a map of suffering, chaos and violence but serene: a face as beautiful as any he had ever seen.

The freshness and newness of it so close to him made him feel an unbearable longing for the times they had never had together. The waste of her life was more than he could bear.

And then she opened her eyes.

They were eyes that had the clarity of an April morning. She looked ahead at first, and then she found him. He moved down, his own face inches from hers. "Lassie?"

Her lips were cracked and dry. They parted, trying to form words.

"Hush. No need tae talk," Jimmy said. He held her hand. It was so cold. "They're coming now. They'll soon have you out of this place and in the warm somewhere."

She lowered her eyes. "It's too late," she said. Her lip trembled and she tried to smile. "It doesn't matter."

Jimmy was desperate. He held her hand. "What, lassie? What doesn't matter?"

"Alfie..." She winced with the pain and faltered. "That he wasn't my little brother. I would have helped him anyway..." She gasped, and clutched her side. "Shit, it really hurts...." She steeled herself. "I've tried everything... to get him away from Spider...but... I've been so weak."

Jimmy's wanted to clasp her to him but she appeared so fragile. "But you did it, lassie. You helped saved the wee lad's life..." From over the brow of the hill, silhouetted against the spotlights of the air ambulance, the shapes of two, then three paramedics bearing a stretcher closed in.

She tried to smile, but her face creased in pain again. She twisted onto her side, pulled her knees towards her middle. Her eyes were shut, tears forced from the outer corners.

Jimmy was desperate. "What is it, lass? Where does it hurt?"

She spoke with a clamped jaw. " Since the train… it's hurt more and more… every day. But I… I …had to find Spider… to try to stop him…"

Her breathing slowed. The last words were half-mumbled, as though she were speaking in her sleep. "The old man who was on the train - he has the book … with your letter inside." She saw the world for the last time. "You'll find me there, " she said.

The armed police officer had him by the arms. "Sir, let them get in."

Jimmy clutched at her arms, as she tried to focus on his face. "No," he said. Two policeman had grabbed his arms and were pulling him away. "Stay with me, lass!" He saw her face for the last time. There was, in her expression, something deep that needed no words. Her lips parted, and then were still. And her eyes were still. And then she was gone.

The rain stopped. The sirens fell silent. The world stopped turning for the briefest of moments.

Above the hill, a second police helicopter hung in the air and surveyed the scene. Over the fields below, stretchers, flashing LED lights of radios, bodies being borne away; and to the bottom of White Hawk Hill, a necklace of cordons, hangers-on and the flashing lights of emergency vehicles.

In the centre of all, middle aged man stepping away from the body of a young woman. The paramedics were crouching around the body, a frenzy of activity. After a while, one of them rose, followed by the others. They moved away. The middle aged man fell onto his knees. He scooped up the her body. He looked, for all the world, like he would never let her go.

PART FOUR

Twenty-Four – two weeks later

"I'm here to see a Mr. Oleg Kowalski?" Jimmy Dunbar lingered at the door of the hospital ward, clutching some garage-bought flowers. He had a plastic punnet of grapes tucked under his arm.

Two nurses behind the reception desk looked over to where another was making up one of the beds. They pointed to him. "Talk to Simon. He had a lot to do with Mr. Kowalski after he was admitted." One of the nurses looked him up and down. "It's Mr. Dunbar, isn't it?"

Jimmy tried to smile. It had been almost three weeks since he had received Oleg Kowalski's call. A call he had failed to return. He nodded. "Aye."

The nurse at the reception stood up. "I was glad to read about... you know. Getting your son back." She nodded, in an unconvincing attempt to reassure. Jimmy Dunbar rested the flowers on the desk. "I'll get Simon over."

Jimmy watched as she went to him. There was a brief word, a glance from both of them in his direction. Simon approached him grimly. "Mr. Dunbar? I'm afraid it's not good news."

Jimmy raised his eyebrows. "Oh?"

"Mr. Kowalski passed away a few days ago. Thankfully, he was peaceful. I'm very sorry."

"I see." Jimmy looked over to the pristine white sheets of the bed that he presumed the old man had occupied. The covers were folded back with a neat turn. He wished that he could remember more of their brief conversation; of how he had been alerted him to the Hope's fate not long after the train accident.

He tried to contain the anguish that swelled in his heart. "I didnae really know him. It's just... well we had this wee telephone conversation and..." He struggled to find the words. "You see, he told me about the accident. My daughter was on the train ."

Simon nodded. "So I understand."

Jimmy looked down at the flowers. "Still. Not much use for these now, is there? Maybe you can find a vase for them? Cheer the place up..." He paused. "Before my daughter..." He couldn't bring himself to say the word. "When I spoke tae her - she'd mentioned something about a book?"

Simon stood still for a moment. "Oh! Yes!" He moved behind the desk. "There was something he had hold of. He said I was to keep it safe if your daughter should she come back for it. I suppose it's right that it's passed on to you now." He lifted a few small boxes and sheets of notes onto the surface, to extract out a sealed and labelled transparent wallet. The slim red and white volume was tucked within. "And... I'm so sorry for your loss."

Jimmy received it with no words.

***

Later that day, during a quiet time, Jimmy slid the volume out of its skin, his fingers moving over the pages that hers had moved over. He wondered what she had made of these, his own words?

He pulled the font cover open, and a folded sheet of paper fell to the floor. Stooping to retrieve it, he could see where it was tearing along the folds, having been opened refolded so many times. Before even opening it, he knew it to be that letter he'd sent all those years ago, the one that Jasmine had kept back from her. His own words shouted back at him.

We can take as much time as you need to get to know each other.

He folded it back up and opened the book of poetry. He could see, as he turned the pages within the book, page after page of his crude verse wrapped in spools and spools of her pencilled annotations; picking apart every stanza, image, word that he'd sketched.

Jimmy's fingers moved over the page, over her notes that spilled over, around and between his rigid lines of poetry. He could feel her soft shadow over his pages, dissecting the metaphors, wondering why he would break off mid-line. Turning the pages, he knew it was the way she had chosen to try to understand him, to be closer. He had found the last of her here, and it touched his heart more tenderly than anything had done.

He closed the book and closed his eyes. He tried to see her again. It was the night when he came to the houseboat: that first glimpse of her, haloed by the drifting cigarette smoke beyond the water.

Jimmy Dunbar felt consumed by the sadness of what had been, and what could never be.

Twenty-Five – An 'Other' Place

What I'm telling you isn't the way it was. It's is the way I wanted it to be.

So.

I'm standing between carriages on a train. The doors are there in front of me.

The place I've travelled from has been, well, let's say a mixed bag. And a person can complain all she likes about the hand she's been dealt, but you know what? In my book, you define your own life by how you choose to play it. Me? I wanted people to be happy. I think I might have made someone a good mum. But my candle was blown out too soon. That's the way of things.

So what to expect from my destination? Sure, I've thought about God, what lies beyond and all that shit – who hasn't? But real life has a habit of getting in the way of thinking about the heavy stuff until it's too late.

Anyway – back to the train. I press the button. The doors slide open. I walk down the carriage taking my time, 'cos, the thing is, I don't have to run away from anything anymore. I can see that it's sunny outside; the light is pouring through the hedges and trees as they fly past, throwing millions and millions of crazy criss-cross patterns over the walls and ceiling and floors – you know – like one of those disco ball lights?

And there's someone else ahead of me. Another passenger. He has his back to me, but I feel I know him. He's very still, and he has the softest, whitest hair you have ever seen. I'm drawn to him straight away – that carriage could have been jam-packed, but he would have been the one I'd wanted to sit with.

I get to his table. His is the kindest face you could ever imagine. He's an old man, but you can see the child in him. And you can feel his love. It's like he knows everything that has happened and everything that will happen. I feel as though he's been expecting me.

"Good morning," I say to him, because that's what I do. My bestest smile. He gestures for me to sit down opposite him.

There are things I want to share with him - the laughs, the tears - but, for now, we're happy to travel in silence, and to look out of the window. 'Cos it's such beautiful morning and both of us feel as though all the good and kind things in the world are moving through us.

We're happy to travel without words. You see, we're heading for the same place, after all.

Printed in Great Britain
by Amazon

21482942R00164